# No Longer Afraid

## PREDATORS MC BOOK 1

### CHRISTINA C JONES

WARM HUES CREATIVE

# Foreword

Please note that this book contains certain elements that may be upsetting to some readers. If mentions of childhood trauma, sexual assault, violence, and the aftermath of such events might be harmful to your mental health, please take whatever appropriate measures you need before immersing yourself in this book.

# Father To Daughter

"If you ain't scared, you either stupid, or ain't got shit to lose. You don't wanna be in either position."

"But you're never scared."

"I'm scared all the time, Tati. I'm just not pussy. Do you understand the difference?"

# Chapter One

## TATI

I understood the difference between being scared and being pussy.

I had a good grasp on the concept even before my daddy had said those words to me, at a solid eleven years old.

Maybe twelve.

It was blazing hot under the sun, and we'd probably be more comfortable *anywhere* else, but we were up on the roof at *Bottoms Up* because that's where it was safe for me. We were avoiding my mother's rage over me getting suspended from middle school for fighting.

I didn't start it, though.

I just finished it.

Mia Minelli was a bully, and I had to make her understand, the rest of the sixth grade might fear her, but Tatiana Tate did *not*.

I wasn't raised to be scared of *no fucking body*.

Now she knew.

And still, I had to get "talked to".

That's how my mother had phrased it. *"Talk to this damn girl, 'cause she not hearing me."*

She was right.

I wasn't.

I couldn't understand why *she* of all people, was so mad about me fighting. *Carmen Tate* was not to be fucked with around here, and everybody knew it. She had a reputation for throwing hands, so… it was kind of an inherited quality.

So how was I wrong?

But then, my Daddy explained it—the fight wasn't the problem, the aftermath was. The attention, the labels, all that. And so, that day, he bestowed upon me the gift of being afraid. Not of people, necessarily, but of… the reverberations.

Every decision we made, every impulse we acted on, every word from our mouths—they all had influence in some way, major to minor.

They had *power*.

As heir-apparent to the second-most powerful role in the *Predators* club, I, even at eleven years old…had to be mindful of the way I wielded mine.

I had to be reasonably "scared" of what I could do.

Of what could be done to me.

Of what could be done to my family *because* of me.

And a whole lot of nuances all in-between.

So… that was the mantra.

*That* was the prayer.

*I accept the wisdom of being afraid, but please grant me the strength to never be pussy.*

Around here?

Anything else could easily turn into a death sentence.

"TATI? IT'S TIME."

The sound of Keira's voice at the office door pulled me from my thoughts, prompting me to turn off my phone screen. An app on the device had served up "memories" from this same day throughout the years, with accompanying pictures.

One of my photo-hating father had my mind soaked in nostalgia, but I shook it off as I stood, shoving the phone into my pocket.

"He's waiting in the inking room," Keira said, nervously pushing a handful of honey-blonde locs out of her face before she continued, "Should I grab some of the others that stayed behind?"

"Absolutely not." I shook my head, meeting Keira's widened eyes with narrowed ones of my own.

No wonder she was nervous.

She knew I wouldn't like that shit.

"He doesn't get an audience," I reminded her as I approached the door.

"But Blue said—"

"Is Blue here?" I challenged her, and she cut her gaze toward the ceiling as she pushed out a sigh.

"No."

"Then I don't want to hear it. Did you follow my instructions?"

She sighed again, heavier this time. "Yes. And I have to say, making him strip to his boxers for a neck tat feels like some kind of ethical violation or something."

I smirked. "So report me to HR. Come on," I said, moving past her, deeper into the maze of hallways beyond the *"employees only"* sign that separated public spaces from private. I'd walked this path often enough that the purposely dim light didn't bother me; my feet knew where to go.

On the way, Keira kept up a running stream of quick conversation, updating me on happenings with the members, meetings, and a bunch of other shit I wasn't really in the right headspace to hear about.

Moments later, we were at our destination.

The inking room—*not* a place for outsiders.

At least, it didn't used to be.

Until *this* motherfucker came along.

"What's up?" Keira asked, stopping with her hand on the handle. "Seriously, Tati, you've been on one about this dude. Do you see something we don't? Catching a weird vibe?"

I huffed. "*Weird* doesn't quite cover it," I admitted, shaking my head.

If only I could articulate what was happening.


AN OPENHANDED MEASURE of suspicion was a healthy characteristic with the kind of life I led. I didn't need everybody falling at my feet, kissing my proverbial ring or any shit like that, but I *did* need a good mental grasp on their motivations.

Their desires.

Those things we all supposedly have that make us "tick".

I needed to know where they stood, the crux of their allegiances, if they existed.

I didn't know any of that about the man waiting on the other side of this door to be treated to a privilege I didn't think he'd earned, not even in the slightest.

I trusted my president though.

My *brother*.

As we entered the inking room, my confidence in *Brandon's* judgement was the only thing keeping me from putting a bullet between Onyx's eyes while he was vulnerable in the tattoo chair.

Instead, I locked gazes with Maite and nodded.

I trusted *her*, despite the nickname of Sketch my father had given her. She was oblivious to my skepticism of Onyx, getting straight to the work in front of her.

Marking the newest member of the *Predators* with our distinguishing ink.

This was usually a big deal—room full of people, lots of shots, music, the works.

A celebration.

But I wasn't really feeling that.

Because of the *other* ink that marked him.

There was one I found especially noteworthy—a ring of thorns around his bicep. Paranoia pulled my attention to the precision of the lines, the depth and richness of it, even in all black.

*Something* told me I should be careful – *very* careful – of a man with a tattoo like that.

He... scared me.

Just on the other side of the wall, the music from the bar was pounding. I latched onto the beat, using it as a kind of soothing exercise. It was early afternoon, probably too early for a bar full of people, but this was Vegas, after all.

Land of the fucking tourists.

I bobbed my head along with the music anyway, relaxing my shoulders, my hands, trying to almost disappear into my place in the shadows, to continue my silent observation. Beside me, Keira leaned in my direction to ask in a whisper, "You *sure* I shouldn't grab just—"

"Fuck off, Keira. Don't you have somewhere else you could be?"

She did not.

"He's quite handsome, isn't he?"

As if I didn't already know, my eyes left Keira and went to his face, as if to check again.

*Fuck.*

He was looking at me.

"If you scowl at me any harder, you might ruin that pretty face," he said, and I blinked hard, my hand instinctively moving to the gun at my waist.

"Damn." Onyx chuckled. "You shoot niggas just for talking to you?"

"I'd need a much better reason than general idiocy to shoot you," I told him, crossing my arms. "Consider yourself lucky."

He smirked. "Am I, though?"

I rolled my eyes but didn't answer.

If I *did* shoot him, nobody except my president had the authority to address it, and I didn't want Brandon on my damn neck about it.

I *hated* explaining myself.

As such, I stayed where I was and kept scowling, letting my gun stay holstered, for now.

Only for now.

My eyes drifted to that ring of thorns on his bicep, the perceived symbol of that offending duality that wouldn't let me relax. He was immersed in ink, actually. Dozens of colorful pictures decorating the landscape of his deep caramel skin. They told the story of a life filled to the brim with experiences, with travel, of loss grieved and instigated.

Those thorns, though...

That was some other shit.

Shit we already knew, because he'd put himself on our radar by beating up a handful of our members at once. They got their ink revoked and he took their place, even with his vague answers about where he was from, who he was, all that.

Brandon was impressed enough by what he could do for us that he let the shit slide.

I... wasn't so easily moved.

I sauntered across the room, feigning interest in the images Maite had used to line the walls of her studio.

I could feel his eyes tracking me, as if he'd been trained to find the largest threat in the room, and not let it out of his sight.

The type of shit my daddy taught me to be wary off.

"You're not about to try to slit my throat or anything, are you?" he asked, as I purposely stepped beyond his peripheral.

"Try? No."

"Wh—*Hey!*" Maite sputtered, outraged, as he pushed up from his prone position in her tattoo chair, turning to lock eyes with me. "Can y'all cut the shit so I can work?"

Ignoring her, he locked eyes with me. "I'm not fond of this game."

The gravity of his tone made me raise an eyebrow. "What makes you think I give a fuck what you're fond of?"

He shrugged. "I doubt you do. But I *do* think you give a shit if I walk out of here and you never fucking see me again, which is what's about to happen. Would Blue be good with that?"

"I'm sure he'd figure out a way to get over it."

"Let's cool down," Keira spoke up, stepping between us. "This is supposed to be a rite of passage, a good thing..."

"Exactly." Onyx nodded, looking past her, to me. "So you get your ass back where I can see you while she's doing this shit, so we can move on."

"*You* watch your goddamn tone with me," I snapped, pushing Keira aside so I could step right in his face, staring him down.

"Tati!" Keira hissed, linking her arm with mine to try to pull me away.

Onyx smirked.

"I accept those terms," he said, his words tinged with mischief in a way that made me roll my eyes as he relaxed again, letting Maite go back to what she was doing.

I conceded to Keira's urging, allowing her to pull me to the front of the room to ask, "Seriously, what is up with you? You've never been so averse to a new member before."

"I don't trust him and I don't understand why I'm supposed to."

Keira's eyes were wide as she shrugged. "Because Blue says so."

"He's not infallible," I countered, even though... he'd never steered me wrong before.

Again, it was the only reason I hadn't simply shot Onyx and left him for the coyotes after he beat up our damn members.

"He doesn't seem that bad... does he remind you of an ex or something?" Keira snickered, making me scowl.

"Why the fuck would you ask me that?"

"Because." She shrugged. "You seem personally offended by his presence."

"Oh I *am*," I admitted. "Something about him is just... I don't know. Unsettling."

Maite was almost done with him, thank God.

I crossed my arms, stepping around Keira to approach the foot of the chair. "What does loyalty mean to you?" I asked him, just getting into what was bothering me instead of letting the question linger in my mind any longer.

Fresh amusement turned up the corners of his full lips. "I was wondering when you were going to stop beating around the bush and just come on out with it."

I rolled my eyes. "That doesn't answer my question. You're getting Predator ink, which for most of us means Predator *loyalty*. I don't know where you stand."

"I stand as a man who keeps his word," he said, his eyes dark and intense as they met mine. "I told Blue y'all had my commitment, so you've got it."

I scoffed, shaking my head. "I didn't ask about your goddamn *commitment*. I asked about your *loyalty*."

"What's the fucking difference?"

"Commitment is in your actions," I explained. "Commitment is easy to come by, easy to *buy*. Loyalty is scarce. Loyalty is... in your heart."

His eyes narrowed. "Well you're out of luck there, sweetheart. There ain't shit but savagery '*in my heart*'. So you can hang up your ideals," he told me. "I'm committed, and I'm a man of my word. You don't have to trust anything else, but you can trust that I'll do what the fuck I said I was going to do."

"What if that's not good enough?"

He tossed up a hand. "Sounds like a personal problem. It was good enough for your president."

Hmph.

There wasn't much I could say to that.

There wasn't *shit* I could say to that.

He was right. It was good enough for my president, so it was good enough for me, and on a surface level... I knew I was giving this too much energy. Hell, I could probably depend on him more than I could depend on a *lot* of other motherfuckers who wore this ink.

The difference was accessibility and insight.

This man, this virtual fucking stranger, had been let in on information plenty of other *Predators* would give their lives to know about, shit that could make or break a whole operation.

In fact, the breaking of an operation was what we were counting on.

It's the whole reason he was here.

"Don't ever fucking call me *sweetheart* again," I told him, because if nothing else, I couldn't let *that* shit ride.

He smirked. "Got it."

*Ugh.*

I didn't say shit else to him while he finished getting his ink, and when Maite was done, she insisted on giving him the whole rundown on aftercare.

Like he wasn't already covered in years of scribbles. Maite wasn't a half ass job kind of chick though.

Other times, I'd appreciated how thoroughly she made sure our members were taken care of; we had an image, a standard to uphold. Now though, she'd prolonged the time I had to spend in this dude's presence, and I wasn't too thrilled about *that*.

I was relieved when it was finally time to escort him out.

"Ladies first," he said, gesturing for Keira and me to exit Maite's studio in front of him.

Only because I knew we'd be standing there forever if I didn't, I accepted the offer well after Keira had already moved, keeping my eyes on him as I stepped out, then waiting for him to make the same move. I wasn't actually concerned he'd do something to me, but I needed to make a point, so here we were.

"I need to go check on the bar. You aren't going to kill him, are you?" Keira asked, and I shook my head.

She didn't move.

"I won't," I insisted, but she still gave me a *look* before she moved on, shouting "*Welcome to the club*," to Onyx over her shoulder before she disappeared down the hall ahead of us.

You'd think *she* was the one that was damn near a decade older, and the boss.

"Tell me something," Onyx said, as we headed up the long hall that would take us back into the bar side by side, neither of us wanting to be ahead of the other.

"You *don't* have to talk to me, actually," I replied.

He stopped walking, so of course I did too. "Do you make everybody get naked to get their ink or was that some type of special treatment just for me?" he asked, like I hadn't said what I did about not talking to me.

I rolled my eyes. "Why are you complaining? You got to keep your boxers on," I reminded him, annoyed by the smirk that had already spread across his handsome face.

The answer to his question though, was no. Most people didn't have to strip down as much as I'd required of him. Because *most* people didn't have tattoos that looked like the shit killers would have.

"Did you get paid for what you did?" I asked, baiting him. I gestured toward his arm with the thorn tattoo, even though it was currently covered by his sleeve.

His eyebrows knit together. "That ain't got shit to do with you, sweetheart."

"Actually, it's got everything to do with me if you're going to be hanging around here. And what did I say about that *sweetheart* shit?"

"My bad, *Tatiana*." He smirked, stepping into my personal space. "You were so much nicer to me when you were recruiting me, even though I'd whooped your members' asses. What did I do wrong?"

"Wrong? Nothing." I put a hand to his chest, making sure he didn't step any closer. "But *this...*" I used the other hand to point to the fresh ink on his neck. "Means closer scrutiny. And those thorns you don't want to talk about? Just make me even more suspicious."

"They shouldn't."

I scoffed. "Try that shit on someone else."

"What makes you so sure I'm *trying something*?" he asked as he moved his face down to mine, oblivious to my attempt to keep some distance between us.

He smelled good, intoxicating, even. The body, the facial hair, the locs, the tats—visually, he was gorgeous. And those deep, damn near black eyes of his were like looking into the abyss.

All that taken together?

It would make a weaker woman melt.

*Even more reason not to trust him.*

I pushed out a sigh through my nose, trying to expel his damn scent. "Back the fuck up off me."

His gaze narrowed; corners of his mouth curled up. "Or what?"

I had my gun unholstered, the barrel tucked under his chin before any verbal response came to mind. I was already sick of the slow smirks with him, and this one was no different.

No.

Actually, it was worse.

It was *mocking*.

Because he didn't believe I would pull the trigger.

He pulled his soft bottom lip into his mouth, digging in for a second. "I don't like having guns pointed at me," he said, raising a thick eyebrow.

"And *I* don't like niggas in my face uninvited," I countered. "I think if we put our minds to it, we can help each other out."

With impish amusement still knit into his features, Onyx raised his hands, taking a step back.

"Tati... is there a problem here?"

No hesitation, I turned my weapon toward the source of the sound, looking down the barrel to find Kev standing nearby, a hand at his back, no doubt reaching for his own weapon.

I looked back to Onyx as I dropped my arm, re-holstering my gun. "*Is there a problem?*"

He shrugged, then gave me a full-blown grin, briefly flashing a mouthful of glittering adornments at me. "I'm good if you are, doll."

*Ugh.*

Honestly, *that* alone was enough to reconsider shooting him. Or at least a little light pistol-whipping.

I didn't get the opportunity for either; he was already headed down the hall, swaggering past Kev and looking him right in the face as he did, without even a hint of a smile.

Kev glowered right back at him. "Ay, you got something you need me to handle?" he asked once Onyx was well past and I'd caught up to where he was standing.

"It's already been handled," I said, waving a hand in the direction he'd gone. "But thanks for offering. What are you doing here?"

He shrugged a bit, scratching at his neck, where his own ink was covered by his collar. "Seeing if Blue was back yet, so I could holla at him."

"About the treasurer role?" I asked, but I already knew that answer.

Kev was a money guy, hence the collar and shit in the middle of the day. He'd been inked about a year or so ago, and even though he'd earned it like everybody else – *almost* everybody else – it still barely felt real to me.

He wasn't quite like the rest of us.

He was... clean cut.

And fine as shit, honestly.

He flashed me an embarrassed grin full of pretty white teeth, and I laughed, shaking my head.

"He won't be back until later tonight, after their run," I explained for the second, maybe third time. "But I promise you, he'll have a decision soon."

He stepped in toward me a little closer. "Will I *like* the decision?"

"I don't know what you like," I countered, wrinkling my nose.

"I beg to differ," he smirked, chuckling when I dodged his attempt to grab me.

"Not right now," I told him. "I've got somewhere to be."

"Later, then?"

I thought about it, then nodded. "Later."

# Chapter Two

## TATI



*Club Allure.*

*Bottoms Up.*

The unnamed dispensary that was going to change our whole trajectory.

All of it was *Predators* domain.

*Predators legacy*, actually.

When Brandon and I had approached the OGs – our fathers – about the dispensary, we'd initially been met with skepticism. The legal marijuana business was brand spanking new, and it was hard to think there was a way to approach it that wouldn't require looking over our shoulders for the cops.

But why the fuck not, if it was being sold either way?

We were told to explain it, so we did.

Told to refine it, so we did.

Told to make an actual plan, so we did.

We never got to actually present it, though.

The opportunity was stripped from us via massacre, with our fathers – the president and vice president of the *Predators* – right on the frontline.

The whole situation was a bottomless pit of questions with painfully few answers and lots of assumptions about culprits, motives, and more.

And there was still a club to run.

Still businesses to develop.

Still a legacy to build, for the children we didn't yet have.

So we pushed on.

I left Keira at *Bottoms Up* to check on the newly renovated space that would become our dispensary.

Not that it really needed "checking on".

It was on the fringes of *Predator* territory, but unquestionably ours, and the renovations had been done for weeks. There was no signage or anything up yet because it wasn't quite ready for all that, but once it was time, that was it.

I liked to think it would've made my father happy.

He would've been cool about it, gruff like he always was. No smile, probably, but he was always so bad at hiding any sort of joy or excitement from his eyes.

Standing in the space that would eventually be lined with display cases, informational posters, plants, and whatever else we could imagine, I could damn near hear him.

"*Whatever happened to just smoking the shit? What are these damn tools? Why the weed need citrus notes, what the fuck is that?*"

And he'd really want to know, too.

No rhetorical questions with him.

I wished he could ask.

"I thought that was you, knew I recognized the bike out front."

I turned around, gun drawn, to find probably the last person I wanted to see draped in the doorway, entirely too comfortable.

"What the fuck do you want, Jake?" I asked, brows furrowed as I glared in his direction.

He swept a hand through his sandy blonde hair, trying a little too hard to appear unthreatening as he took a step forward. "Honestly, to offer my condolences."

"A little late for that and you've got a lot of nerve anyway," I hissed. "Tell me why I shouldn't put a bullet in your head for what your folks did to mine."

"We can start with the fact that you've got this shit all wrong," he insisted, holding up his hands. "I'm sorry for what happened to your dad, but I swear to you—it was *not* us."

"It sure as fuck looked like it was."

He nodded, eyes wide. "I know what it looked like. But we've never had any problems, not... beyond the usual."

I huffed. "Beyond the usual racism, right."

"*I'm* not like that!"

"I don't *give a fuck*," I countered. "All I know is, what should have been a quick – unavoidable – detour through *Marauders* territory ended up with half the people I know dead. An act of *war*."

"That we didn't initiate; be reasonable, Tatiana," Jake said, taking another step in before I held up my hand.

"Don't you come any closer to me, talking about some goddamn *be reasonable*. The fact that we haven't already wiped you motherfuckers off the face of the planet is as *reasonable* as it gets," I spat. "But you keep your eyes open."

"How do I prove we didn't do this?" he asked, earnestly—or at least, feigned it. "We don't want a war with the *Predators*."

"You say, standing *uninvited* on *Predators* territory."

"Territory that borders ours; it should be neutral."

"Well I say it's not," I told him, with a smile. "If your people didn't do it, who did?"

"I don't know."

"Not good enough."

"It's all I've got." Jake shrugged, frustrated. "I don't know who'd be bold enough – *stupid* enough – to pull something like this, but we've got all the same questions you have," he explained. "We've tried to get security footage; everything is destroyed. Hell, we even talked to our members; nobody with our ink was anywhere near where it happened."

"Witnesses put riders with your patches near the area; that's from the police report," I reminded him. "LVPD is useless otherwise, but they at least gave us *that*."

"Which should be suspicious to you, honestly," he disputed. "When have those fuckers ever been so forthcoming?"

*Hm.*

He had a point there.

Truthfully, that little nugget was the thing that compelled us to pump our brakes a bit on this "war" and seek more information first. In the meantime, we were gathering resources, rebuilding our structure, and moving on with getting business handled.

We'd get our lick back, without question.

We just needed to be certain we hit the right person.

LVPD cooperating with the families of dead Black bikers to implicate white ones was shocking at best, convenient at worst. If they had proof they wanted to act on, arrests would've been made, and they'd have handled their own shit.

Giving us that information – supposed witness who'd seen *Marauders* riders kill *Predators* in a bloodbath on the outskirts of town – could easily be a setup.

Get us to take them out, then arrest us for doing so.

Two birds with one stone.

This was a situation we had to be smart about.

"Tatiana, we have an opportunity here," Jake said, taking a chance on moving closer yet again. "It's why I stopped when I saw your bike."

I rolled my eyes. "You didn't stop 'cause you saw my bike. You have this building being watched and someone let you know I was here alone."

He didn't deny it.

Couldn't.

"Either way," he continued, "An opportunity is still in front of us, an alliance between our clubs. Groundbreaking shit, like my father, grandfather, could never imagine."

I laughed, right in his damn face. "Yeah, mine either, considering your father and grandfather would've strung mine up from trees before *ever* considering an alliance."

"I'm trying to be better than them."

"Good for you. The *Predators* have no interest in being part of your process," I told him. "You wanna be *woke* or whatever the fuck? Nice. Have fun with that. But we'll never mistake you and yours as anything but *ops*."

A sudden commotion outside pulled both of our attention away from each other to the window instead. Of course Jake hadn't shown up alone, his father was president of their club, and Jake himself was more than just a member, based on the *Road Captain* patch on his jacket. He had muscle with him, like I should, honestly.

Especially with the current circumstances considered.

There were five bikes out front, mine, Jake's, plus three others, none of which held a rider. Looking out a little further, I could see two large bundles slumped on the pavement...

Bodies?

Beside me, Jake went for his weapon, but mine was already drawn.

"Uh-uh," I told him, aiming right between his eyes. "Hands up."

"What the fuck is this?" he asked. "Some kind of ambush?"

"You tell me," I demanded, as a loud thump echoed from down the hall. "What the hell is happening?"

"*I don't know.*"

My grip tightened on my gun as my heart raced, wondering what was about to happen. It was silly of me to have come alone when I could've easily grabbed a few enforcers.

It was funny, almost, that I'd chosen solitude because I wanted peace.

This was quite the opposite.

The sound of footsteps coming toward us made me employ a subtle switch, aiming there instead of at Jake as I backed away, keeping both possible sources of danger in view.

"*Are you fucking kidding me?*" I muttered to myself when Onyx appeared in the doorway. He locked eyes with me briefly, then looked to Jake.

"Are you gonna be cool, or I gotta kick your ass too?"

"I'm at the mercy of Ms. Tate right now, so I'm not making any sudden movements," Jake answered, shrugging. "You killed my guys?"

"Nope. Just a little nap."

Jake let out a breath. "Suppose I should thank you."

"Not unless Tati says you can walk away from here. There's still time for this all to end different," Onyx said, with none of the good humor or jesting he'd employed with me before. His eyes were cold, shoulders tense, clothes splattered with the dark red evidence that he'd done whatever he might be accused of.

He was terrifying.

Jake saw it too.

He looked to me, his icy blue eyes wide and desperate.

He didn't want to die today, and I didn't want him to, not at *Predator* hands, at least.

"Get your guys and get the fuck outta here, Jake," I told him. "And don't venture into any of our shit again."

He didn't hesitate.

Neither Onyx nor I said a word as he scrambled down the hall, stopping to gather one of his people; the noise we'd heard down the hall. Moments later, they'd stumbled outside, in full view of the window as they woke the other two from their "naps" and hopped on their bikes to peel off.

It was a wonder they were even able, looking at the state of Onyx's hands and clothes.

"Every situation doesn't require a barbaric approach, you know?" I asked, turning away from the window. "Was finesse even a consideration for you?"

"My vice president was outnumbered and alone." He shrugged, wiping the back of his hand on his jeans. "So... no."

I rolled my eyes, trying to shake off the reality of his words. Would Jake have done anything to me? Probably not.

But the chances *weren't* zero.

"What are you even doing here?" I asked, trying to shift the subject. "Did you follow me?"

He shook his head. "No. I was told to report to you, couldn't find you, so I asked Keira where you were. She said you were here, so I came here."

"Who told you to report to me?"

"Ozzy."

I nodded.

Ozias was *our* Road Captain, and if Brandon hadn't taken Onyx on their run, the next best thing that made sense was sending him to me for marching orders.

But that didn't make me any happier to be bothered.

"Where's your bike?" I asked, suddenly realizing mine was the only one still parked out front.

"Safe."

I met his gaze, eyes narrowed, already knowing there was no point in challenging his none answer.

*Whatever.*

"Clean up whatever mess you've made here, then clean yourself up. I'm going back to *Bottoms.*"

*Bottoms Up* was right on the outskirts of Vegas and had a reputation. We were open to everybody and caught a steady stream of curious tourists and ninety-nine percenters with no interest in smoke. Occasionally there was a ruckus; especially if people got mixed up in some shit they hadn't expected because they didn't know better.

The regulars knew to give the club members a wide berth.

These other folks though...

Well, there was a reason I got a text from Keira giving me a heads up that a swarm of *Predators* were coming in hot.

"They're on the way," I relayed to a couple of servers Keira hadn't already notified, and they knew what to do; make sure the people who weren't trying to be around for whatever energy the *Predators* were bringing with them... weren't around.

I stopped to tell a group of glammed up women wearing sashes and tiaras. "Hey, we've got a bit of a rough crowd coming through."

The one with *the bride* emblazoned diagonally across her barely-there dress blinked at me, then flipped a handful of waist-length, impressively straight tresses over her shoulder. "Good, that's exactly why we came, sis!" she announced, earning a chorus of sorority calls from the women surrounding her. "We was waiting on them *at the doe!*"

Surprised, I grinned. "You sure? 'Cause um... I know a few motherfuckers that are gonna see your impending title across your chest and that ring on your finger and consider it a challenge."

"*Good.* Send them niggas straight in this direction," she said, her friends hyping her up with a collective "*yesssss bitch!*" that made it clear I was missing some context.

But it wasn't my business.

"Where the hood niggas at?!" they started chanting, making me laugh.

"Hey Erica!" I called over to the bartender, getting her attention. "A round of shots for these ladies, on me." That won *me* an appreciative ovation of my own, and I chuckled as I walked off, toward the front of the bar.

"Yo, why you hyping them up?" Kev asked, reminding me that he'd been trailing along behind me since he'd arrived after work. It seemed like a week had happened since I told him I would see him "later", instead of just a few hours.

I sighed, shaking my head, and giving another table that didn't look like they were about that life a quick warning before I answered. "They're having fun. You got something against fun?"

"Getting ran through the night before you marry some poor chump is *fun?*"

I stopped to turn in his direction and crossed my arms.

He was lucky he was fine.

And his dick was big.

'Cause otherwise...

"What do you think the groom is doing right now, assuming he's in Vegas too, if it's the night before the wedding?" I asked. "Taking in a show? Hitting the poker tables?"

Kev sucked in a breath, his eyes moving wildly as he tried to come up with *something*.

"*Exactly.*" I chuckled, turning to continue on my way. "That nigga is without question, balls deep in stranger pussy, and it's probably a regular occurrence. She can do hoe shit with her friends if she wants. As a matter of fact—*Erica!*" I yelled across the bar. "*Make it a double.*"

"Can't believe you're encouraging that," Kev muttered, following me outside, where I stopped again, waiting for him to approach me.

"I think you *can* believe it," I said, reaching out to take his pretty ass face into my hands. Copper skin, strong features, lush facial hair...on a shallow level, he really had *everything* going for him. And really, that was about as deep as I wanted to take anything, with anybody. "My indulgence of said *hoe shit* is exactly how I ended up taking *you* home. Did you forget?"

"Chill with that, Tati."

That's what came out of his mouth, but the smirk on his face said different as he used the back of his hand to wipe a sheen of sweat from his brow, courtesy of the dry Nevada heat.

Occasionally, Kev needed a little reminder of how this thing between us had started and that this was as far as it would ever go. I wasn't his ol' lady, his girlfriend, nothing of the sort. It was a stretch to call it "dating", even.

We were having fun, that was all.

Movement on my other side made me look up, just as Onyx approached, hands tucked into the pockets of his jeans.

Clean ones.

I wiped my interaction with Kev from my features to put displeasure on my face. I didn't need this man knowing he had the power to affect me.

He did, though.

It was like a switch had flipped once Brandon decided to bring him into the fold. Before that, I hadn't really cared about "Onyx" enough to be bothered by him. He had value he could add to the *Predators*, and that was that.

Now though?

Everything from the easy swagger in his step to that *goddamn* black cross dangling from his ear – the type of thing that would've looked foolish on anybody else, but only added to *his* cool – irked the shit outta me.

His superhero antics at the dispensary earlier had only irritated me further.

"Is this the tradition or something?" He grunted the question, arms crossed, not actually looking at me. "Coming outside to wait for the soldiers to return from war?"

"Who looked at your light-skinned ass and named you Onyx?" I asked, instead of answering his question. I watched his face for a reaction and I wasn't disappointed.

His eyes went wide in surprise for just a flash before he schooled his features back to neutral; he either couldn't or didn't care to cover the entertainment dancing in his eyes though. "Internet fan club."

I blinked. "Seriously?"

"Nah," he chuckled, shaking his head. "It's just... my name, I don't know."

"That's on your birth certificate?"

"I said I didn't fucking know," he growled, his volume rising in tandem with a lowered timbre.

"Ay, watch your tone." Kev spoke up for the first time, even though I'd felt him observing the whole conversation, felt his disquiet.

Onyx raised an eyebrow at him, the amused glint in his eyes gone now, replaced with a kind of sinister irritation that made me shift positions, bringing his attention back to me.

He'd fucked up three guys with no issue earlier.

I didn't even want to think about what he'd do to Kev.

"I'm not trying to offend you," I told him. "Just asking."

That dark, intense gaze shot back to Kev for another moment, almost like a warning before his regard came to me and stayed. "The mythology behind the name is conflicting," he said, shrugging. "Some stories say Onyx is the manifestation of a demon; imprisoned in the stone during the day, and at night... wielder of terror and nightmares."

I swallowed. "And others?"

"Consider it a symbol of protection from evil. There's harmony between the layers under the surface."

My eyebrows lifted, but I didn't dare tear my eyes from his. "And where do you stand? What definition do you identify with more?"

He looked away, his jaw tight as his attention settled on the road. "My mother looked at me and decided one or the other, and she ain't around to ask anymore. So who the fuck knows?"

I frowned.

*I* wanted to know.

But my ears had picked up a familiar sound; the proverbial boys were back in town. "*Boys*" being a genderless collective term for everybody who'd rode out with the *Predators* today.

In just a few moments, they'd rolled up loud and chaotic to surround us, gassing their bikes, whooping and hollering, doing tricks to put on a show for the patrons who stuck around for exactly this, who'd slowly started coming out of the bar.

I was looking for one bike in particular in the crowd though.

*Brandon.*

Immediately, my shoulders grew tense, waiting for his report. He and a select few had much more discreet business to tend to while the others were at some rally or some shit, creating plausible deniability for anything they might get into. He pulled up right in front of me, barely stopping before his helmet was off and he was giving me a subtle nod to let me know that his task had indeed been taken care of.

Good.

*Good.*

I blew out a sigh of relief, ready to head inside for a full debrief as Gavin and Teo pulled up too. As usual, Gavin was living up to his nickname – Ghost – not really with all the revelry and attention. My beloved pretty boy Teo though, he was all smiles as he hopped off his bike to bump fists with me and Kev before he waved to a group of women in the crowd a few feet away, setting off... chaos.

"Ay, Blue, how did she perform out there today?" Kev asked, attempting to use his bike as a reason to make conversation, or rather, get Brandon's attention.

Brandon frowned, confused. "Uh... about the same as usual," he shrugged, tucking his helmet under his arm before motioning for me to follow him back inside, to the office. "I'll catch up with you later man," he added, making it clear to Kev that he wasn't invited to the meeting.

But then he hesitated.

He looked back at Onyx, considering him for a moment before he motioned for him to follow too.

"Seriously?" I muttered, reacting before I could catch myself. With a crowd around, it was probably unwise, but... fuck it. This was the stuff that pissed me off.

Brandon raised an eyebrow at me. "Speak your mind, Tati."

"We don't know this motherfucker like that," I said, not caring about the eyes on me as I gestured in his direction.

"This afternoon didn't make it clear I was reliable?" Onyx asked, and Brandon looked to me.

"What happened this afternoon?"

*Ugh.*

"Ran into Jake Lincoln, it was nothing," I assured, knowing Brandon didn't need even another *milligram* of a reason to go after the *Marauders*. "Onyx decided to fuck up his muscle, like a damn hooligan, unprompted."

"That's exactly why I should come to the meeting," Onyx suggested. "So you can keep an eye on me."

I huffed, shaking my head. I understood the potential value Onyx could bring, with his – supposed – special skillset. But he hadn't proven shit other than his ability to throw a punch yet.

He shot a taunting smirk in my direction, knowing his invitation into our committee meeting was irksome.

Brandon's mouth twitched, and he shrugged. "I agree. What better place for him to be?"

"Of course you do," I huffed, then started inside, to go to the damn meeting, pissed. Twenty minutes later, I left the damn meeting pissed too, only to run straight into Kev, lingering at the hall entrance for my attention.

Or maybe Brandon's.

I mostly ignored him, heading straight for my bike. It was no surprise when he followed though.

"What was that earlier?" he asked, starting as soon as we'd made it outside the *Bottoms* doors.

I groaned. "What was *what*?"

"You asking that nigga what his name meant and all that?" he said, moving to get in front of me, impeding my path. "You flirting right in my face now?"

I pinned Kev with a look that held back none of the disgust I was feeling in the moment. "I'm *not having* this conversation. I'm not in the mood so you can fuck off," I snapped, moving to get around him.

"Hold on, damn," he countered, catching me with an arm around my waist. His dick against my stomach was the only reason I didn't shove him off. "I'm not trying to be on any bullshit with you, Tati. But if you had somebody trying to play a little too close to your position with Blue, you telling me you wouldn't be trying to see what was up?"

*Shit.*

That... hit a little too close.

I sighed, forcing my gaze to his face. "I get it. But me and you are *not* the same thing as me and Brandon. I made it very clear what *this* was going to be, from the start."

"I hear you, okay?" he crooned, dipping his head to put his mouth to my neck. A moan escaped my throat when he pushed my braids aside for better access, doing a little thing with his tongue behind my ear that I felt right between my legs. "Let me make it up to you?"

Before this... before the meeting with Brandon *and* Onyx, I'd already decided I was going home alone tonight. And I probably still should.

But then Onyx stepped outside, immediately finding my eyes across the busy parking lot, and smirked.

I felt *that* between my legs too.

*Shit.*

"Fine," I told Kev, breaking my gaze with Onyx. "Meet me at my place."

I pushed off him, frustrated at how hot and bothered I suddenly was.

Even *more* than I'd been about just Kev.

I didn't look back for anybody as I made my way to my bike, donned my helmet, and took off, eager to leave all the annoyances from the last few hours behind.

# Chapter Three

## TATI

"Some say Onyx is the manifestation of a demon; imprisoned in the stone during the day, and at night... wielder of terror and nightmares."

"And others?"

"Consider it a symbol of protection from evil. There's harmony between the layers under the surface."

I went to sleep with that shit on my mind, and woke up with it too, staring up at the shadows of my ceiling in the dark.

Pondering.

I had no idea what was under the surface with Onyx, but whatever it was...it was there in abundance, bubbling up and ready to spill over, no matter how outwardly controlled he seemed.

I felt it.

And more than that, I saw it in his eyes.

I just didn't know what *it* was.

That's what gnawed at me.

Beside me, Kev stirred, spurring me to slip away, leaving the bed before he had a chance to try to pull me close.

I didn't need to *cuddle*.

I needed to *think*.

The leathered granite floors were a welcome contrast against my bare feet as I padded down the hall, in no hurry to get anywhere. What I needed was quiet, a moment of stillness in the midst of so much happening.

There was always something *happening* lately.

To be expected, I guess, as *Predators* vice president, but this level of responsibility, so suddenly… it was enough to overwhelm anybody. Brandon and I had still been in the process of being groomed for our positions.

Being shoved out of the nest in the manner we had wasn't ideal, to say the least.

But there was no room for our anxieties, only… action.

*Swiftly.*

Not only was there the club to be run, with its own politics and rules and culture, there was the *business* to run as well, with multiple holdings in the works.

Legitimacy was paramount.

We were finishing the work our fathers started, of having something concrete. Yes, the club had survived this long based on the usual sources of income, but if we could finish putting the processes in place for our members – and shit, other people too – to actually build something?

It would be groundbreaking.

It was just *so much* work.

Which was why, instead of curling up next to the handsome man in my bed or waking him up to request his head between my legs, I found myself outside on the balcony, staring off into the sky as I watched the sun start its daily masterpiece. As colors crept across the atmosphere in ombre streaks, my mind drifted from their general splendor to how beautifully they might blend on a canvas.

Or on the skin.

So I was right back to tattoos.

Right back to Onyx.

*His* canvas.

There *had* to be a reason that thorn tattoo bothered me *so much*… had I seen it before, on someone else? When I closed my eyes, there was a memory that lingered just on the fringes of my peripheral thoughts, one I couldn't bring into focus.

Frustrated, I let my eyes pop open, glaring across the painted sky.

I needed more details.

Details I didn't have.

*Shit.*

*I bet Tali would remember…*

I closed my eyes again, my hand going to my neck to feel for the trinket I kept there, a gift from my baby sister, from what seemed like a lifetime ago. The tiny carved rose had been a joke, an ongoing one, based on me having "saved her life" when we were kids.

*Such a silly ass story.*

We were running one day, after school. Not for sport, or for fun—just running.

Why?

Who knows?

But we got so wild that we messed around and ran into this mean ass lady's rose bushes, which hurt like a bitch. I had to untangle Tali, her hair, her backpack, all that.

I had to punch that lady in her face 'cause she tried to grab Tali.

Then we were running again, while she chased us, screaming.

*That* memory made me smile.

I ran my fingers over the smooth stone rose carving, feeling the familiar ridges and grooves, still marveling over the detail of it all.

But then another, *different* memory struck.

My eyes went wide, shoulders tense as I snatched my phone from the pocket of my robe and navigated to one of my contacts to hit the *call* button. The phone was barely answered before I started talking.

"Hey... do you remember telling me about this client you covered up a rose tattoo for?" I asked Maite, heedless to the time of morning as I excitedly spouted the question into the phone.

I *needed* her to remember, so I'd know the thought wasn't something I'd made up. She was probably cussing me out in her head, but all I had to endure was a long, exaggerated yawn before Maite confirmed, "Yeah, some drunk chick talking about assassins and shit like she was in witness protection. I shouldn't have inked her with liquor in her system, but she seemed desperate. And she was fine. But how do *you* remember that? It was like a year ago. Maybe two."

"I remember a lot," I told her. "It's kind of an important quality considering..."

"Right," she agreed. "Working with *these* niggas. You know what I always think about though? That girl swore afterwards she was just fucking around, but... I don't know. A while back, I read on the internet about some secret society shit. All the women got tattooed with a rose."

My eyes went wide. "Like an article? Is there *any* way you remember the site?"

"Nah, like...like a story. It's one of those sites where people upload whatever they want for folks to read."

"Like fucking *Wattpad*, Maite?!"

"Wattpad has some good shit! A lot better than some of the so-called New York Times Bestsellers," she started up, and I shook my head like she could see me.

"I'm not debating *that* girl, damn! I'm saying I thought you were... giving me some factual information. *Nonfiction*."

"Oh. My bad. Nah, I can't vouch for any of that. But I don't know... it's just real coincidental to me. Real convenient, you know? She's drunk and spills all her beans, then she sobers up a bit and now all of a sudden it's *tee-hee I was just playing*. Story is posted on the internet, starts to gain a little interest, and all of a sudden it's scrubbed down. Can't find it anymore. Which pissed me off, 'cause I was *not* finished reading."

"Please stay focused," I said. "This client, do you remember her name?"

"Nah, she was a walk-in at the shop, and you know how that goes. I think she was a dancer though."

"A dancer like in a show? On the strip?"

"*Nah*," Sketch laughed. "Like a *stripper*. At the titty bar. Maybe even *Allure*."

"Well if you remember her name, or *any* other information, let me know as soon as possible."

"Yeah that's no problem Tati, but... what is this about? What made you ask me that?"

"Just curiosity," I said although that was far from the case. I didn't need anybody else in on my theory before I had a chance to fully flesh it out.

*Rose*s, rings of thorns...

The two went hand in hand, right?

It fit too perfectly together to *not* mean something.

And I was determined to figure out what that *something* was.

For now though, I got Maite off the phone and let her go back to sleep, since it was painfully early in the morning. I was too keyed up – and too disinterested in having Kev's hands on me – to go back to *my* bed.

So I set my sights on a different task, heading to the studio space in my house to work on a new batch of rose quartz... playthings. It was a hobby of mine that required a bit heavier machinery than many other crafts, but I didn't mind that part.

Creating this moody space had been a pleasure—the exact right lighting, the display shelves, space for all my tools and raw materials lining the walls.

I loved working with stone, taking the rough uncultivated chunks and molding them into something unique, beautiful, and... pleasurably functional.

Not what Tali had in mind when she'd first introduced the rose quartz and other precious crystals to me.

She had been all the way in it, knew all their meanings and functions, was convinced in the ways they could help your chakras and shit. I wasn't so sure, personally, but *she* believed, and Tali believed in so few things I felt compelled to support her in it.

We all had.

Even with my father's general mistrust in what he considered "*woo-woo shit*"; he'd worn a hunk of rose quartz – one of Tali's first jewelry pieces – around his neck every day because she gave it to him.

And who was going to have a damn thing to say about Gerard Tate's pink necklace?

No fucking body.

That was who.

And even if they did, he wouldn't have cared. He would've given it the same treatment he gave all direct disrespect, broken some assortment of bones and kept on trucking, mad that he'd had to beat somebody up while wearing Tali's charm.

*"I thought you said this shit was supposed to take away negativity and boost conflict resolution. Then why was I fighting motherfuckers all day, huh?"*

We heard that once a week, easily, usually with Tali wrapped in a bear hug in his thick arms.

*"You're too mean, Dad. I don't think it's any match for you."*

She was probably right. He was *never* mean to us, always fiercely loyal to family. Anybody else though... they could get it.

I shook my head, blinking back tears over the stark reality that I didn't have *either* of those two now. My fingers went back to my necklace; a talisman Tali had carved herself, after having worked with the medium for a while.

It was supposed to bring me inner peace, and love.

I hadn't quite mastered either of those yet.

The *sensual* element of it all though... I'd definitely been all over that, a fact that if Tali knew would have her so scandalized.

Or would it?

Especially considering who she'd been with before...

"Tati!"

The sudden intrusion of a voice in my space made me jump, and I looked up to see that Brandon had invited himself in.

"I've been meaning to tell you, the rose quartz nipple clamps in that set? You were really in your bag with those."

I rolled my eyes. I was caught off guard by his – uninvited – presence in my workspace, but definitely not surprised by it.

"The words coming out of your face imply you thought I was waiting on an update," I quipped. "As if I *wanted* that information. And we both know that's not true."

"What?" he asked, coming to stand right beside me, and leaning down, peering at the small ring I was creating. "I thought every small business thrived on customer satisfaction surveys. *Especially* satisfied." He winked at me.

"I really hate you," I replied, making him laugh as I put my tools down and straightened up, turning to look him in the face. "Why are you here anyway?"

He raised an eyebrow at me, shaking his head before he gestured at his clothes, a full-blown suit, much more formal than his usual jeans, t-shirt or crew neck, and fresh sneakers. "We've gotta swing by *Allure*, then got a meeting at *Reverie*... remember?"

I frowned, then reached for my cell phone to check the screen for the time.

"Oh shit!" I hurriedly removed my gloves, tossing them beside my protective apron. "*Shit*. Give me like twenty minutes," I called behind me as I rushed out of the room.

Brandon chuckled. "Tati, relax. It's not the end of the world if we're a few minutes late."

"It's not a great impression to set with people we need help from though," I countered, stopping at my bedroom door.

*Shit.*

I'd forgotten all about Kev on the other side, and the chances of him *not* slowing me down were slim to none.

"I already handled your lightweight," Brandon said, laughing, from right behind me. "Sent him on his way. You're welcome," he said, as I peeked into the door to confirm what he was saying.

"*Thank you*," I told him, on the other side of a relieved sigh that made Brandon suck his teeth.

"Why are you even fuckin' with Kev?" he asked. "He's... a bit too low on the totem pole if you know what I mean. It's not..."

"A good look? Like the princess of *Hamilton Luxury Transport*?" I teased him.

Not because I didn't think Nessa Hamilton was a good look for him; she *absolutely* was. In the short time they'd been doing whatever they were doing, I could already see a tiny change in him.

For the better.

He wasn't as reckless, which was important for the current climate.

"I ain't saying you gotta get some oil baron or something like that, it's just… I'on know. He's a little corny. Why you think I don't want him near the *Predators* money?"

I nodded, because… well… Kev *was* a little corny. But he was fine, which served my purposes, and good with numbers, which could have potentially served the club. I understood why Brandon didn't want him in the treasurer role though, even though Kev had campaigned hard for it.

It was more likely to go to Gavin, who was like us, a legacy member, whose father was one of the OGs in the club. He was great with numbers too; his father had served as treasurer before the day we quietly referred to as *The Fall*. But, more importantly, nobody fucked with Ghost.

With a nickname like that, who would?

Kev, on the other hand was… approachable.

"You act like I'm marrying him or something," I quipped, heading to my closet, grateful I'd already showered the night before. "He's a good time, not a long time, and I like to think everybody is clear on that."

When I popped back out of the closet, Brandon was shaking his head.

"I don't think you realize it, but the same way you like to point out to me that women are attracted to power, so I have to be careful? These dudes are out here on the same second gentleman shit," he said, dropping to a seat on the bench at the end of the bed. "*Treasurer* my ass. That's not what he's really after. He would do anything I told him to do if it meant a chance at being close to the head of the *Predators*. You need to be careful too."

I propped a hand on my hip. "It's really funny you mention that, considering how trustful you are of Onyx."

Brandon dropped his chin to rest on his fists, elbows propped on his thighs. "Yo, what is up with you and him? When I first told you to recruit him, you didn't have any problem with it. You saw the vision and you were down. What happened? Do you know something I don't?"

"No, I just think I *see* something you don't. He's dangerous."

"*Yeah*." Brandon laughed. "That's the whole fucking point, Tati."

I groaned. "I get that part. But there is *something* more to it. And really it's… it's not even that I think he's going to betray us, or anything like that.

The problem is... I don't *know.* If we were paying him and I knew I could only trust him as long as the money clears, cool. I can live with that. If we were just hiring him to do a job. But you've welcomed this motherfucker *we don't know* into the fold, and I don't like that shit. I can't get a good read on him."

Brandon pushed himself up from the bench, sighing as he walked up to prop his hands on my shoulders. "I get it. I promise you; I do. But I'm telling you, we need him. I don't know what the fuck he was into before he ended up in Vegas, or *why* he ended up in Vegas. But I know that motherfucker is a killer, and with these white boys lurking around..." He shook his head and dropped his hands. "I don't know. There's some shit going on, a different energy that I don't fuckin' like. What made Jake think he could walk up on you in *our* shit like it was nothing?"

"He claimed he wanted an alliance," I told him. "I didn't get the vibe he was looking for trouble."

"Onyx said he didn't like the energy."

I shrugged. "That's how he saw it. How *I* saw it is...I think Jake is scared. I don't think he – or his folks – want a problem with us, and yet... somebody shitted in their laps."

"So you don't think they're the ones who ambushed our people?"

"I think it's too convenient to be as it appears," I answered. "It adds up so well that it doesn't add up."

Brandon nodded. "As much as I want blood for this shit... I gotta keep it a buck. It never sat right with me that they would waylay *Predators* in the first place, you know?"

"Yeah," I agreed. "Any other time, all they do is make their meth, drink, and... hunt in the woods and shit. They were never the type to want any real smoke with us."

"They would never even run up in our territory," Brandon added. "But now they're ambushing us? When our people were where they were on some traffic detour bullshit? Getting close enough to take out the head? Something is *off* with that. Which is exactly why we need a dude like Onyx on our side while we figure it out. You feel me?"

"I do."

"Aiight," he said, chucking me under the chin. "Get dressed then. Can't have you beside me all bummy in your pajamas and—ay!" he laughed, dodging the jab I sent in his direction.

"Fuck you," I told him, and I headed to my bathroom with my clothes. "You could at least make some coffee or something."

"So you can blow up these rich people's bathroom? I think not!" he called through the closed door, making me laugh.

I really *did* have to get ready.

I made it quick, thanking God and my mama for my hereditarily clear skin, which meant after my hygiene routine I could just pop on tinted moisturizer, mascara, liner, and lipstick, and look polished. My braids went up in a neat bun. I'd chosen slacks and a blouse that were both tailored to my curves, and a higher heel than I'd normally bother with; all for the aesthetic.

The Whitfields weren't really our kinda people.

Not even in a bad way, they were just... on some Black royalty shit that wasn't really how we got down. Gerard and Jesse – my father and Brandon's – had been good friends with Daniel Whitfield.

Kingston Whitfield's father.

The lifestyles between them were so vastly different that I never quite understood it. Brandon and I weren't trying to be cool with the Whitfield kids growing up either. Not because we didn't like them, we just didn't have shit in common.

As adults, we had a healthy respect for each other, but rarely crossed paths.

Until now.

The quest for legitimacy – and legacy – was one the Whitfields were keenly familiar with. Kingston's current reign at the head of their empire was the *first* completely unsullied by questionable legalities. It was a ball *Daniel* had set in motion though—a lesson Jesse and Gerard drilled into me and Brandon when they first started grooming us to inherit the president and vice president roles.

At the time, I'd found it strange; we both had, actually. We were barely thirty and had every belief our fathers would live a good long time, barring illness or other extremes.

Now... I wondered if they'd known something we didn't and opted not to share.

What could that *something* have even been though?

"Tatiana, let's go!"

I rolled my eyes at Brandon's admonishment then stepped out of the bathroom, stopping through my closet for jewelry and one last look in the mirror before I went to find Brandon.

In my kitchen.

Holding up a to-go cup of coffee he *had* to have brought with him.

"You look good. Let's go."

# *Chapter Four*

## TATI

"Welcome to *Club Allure* , what fantasy can we indulge for you today?"

I rolled my eyes at the greeting purred in our direction as we strolled through the front door, knowing the dramatics from the beautiful, skimpily dressed woman approaching us wasn't for *my* benefit.

As suspected, she barely acknowledged me, her eyes glued to Brandon, who chuckled. "None today sweetheart, but I appreciate the dedication."

"Are you sure? Because—"

"Where is Dove?" I interjected, knowing we didn't have time to go back and forth with the hostess.

She sucked her teeth. "I'm trying to offer an experience Tati, damn."

"We don't need it," I reminded her. "You know that's not why we're here."

"I'm supposed to stay in character," she complained, directing her words to Brandon to save her.

He stepped forward, leaning in a bit in a way she couldn't help mirror, wanting to be closer to him. "If you *really* wanted to give a good customer service experience, you'd remember to always cater to the *woman* when a couple comes in. Remember?"

I smirked.

Of course she remembered.

She just didn't like *me*.

"Of course!" she sputtered. "I just—"

"Girl close your mouth," I quipped, heading past her toward the back. "I don't give a shit personally, just make sure you're doing right by our customers."

"I always do; ask Kev."

I stopped, turned, met eyes with Brandon, who gave me a subtle shrug as a grin spread over my lips. I looked to Sanaa, taking in the shitty smirk on her face, and smiled wider as she found the nerve to add on.

"Tell him we miss him around here. He was one of my favorite customers," she said, propping a hand on her hip.

"I'm sure you can tell him yourself. I know what you do with your *favorite customers*." I laughed as her eyes bugged. "Dove wanted to fire you, but since you weren't doing it *here*, I had her cut you some slack; what, you didn't know that?" I asked, tipping my head to the side as her gaze dropped.

I reached out, grabbing her chin to make her ass look at me. "You didn't know, did you? Which is fine. I just want you to understand that you're only here because I allow it; and I allow it because you are completely inconsequential to me. If Kev wanted to come see you he would, babe. There is *nothing* stopping him or his dick from giving you a call if that's what he wants to do. And there is literally *nothing* I care less about. Okay? Just so we're on the same page."

I didn't give her a chance to respond to that before I walked off; there was nothing she *could* say, really.

Nothing I cared to hear.

What I cared about was talking to Dove, the manager, about expansion.

We found her in the back, busy as usual, counting off liquor bottles for inventory.

"Hey gorgeous, hey handsome!" she greeted, barely looking up from her task. She was in the middle of a count, so we waited, not wanting to interrupt. Dove was an absolute *beast* about the numbers and got bitchy when anything was off.

*Perfect* manager.

"Okay, you're late," she mused, once she was done tapping in numbers on the tablet she was carrying around. "You're throwing me off my damn day."

"Our bad, sweetheart," Brandon grunted at her, knowing she had a particular soft spot for his handsome ass. As expected, her dramatically enhanced eyelashes fluttered as she reacted to him, shaking her head.

"You're the boss man, so I guess it's fine, *this time*," she purred. "How can I help you folks today?"

"Did you get a chance to check out that new club we were looking at?" I asked, drawing her attention to me. Instantly, her nose curled up, and she used one long acrylic nail to flip a bright blue tendril of wavy hair from her face.

"I did."

"And?"

"*And*," she huffed, turning away from me. "That shit is no *Club Allure*, I can tell you *that* much."

Brandon chuckled. "Nothing is gonna compare to what you've done with *Allure*, sweetheart. We're trying to figure out if you can repeat the phenomenon."

"I can do anything I put my mind to," she countered.

"Okay but *will you*?" I spoke up, pulling her attention back in my direction. "We're ready to write the check to buy the current owners out *today*. But not unless you're telling us we can depend on you to work your magic."

Instead of just answering, Dove pulled a vape pen from her pocket, taking a long inhale from it.

For dramatics.

And the *only* reason we were putting up with it was because she was damn good at what she did.

Brandon's father was the one who had hired her, poached from one of the clubs on the strip. There, she'd been grossly under-utilized, but the *Predators* had immediately seen the potential.

Dove was the kind of woman that commanded attention and demanded respect without saying a word. She'd been a dancer – and less-than-legal variations – herself, so she knew the ropes. Knew what was needed, knew how to make sure the staff was well taken care of.

Before bringing her on, *Club Allure* was the run-of-the-mill strip club— safe enough, clean enough, entertaining enough.

Over the course of six months, she'd turned it into a whole damn destination, one of the most popular outside the Vegas strip.

It brought in the kind of money we needed to be trying to replicate.

"Name your price, babe," I told her, knowing we still had another meeting to make it to. She was right; we were late, which meant we couldn't spend time wooing her into it, going over facts and figures.

It was either yes or no.

And it needed to be yes.

"I need an assistant," she said, meeting my gaze.

"You already needed that," I shrugged. "You want us to find one, or you're doing your own hiring?"

"I'll do my own hiring."

"Fine. You need an assistant manager too. For both clubs," I said, already knowing she'd shake her head before the movement started. "You're one woman, Dove, and you're already stretched thin."

"That's what the assistant is for. That's all I'll need."

"Brandon," I huffed, turning to him for backup. "Can I get some reinforcement here?"

"We can't have you burnt out, D," he agreed. "How about *one* assistant manager, so there's always somebody at one of the clubs?"

She sucked her teeth. "Fine. But y'all gotta find them. It can't be anybody that already works at that other club; obviously they don't know what the fuck they're doing."

"*Obviously*," I agreed. "What else?"

"Gotta be a man; it's already too much pussy around here. Nobody that's gonna be fucking the dancers either," she added, and I nodded.

"No heterobros, got it," I told her. "I'll put Keira on it, see if she knows anybody with ink that might work."

"What about Kev?" Brandon asked, and Dove and I *both* looked at him like he'd lost it. "Shit, my bad," he shrugged. "He needs something to do though."

"*Not* this," I countered. "He'd turn this place into a mad house."

"He's a little too pretty to be around here, have the girls forgetting all their training," Dove added, shaking her head.

"Keira will get it sorted," I assured, after another quick side eye at Brandon. "Thank you; this means a lot to us."

Dove nodded. "Jesse was good to me, never got handsy, gave me a chance nobody else would. Anything y'all need from me, you've got it," she said, then let us know she had to get back to her inventory management.

And *we* needed to get on to our next meeting.

"WHAT THE HELL are you thinking about so hard over there?" Brandon asked, a few minutes away from *Reverie*. "You've been quiet the whole ride."

I sighed, already knowing what the response would be if I answered truthfully, but I did anyway, keeping my eyes focused on the buildings passing on either side of the street. "Tattoos."

"Damn," he shook his head, navigating our last turn. "You're back on that?"

"I was never *off* it," I admitted, staring at his profile as he peered into traffic. "And I won't be, until I know what I want to know."

"Dog with a damn bone."

"And what about it?"

Brandon chuckled. "Nothing, damn. I'm just... do you even have any evidence? Any theories? Other than your gut?"

"The OGs taught us that trusting our gut was everything," I countered.

"So your gut is telling you ol' boy is bad news?"

"He definitely is for somebody."

"But not us?"

I sucked my teeth. "Nigga I don't *know*," I huffed. "I keep telling you; that's the damn problem."

"Okay, so like I said, do you have evidence?"

"You know I don't have evidence," I said, with a light mush to the side of his head that made him swat my hand away. "I might have a theory though."

"Well let's hear it, the two-minute version," he added, gesturing toward the *Reverie* entrance ahead.

Considering how ill-conceived it was... I really only needed *one*.

"So now you're telling me you think *anybody* with a rose or thorn tattoo is a fucking assassin, Tati?" he asked, incredulous, after I'd given him the rundown of what I was thinking after my conversation with Maite. "You've been watching too much TV. Or reading too many of those fucking books. One or the other."

"*Former* assassin," I corrected. "And, no, not everybody. Not every rose. A specific one, in a specific spot. Or a coverup, in that spot. And I'm checking biceps for thorns too."

"That is paranoid as fuck." He laughed. "What, you're gonna walk around hemming up random bitches 'cause of their ink?"

"Random ones? No. And if I'm right... the ones with *that* ink aren't exactly the kind of bitches I could hem up."

His eyes got big. "Damn, you think they tougher than you?"

"I think they're fucking killers."

"Former."

I shook my head as he pulled the car up to the valet. "Former assassins, as in they don't do it anymore. But once you've killed..."

"Always a killer," he muttered, the last words of our conversation as we stepped out of the car. At most places, we wouldn't do this valet shit; it left us too vulnerable.

But this wasn't most places.

We trusted the Whitfields enough to know we were good here, a comfort level that was confirmed by the warm, familial greeting we got from Kingston Whitfield himself as soon as we crossed the *Reverie Casino & Resort* threshold.

With his fine ass.

He was clean cut, privileged, well-spoken, all that jazz. He was Kev, except without the corniness. In another lifetime, I would've made him and his dimples my personal playground. In this one, he was a family man, and I respected that. It was all daps and hugs and asking after parents for a few minutes before he gestured for us to follow him.

"Let's talk business," he said, turning to lead the way.

Yes.

*Let's.*

While our territorial dispute with the *Marauders MC* had required enlisting the help of the Whitfields as well, this wasn't that, which was likely why Onyx hadn't been invited to tag along. *This* meeting was about the dispensary, a venture that could triple our annual revenue.

We just had a little licensing problem.

Meaning no one wanted to give us the appropriate fucking licenses.

They wouldn't dare turn down the Whitfield name though, so the unlikely friendship between our fathers was actually working in our favor. It didn't come without a bit of give and take; Kingston wanted stakes in the business, which was fine.

We'd all eat.

As we approached his office, I couldn't help noticing the security trailing just out of our sight lines, blending in with the crowds, staying discreet, but definitely following. I'd always thought that shit was so pretentious, hiring security for yourself like you were a damn celebrity.

The death of my father had me thinking twice.

There was always somebody who wanted what you had; somebody willing to do whatever it took to get it. And if not that... maybe they just wanted your ass gone, for whatever reason.

It was never a bad idea to have somebody watching your back.

It could wind up being the very thing that kept you alive.

I barely blinked over the appearance of Alicia – also known as Ace – the formidable head of the Whitfields' security, who'd branched out to a security firm of her own. I knew she was also a family friend, had been with them a long time, even though she was basically the same age as Kingston; just a few years older than me and Brandon.

Her ass had *always* been menacing, and now was no different.

Even with a pleasant smile on her face as she stood back, watching us get patted down, she carried a distinct air that she could kill you like it was nothing to her. And somehow, the fact that she was beautiful just made it more alarming. Just glancing at her, you might not know she was security; she was dressed more like a guest of the hotel. Chic black pants, simple white top, draped blazer, immaculate silk press... nothing to indicate just how dangerous she was.

She walked into the office with us, pulling King aside to say something.

"*Look*," Brandon muttered to me, with a quick, subtle gesture toward his own chest before he tipped his head toward her.

I followed his gaze to where she and King were talking, watching as she pushed her hands into her pockets. When she did, it pulled her blazer back, the camisole underneath offering a clear view to what Brandon was trying to show me.

It was just a peek.

Just a *corner.*

But it was definitely there.

*A goddamn rose tattoo.*

Quickly, I glanced away, giving him a wide-eyed look. A moment later, Ace gave us a nod as she left the office, breezing past us like she hadn't just blown my damn mind.

I tried to pay attention.

I really did.

We talked about expanding the gentleman's club, we talked about the dispensary, we talked about the potential for opening other bars like *Bottoms Up.*

But my head was reeling.

I couldn't keep myself from standing from my seat, declaring that I needed a moment before stepping out of the office.

To find Ace standing right on the other side.

"Can I help you?" she asked with a smile, probably thinking I needed the bathroom or something.

That's what I should have answered with.

*That's* where I should've gone.

But no.

"Your tattoo," I blurted, gesturing toward the spot, just above her armpit, even though it was covered now. "What does it mean?"

She stared at me for a moment, her eyes searching mine before she answered in a tone suddenly much cooler than what she'd greeted me with before. "It's just a flower."

"No, it's not." I shook my head. "And I need to know what it *is*."

Her gaze narrowed. "Why?"

Alarms went off in my head, and it struck me how incredibly stupid this was of me to confront her in this manner, alone.

Idiotic, honestly.

But I was out here now, and I couldn't *un*say the words.

"I need to know if it's related to another tattoo. A ring of thorns," I answered, pointing to my bicep like I had one.

A second later, she had the throat of my pretty blouse clutched in her fist, dragging me right up against her.

"Start talking, *right now*," she demanded, in a tone that invited no argument. "Tell me what you know and how you know it, about *that* tattoo."

Trust was no simple thing.

No simple *feat*.

Immersing yourself in an unfamiliar reality – one where trust was not only coveted, but *necessary* – was a challenge that easily rivaled some of my most harrowing missions in *The Garden*.

I'd been conditioned to expect attacks from all sides.

The same person I relied on to cover my ass in one operation could be the wielder of my demise in the next, best not to get *too* comfortable, with anybody.

Here?

That was blasphemous.

"You ain't tell me boss lady made you get your ink alone," Ozias hollered across the room at me as soon as I walked through the door of the clubhouse, a nondescript building tucked into about a mile of self-storage. From the outside, it was aggressively ordinary, brilliantly camouflaged to the stranger eye.

Beyond the gates though, concealed in an outer façade of run-down aluminum siding and ragged garage fronts, was an impressive sprawl of motorcycle lots, shooting ranges, bunkhouses, an arena – and a training area for it – and of course, the clubhouse.

It was decked out with tables, couches, TVs, a stocked bar; everything you could want to maximize kicking it without ever leaving the clubhouse, if you didn't want to.

I guess for when the club was in a more insular mood.

"I didn't think it was something I needed to lead with," I answered, stopping at the pool table that was essentially Ozzy's desk. I'd quickly realized he was always either here, or on the road, rarely any in-between. "It mean something I don't know about?"

"It means she doesn't fuck with you," he chuckled, in the grizzled rasp I'd come to expect in my short time of knowing him. As *Predators* road captain, he was the one who gave everybody their marching orders, even though that wasn't a "typical" structure.

Not that they did much in the "typical" way.

"So does that mean *nobody* fucks with me, since she doesn't?" I asked, watching as he lined up a shot in his solitary game.

He took his shot before he answered, picking up a fat cigar from a nearby ashtray to accompany his words. "That ink means can't nobody fuck with you, but *we* all fuck with you, you know what I mean?"

"No."

"Really?"

Shaking my head, I chuckled as I answered. "Nah, I follow you, but... I need to know what Tatiana's approval means around here. Obviously y'all respect her, and her word is law, but if she don't fuck with me..."

"Just means I shouldn't have sent you to check in on her, better if you keep your distance until she mellows out."

I raised an eyebrow. "How long does that usually take?"

"Well..." Ozzy stood back, surveying the balls still scattered on the pool table before he laughed. "She's been pissed at me since *The Fall*, and I've known her most of her life, so depending on what you did... might be a while."

"I haven't done shit to her," I immediately replied, shrugging. "What did you do?"

He pushed out a heavy sigh, then shook his head. "I didn't have a crystal ball."

"What does that mean?"

"I didn't anticipate the attack that took her daddy," he explained. "And some others. The only reason I wasn't out there too is 'cause I had a bum leg and couldn't ride. Otherwise..."

He drew a thumb across his neck, indicating that he would be dead too and I nodded.

"I thought it was out of the blue, no intel could've predicted it?" I asked.

"I didn't say she *blamed* me for it; I said she was pissed about it," Ozzy said, as if that shit was some sort of explanation.

Maybe it was.

Just some shit I didn't understand.

"Should I be worried about that? Her being pissed at me for a reason I don't understand?"

He smirked. "That's why I said it's best to stay out of her way. You're inked, so you're good with everybody. But she ain't everybody, so you ain't good."

"Meaning?" I insisted, just wanting a clear answer, but he shook his head.

"Meaning, stay out her damn face as much as you can."

I sighed, knowing it was pointless to press the man for any further answers on that front. "Okay... so what do I do instead?"

"Go see Retta, a couple doors down. Get her to put your package together."

"Bet."

I didn't linger, waiting for more cryptic advice from Ozzy; he was an old head, and clearly set in his methods. It made the most sense to me that I should be reporting straight to Blue. He was the damn president of the club, and he was the one who'd brought me on. He was the one who'd sanctioned my ink, without me going through whatever their usual process was.

But, with him handling business over the last few days, it had been troublesome getting in front of him.

I was patient, though.

Mostly, things were going as I'd anticipated. I'd gotten their attention and had already been invited into the fold. So far, the only kink in my plans was the mistrust from Tatiana, which I hadn't really accounted for.

I'd expected Blue to be the one with the trust issues, not her.

Not that it really mattered.

Her faith – or lack thereof – didn't really factor into my plans.

This shit wasn't about her.

Wasn't *supposed* to be, at least.

For unknown reasons, her skepticism actually... *bothered* me.

Had I lost my touch?

The fall of *The Garden* had meant the end of any missions, no continued trainings, but damn... was she not buying into my role?

Or was it that for the first time... I wasn't really playing a role at all?

There was no dossier to hide behind, no alias to get lost in, I was just... a nobody, at least by their standards. Some lonely outsider seeking a place in the world to belong. A drifter searching for a motive to stick around.

I was all of those things.

But also, none of them.

I'd gladly fulfill my personal mission and move on, with no thoughts of these people in my rear view.

That was the objective when this place had first landed in my sights.

When I'd closed my eyes last night though, my thoughts had been less about the release I'd feel when my objective was complete, and more about the angry vice president of the *Predators*.

She sure was comfortable with that damn gun.

*And I sure was comfortable with her.*

I shook my head, clearing away the thought as I headed where Ozias had sent me, to the armory, to talk to Retta. For obvious reasons, her domain was next to the gun range, my next destination.

My thoughts had strayed so far from my objective that clearly I was rusty.

Shooting up a target was a great way to get refocused.

Vegas was good for disappearing.

Crawling with tourists and gamblers and junkies and nomads, you could easily never see the same face twice if you played it right.

Unless maybe someone was looking for you.

And even then, if you were smart enough – good enough – you could live a life of perfect immersion with the crowd. You just had to understand... there was a certain art to being watched.

You had to be ready to fluidly navigate between genres at any time, whatever fit the situation you'd found yourself in. Maybe a guileless baroque era piece—no nuance, just a subject laid bare, offering a knowing smirk. You knew you were being watched, and the watcher knew you were aware.

A very classic style, admiral.

Personally, I had a penchant for performance art.

The elegant equilibrium of maintaining natural movements; no hesitations, no embellishments. The precarious willingness to take your eyes off a target that might be trying to kill you, while not eschewing the disinterested sort of eye contact one might unconsciously make. Curtailing the impulse to drop a motherfucker and coax out all your antagonists, just get the shit out of the way.

All a beautiful challenge I welcomed, even when I wasn't in the fucking mood, because I didn't have much of a choice in the matter anyway.

This was happening.

*Bottoms Up* wasn't exactly a dive bar, but it was no upscale place either. The kinda spot where you weren't *likely* to get shot but there was always a chance.

That was part of why I liked it.

Aside from the obvious proximity to the *Predators*, it was just my kinda spot, purely on the likelihood of shit popping off.

I just hadn't expected *this*.

Apparently, I *had* lost my touch.

I feigned another swig of my midday beer – too early to drink anything harder – knowing it wouldn't do to add anything more to my current low-level inebriation. After I was done shooting shit up at the range, Ozzy had sent me over here to act as additional muscle for Keira – club secretary – who was managing the bar.

She was the one who'd put the beer in front of me.

Another mistake on my part.

I was good, but the *Rose*s and probably a couple *Thorns* that were currently scattered throughout this bar were just as good—probably *better*, with no alcohol tainting their vigilance.

*Shit.*

Where had I gone wrong?

Whose attention had I gotten at such a level to warrant *this* response? I shook my head, realizing their presence meant this place was burned as a spot where I could relax; a damn shame because I really liked *Bottoms Up*.

Randomly, the fresh new ink on my neck itched, reminding me of my new allegiance. I put a hand to it, but didn't scratch, not wanting to fuck it up.

As if the whole idea of all this wasn't already fucked up.

Had I *really* expected this shit to work in my favor?

"Is that good?"

I looked at the beautiful woman who'd slid onto the empty barstool beside me, gesturing at my beer. Some craft shit I was probably enjoying a little too much.

I nodded, taking her in as I returned her smile.

Natural hair twisted into thick ropes framing a deceptively pretty face, big brown eyes.

*Fine*, honestly.

"I'll have your neck snapped before any help can get to you, sweetheart," I leaned in and told her, cutting through the bullshit as I met those big, pretty eyes with mine. "But that's really not how I wanted my day to go."

A full-blown smile, none of the flirty shit spread across her face then. "I'm sure you think so," she said. "But it's a good thing we don't have to test that theory, huh? My boss just wants to talk to you."

"Fuck you, and fuck your boss," I told her, shaking my head. "People who just want to talk make a phone call."

She nodded. "I get it. I had the *exact* same reaction before I was brought into the fold. I didn't trust shit, because why should I? Submitting to *just a conversation* went against every damn thing I was taught."

I stared at her, knowing exactly what she was doing. It was the same thing I would do if I was on the other side of this exchange.

Still.

"Your persuasion tactic isn't working."

"It's not a persuasion tactic," she countered. "I'm just telling you what I know. You don't need to be persuaded."

I raised an eyebrow. "And why is that?"

"The conversation isn't a request," she scoffed. "You're *going* to have it. It's just that you could make it easy, or *we* can make it very, very hard."

I ran my fingers along the condensation of the glass bottle, using the moment for some necessary mental calculation. "Was there any scenario where you thought I'd choose easy?"

She grinned and shook her head. "No. But it was worth a shot."

"Is your employer the type to make a scene in a room full of people?" I asked and the *Rose* shook her head.

"Nope. I'm sure you can get past us in here—make it outside," she admitted. "But you won't get any further."

"I think you're underestimating me."

She shrugged. "Maybe."

"How many of y'all are there?" I asked, and she laughed.

"Now why would I tell you that?"

"Aren't we family?" I asked. "Grown on the same farm, all that jazz..."

She chuckled. "That's cute. *You're* cute. We'll revisit that *family* thing after you talk to the boss."

As if that was ever going to happen.

Willingly, at least.

I pushed away from my seat with no preamble, heading toward the back of the bar.

"Oh, we're starting now?!" she called after me.

Yeah.

We were starting now.

I was much more familiar than they could possibly be with the maze of hallways and doors that lay beyond the main room of *Bottoms Up*. It was a smart design, laid out that way for the *Predators* to use as a quick getaway if they ever found themselves in need of one.

Here I was, in need.

Surely my former companion seedlings had done some recon, but I had to take the chance that maybe they hadn't had time to do enough. They were on me before I even got to the back, but I was quick—it only took a few doorways before I'd lost them in the maze.

But I knew that was only the first step.

Briefly, it crossed my mind to engage some of the *Predators* for help, but I couldn't drag them into this, not with trained killers. I was on my own, the same as it had kinda always been.

At least when I was being smart.

I had to assume my apartment was burnt, even though I didn't have any hints as to what had put me on their radar. I had a room at *The Drake* I could use to lay low for the night, but that was deep in the middle of the action —*Bottoms Up* was on the outskirts.

I still had to actually get there.

I made my way to a side entrance of *Bottoms* that I knew was camouflaged on the outside to blend in with the other bricks. I eased it open slowly, but there was only one direction I could check for danger on the other side.

I had to take a chance.

I took a deep breath, steeling myself to get ready to run, hoping I could make it either to my bike, or someone else's. If I had to borrow one, I'd make sure it was returned to the owner.

I was two steps out the door before they were on me.

I easily dodged one attempt to grab me, and then another, sacrificing my line of sight against the third. He caught me with a jab I ate like it was nothing, then sent one right back.

If these were regular people, I could have handled it with no problem.

But they weren't.

We had the same training, the same discipline, and I was severely outnumbered. I couldn't have expected it to go much differently than it did.

There wasn't any type of training that would have made me impervious to the electric current from a taser as it coursed through me, snatching away my ability to move or fight back. I dropped to the ground, stripped of control over my limbs.

I knew the needle was coming before I felt the jab, and there was nothing I could do to combat it. The last face I saw was the woman from the bar, gazing sympathetically at me as whatever was in the syringe started its quick course through my blood.

"I know it sucks," she said, "but it's the only way to ensure no more fighting between us. Nobody gets hurt this way."

I understood that.

I did.

But I was still on the ground, injected with foreign substance without my consent, all in service of conversation I didn't even want to have.

So I was sure she didn't take it personal when I used the last of my faculties to look her right in the eyes, and tell her one more time...

*"Fuck you."*

# Chapter Six

## NYX

I groaned as I peeled my eyes open, forcing them to stay that way so I could take in my surroundings.

*Good job, Nyx.*

*Another fucking windowless room.*

My head was fuzzy, limbs sluggish, but a quick check didn't reveal any swelling, no cuts or gashes. Which I took to mean I had *not* gotten my ass kicked while I was unconscious.

A good sign.

Maybe.

It could also be a way of giving me a false sense of security. I'd woken up mostly intact, but I was still in a room with only one way out, a single door, probably locked.

I was familiar with this kind of room.

I'd *put* people in this kind of room.

The table was bolted to the floor, but the chair was not. I didn't see any mechanism for locking someone's hands to the tabletop, surprisingly. I had done enough snatch and grabs to have a firm grasp on all the tips, tricks, tools, and toys.

I just wasn't sure what methodology was about to be employed *here*.

A sound just outside the room told me it was time to find out.

As the door swung open, I forced my heavy eyelids to stay open, trying to pull on any readiness for whatever I could muster.

The woman who walked in was... familiar.

Painfully so.

Whatever drugs they'd given me, I was still foggy to the point of discomfort, so I couldn't immediately bring it to mind. I *could* catalog the details of her though, filing them away for what would hopefully be another day in my life.

Tawny skin, athletic build, nice face. Her long hair swung behind her in a single braid as she turned away from me to close the door.

I shook my head, ignoring the steady pounding inside my skull. "You think I don't know exactly what you're doing?"

"What am I doing, Nyx?" she asked, moving to take the seat across from me at the table.

*How the fuck does she know my name?*

"You're trying to make me think you're not a threat," I told her, eyes narrowed. "Make me think you're stupid enough to turn your back to me when I'm unshackled. But I know better. How many motherfuckers are on the other side of that door waiting? Ten? Twenty?"

She shrugged. "I *do* have a lot of operatives here at my compound, and I like to think the vast majority of them would be pretty upset about it if you decide to lay a hand on me. But you're wrong about why I showed you my back," she noted, smiling. "It wasn't because I want you to think *I'm* not a threat. It's because I trust *you* not to be a threat to *me*."

"That's stupid," I quipped, and she laughed, shaking her head.

"I can understand why you'd think so, but I think your brain just needs to settle in with it a little more," she said. "The sedative will wear off. I don't believe you would hurt me at all."

"Enlighten me," I said, tipping my head to the side, my muffled thoughts working overtime trying to pinpoint who this woman was.

"I'd like to think I raised you somewhat. As much as any of us were *raised* rather than... constructed."

My eyes narrowed even further, sharp pain coursing through my head as I absorbed her words. I had to look away, had to close my eyes for a moment to give them a break, but when my gaze returned to her face, it was like I could see her more clearly now.

It provided no comfort.

My mind *still* wouldn't produce the direct connection of who the hell this woman was.

"I've been away from *The Garden* a long time. A lifetime, it feels like," she corrected herself, "Before I went back to take it down. I remember you—the angriest little motherfucker I'd ever seen. They sent you to me because the men couldn't tame you. No matter how much they abused you, you wouldn't break. So they thought you needed a mother figure. And I favored yours, they said. A different kind of torture."

*Shit.*

I closed my eyes again, trying to shut away the sudden rush of grief and rage and... knowledge.

I knew now, who she was.

Knew why my brain was fighting so hard against it.

"You left me," I grumbled, my fists clenching tight against the cold metal surface of the table.

A deep breath rushed from my lungs after those words—my most immediate coping method to manage this abrupt, dizzying blast of emotion. I was fighting hard against the childish urge to lash out in violence, an impulse I'd long conquered, but her words had brought me right back to a moment in time I'd worked hard to suppress.

It took her a moment to respond to that, and when she did, there was a strain in her voice. "I did." She nodded. "But I hope you know it wasn't because I had a choice."

"Why then?" I asked, finally meeting her eyes so I could glare into them directly. "Huh? You were one of the only people in that place who ever gave a shit about me, and then one day you were just... gone."

Her gaze was... soft.

Nostalgic.

It pissed me off even more.

"Nyx, I'm surprised to hear you cared so much." She countered my words, with the hint of a grin playing at the corners of her mouth. "As many times as I had to whoop your ass to make it clear I wasn't going to let you whoop mine."

I shook my head. "I *let* you win," I claimed and she laughed.

"No you didn't," she insisted. "You couldn't back then and you can't now."

I grunted, knowing she was trying to provoke me at this point. "If this is supposed to be a happy reunion, you've got a funny way of showing it."

"I never claimed happy," she said, her tone losing the amused edge. "But a reunion... yes. It's definitely that." She laced her fingers together, leaning over the table a bit. "What are you doing in Vegas, Nyx? Why are you here? You here for me?"

"Why the fuck would I be here for you?" I snapped. "You *left* me," I told her, jabbing a finger in her direction—an emotional slip I instantly wished I could take back.

I wasn't a fucking kid anymore; I was a grown ass man.

I was supposed to be beyond *this*.

"Because *The Collective* said so," she snapped right back, glaring at me as she reclined in her chair, arms crossed. "I was nineteen years old, and still under their control. What the fuck was I supposed to do?"

"The same thing you told me to do, *fight*."

She stared for a moment, and then asked, "And why the fuck do you think you're free now?"

My eyebrows went up. "Oh yeah, that's right. *The Mighty Garden*, taken down by the long-lost heiress of the Pelletiers," I grunted, not bothering to keep the cynicism from my voice. "I heard the rumors. That really was you?"

"I'm here aren't I?" She gestured around us. "This compound is full of *Thorns* and *Roses* who found their way to Vegas. Who found their way to *me*."

"Well isn't that just a fucking hallmark card?" I countered with a smirk. "A house full of sons and daughters you could never have on your own, right?" I asked, wanting her to feel even an ounce of the same hurt I was.

Too bad I felt like shit as soon as the words were off my lips.

I saw the way that jab hit her.

Harder than intended.

Worse than she deserved.

Briefly, her eyes closed and then a cold sort of smile spread over her lips, just a flash before she suppressed it.

"I understand that you're angry," she started, deadly calm. "You were twelve when I left, and for years, I was the only semblance of a maternal relationship you knew. And then I was gone. You get to be angry about that." She nodded. "But I need you to remember... I was a fucking child too. 'Trained', abused, used, *just like you*. I'm not the enemy."

"You're right," I conceded, hands raised. "That shit was uncalled for. I'm sorry."

She shook her head, blowing me off. "Don't be. Honestly, if you want to be angry with me... you know what? Okay. You wouldn't be the first person."

For a long moment, we just looked at each other, neither of us speaking.

"What are you telling me any of this for?" I asked, finally breaking the silence.

"I'm telling you this as a preamble to the fact that although I understand

your anger... I'm still gonna need some answers from you. For example –
*again* – why are you in Vegas?"

"I like the sounds the slot machines make," I answered, offering her a
grin.

From the look on her face, she wasn't amused.

"Look, I can't force you to join us. But I *cannot* have you running around
this city without knowing your motives." She shrugged. "I have people to
look out for. You understand that, right?"

I frowned. "I'm not here to disrupt your precious family, if that's what
you're concerned about," I told her. "I've been laying low; I haven't bothered
anybody."

Her eyebrows shot up. "You haven't bothered anybody? I heard you beat
five or six niggas up," she said, tossing her hands. "Broken bones, all that." She
laughed. "I bet *they're* feeling quite bothered."

"They started it," I said, even though it wasn't *quite* the truth and already
knowing what her response was going to be.

She laughed. "That was always your thing wasn't it?" she asked. "*They
started it.* No matter that you had the power to walk away. *They started it*, so
you had to finish."

"You're damn right I did," I grunted, really not appreciating her tone.
"You've got a lot of nerve, being on this maternal energy with me."

She sighed. "You're right. I don't have any license to take that tone with
you anymore. But the fact remains... you running around Vegas doing God
knows what is a liability for me and the reputation I've built."

"That sounds selfish as fuck."

She shook her head. "No—I'm worried about my people that I brought
here. They came in because they want peace. They don't want to be hunted;
they don't want any trouble. But if somebody with *that* on their arm," she
said, pointing at my thorns, "*The same ink they wear,* is going around causing
trouble, what do you think it tells the world about them?"

"Not to fuck with them," I countered, and she nodded.

"Yes, but in more than just the way you're implying, which is what I need
you to get. Don't hire me for a job. Don't say yes to a date. Any number of
things. You should know, these people have been through enough. *You've*
been through enough, Nyx. Believe it or not, you need people. Let me help
you."

"Appreciate the offer, but I think I'm good," I said, shaking my head. "I
made it this far. I'll be okay."

"It's not about being okay, it's about thriving."

"I don't give a shit about that," I admitted. I wasn't there mentally—wasn't anywhere close. "You've got all these questions about why I'm in Vegas, how about you tell me how you found me?"

She sighed, then pointed at her neck, and for a moment I was confused, until a little itch reminded me of my fresh ink.

Shit.

"Okay, but *how*?"

"You attracted the wrong person's curiosity," she answered. "Consider yourself lucky I was filling in at *Reverie*, because if ol' girl had asked a different *Rose* about her ink, she might be pushing up daisies right now."

I frowned. "What the fuck are you talking about?" I asked, even as my brain tried to pull up an answer of my own.

*Reverie?*

Blue had a meeting there earlier, him and Tati...

*Fucking Tati...*

I knew she had her issues with me, didn't trust me, but damn.

"You made her suspicious," Alicia said, as if she'd heard what was going through my head. "A woman like that gets answers, one way or another. With the right training, she would have made a good *Rose*, honestly."

"So she ratted me out?" I asked, my mind racing with unknown information.

"No," she answered. "She asked a certain question to a certain person. A question *you* put on her mind. So you kinda ratted yourself out."

"Yeah," I scoffed. "If you say so. Where is she now?"

Alicia raised an eyebrow. "Why? What are you going to do? It's not *her* fault you got caught. The blame for that rests solely on you."

I huffed. "What? You think I'm going to do something to her? You think *that's* why I'm asking where she is?"

"Isn't it?"

"No," I insisted. "I'm trying to make sure *you* didn't do anything to *her*."

She shook her head. "We have a policy against harming innocents around here. Which is part of why, again, I'm going to need certain assurances from you before I let you walk out of here. I know Brandon Garrett brought you on as muscle for his war with the *Marauders*."

I rolled my eyes. "*Blah, blah, blah, stop the gang violence, blah, blah, nobody else has to get hurt, blah, blah, blah.* I'm guessing your spiel is going to go something like that?"

"Nope." Alicia laughed. "The *Marauders* are racist assholes; I don't care if they die or not. What *I* care about is the collateral damage this little rivalry leaves in its wake."

"So that's what you're on now, some save the world shit?"

"No, not at all. Last year a politician named Tommy Turner put a hit out on his mistress. Who happened to also be the mother of his child."

I blew out a sigh and shrugged. "Okay. What does that have to do with anything?"

"He used a *Thorn* to do it. Isaiah."

My eyes went wide. "Isaiah as in…"

"Yeah," she nodded. "Isaiah as in your little rival-slash-homeboy from back in *The Garden*. He wants to see you, by the way. He tells me that y'all lost touch a while ago."

"We didn't lose touch, we were…" I stopped and shook my head.

*Separated,* was the word for it.

I clenched my jaw, mentally brushing aside the feelings associated with all that. "After *The Garden*, I went radio silent, because *that's* what we were supposed to do if we didn't know what the fuck was going on. Not pull together a convent."

"I called it a *compound*," she corrected me, laughing. "Not a convent. But anyway, your friendship with Isaiah is not really why I brought it up. Since that incident, the air in Vegas has just been feeling… ominous. It doesn't feel like anything I've felt around here before."

"Alicia, what are you saying?"

She was quiet for a long moment, and then looked me in the eyes. "You know who Renard Belrose is?"

My whole body went tense.

She knew the answer to that.

"How could I not?"

I hated the sympathy in her eyes when she nodded. "Right. Well… do you remember when you'd just come to *The Garden*? You were probably around nine years old…"

"How could I forget?"

"I don't mean in general, Nyx," she explained. "I'm talking about something specific. It would've been the first time you met Renard. He came to visit Etienne."

*Shit.*

All these years later, as a free, grown ass man, and their names still sent a tight feeling through my chest.

"Yeah, I remember," I assured her. "He wanted to take me with him and

Etienne wouldn't let him. But it never felt like it was about protecting me. It was more like…"

"Protecting an asset," Alicia filled in for me. "Something was *off* with Renard. I mean, the whole thing was fucked up, but *him* especially. Did you know he was the one who started *The Garden*?"

I shook my head. "No. Why would I?"

"You're right," she agreed. "It's not common information. I'm not even sure I'm supposed to know. It just keeps playing in my mind. I overheard them arguing about the direction of *The Garden*. Etienne seemed kind and merciful, compared to his brother."

"Now *that's* hilarious," I scoffed. "You must not know how shit started going down after you left."

She shook her head. "No, I'm well aware. Don't get me wrong, Etienne Belrose is an evil motherfucker. But Renard is worse. And that's frightening."

I chuckled. "What, you think you're going to say his name in a mirror five times and he's going to appear?"

"I think he's already here," she said, and the smile slipped off my face.

"I… thought he was dead."

"So did I," she nodded. "But those evil old men… they always hang in there for the long haul, don't they?"

I leaned in over the table. "What makes you so sure?"

"I'm not *sure*," she clarified. "There are rumors of him being stateside. I don't know if he's here for revenge against me for taking his brother down, or to rebuild *The Garden*, or just to see the sights… I don't know. But what I *do* know is, we have to be careful. We have to watch out for each other."

"So then what was that about not wanting any collateral damage, not wanting me to be a bad example of the ink and shit?"

"All of that is still valid," she said. "It's part of looking out for each other. We can't make ourselves unnecessary targets. Renard Belrose comes here, what do you think is going to happen? You think he's *not* going to buy the police? You get arrested with those thorns on your arm, *what do you think will happen?*"

I shrugged. "I'm not afraid to die."

She leaned across the table too, getting right in my face. "He's not going to kill you, Nyx. He's going to *play your song*."

*Shit.*

I blew out a sigh.

I didn't want to let it show on my face, but honestly… that shit sent a chill up my spine.

"What is it you want from me?" I asked her.

"I want you to be safe. I want you to be whole."

"That ship has sailed. What else?"

Her eyes narrowed. "What are you doing in Vegas?" she asked me again.

"I told you, I like the casinos. And I made a few friends." I shrugged. "Came for the slot machines, stayed for the brotherhood," I said, smirking as I pointed at the *Predators* ink on my neck.

She stared at me for a long moment, then shook her head. I could tell she wasn't convinced, but I wasn't sure I needed her to be.

"I'm not going to have anybody watch you, Nyx," she said, after a moment had passed. "I don't think you're telling me the whole story, but I don't get the feeling you're here for any trouble either. With your *former* brotherhood that is."

I scoffed. "We weren't a family, Alicia. We were trauma bonded victims."

"I choose to see it differently." She pushed up from her seat, still staring at me. "I like the locs. And the earring," she said, setting off a weird feeling in my chest. She tipped her head to one side, peering at me, then the other, then grinned. "You never did get the other side pierced I see."

"Don't read into it!" I called after her, as she flung the door open and headed out.

"I think I'm going to read *everything* into it." She laughed, noticing that I'd hopped up too, and had followed her. "You're free to go," she told me. "Your bike was just brought up from the garage."

I frowned. "*How the hell...* never mind," I said.

Honestly it would have been more of a surprise if they *hadn't* identified my vehicle.

I stopped my exit to turn and look her in the face. "You never said what you did to Tati."

Alicia smiled. "She's beautiful, Nyx."

"What the fuck does that have to do anything?" I grunted. "*Where* is she?"

If something happened to her, the *Predators* entire focus would shift to *that*, which wasn't what I needed.

She shrugged. "How the hell should I know? The bar, the clubhouse, or home, or... wherever else the *Predators* hang out, I guess. But hey, don't take *your* mistake out on her."

*Funny.*

Tati was too precious to Blue for me to fuck with like that.

"I won't." I breezed past her through the door.  The first place my gaze went was up, to the sky, finding my map in the stars.

"There's a tracker on my bike, isn't there?" I asked.

"I don't need to track you, Nyx. I trust you. And... I've got a feeling *you'll* come back to *me*."

I climbed on my bike, and shook my head before I took off, tossing one last statement over my shoulder.

"I wouldn't count on it."

# *Chapter Seven*

## TATI



That question played in my mind over and over, hours long after I'd made the mistake of opening my mouth.

I didn't know what I expected the outcome to be when I'd asked Alicia about that tattoo, but it certainly hadn't been getting snatched up and fearing for my life.

Though in retrospect... it's exactly what I *should* have anticipated.

And I didn't even end up with any answers, not direct ones at least. If anything, I had *more* questions now, based on the questions she had asked *me*.

*How long has Nyx been in Vegas?*

*Why is he here?*

*Who has he been talking to?*

*What do you know about him?*

I didn't know *anything*, not really.

My curiosity was cured though.

As much as I wanted to know about Onyx and those thorns on his bicep, I was *much* more interested in keeping my damn head attached to my neck. Alicia had sent me back into that meeting like it was nothing, and I played it off in front of the men like everything was cool.

For hours.

Kingston had lunch brought in, and we talked more, made plans, all that, until *finally* we could get the fuck outta there. Brandon was hype about business happenings, yammering away about it all when we first got back in the car, but once we were well away from *Reverie*, I explained the situation to him.

"Why the *fuck* would you say something to her about the ink, Tati?!" he asked, eyes wide. Already, he was reaching under the seat, looking around as he navigated traffic to make sure we weren't being followed.

"She doesn't give a shit about *us*," I tried to tell him, but he shook his head.

"How are you going to say that as if you didn't get hemmed up?"

I blew out a sigh. "For information about Onyx, nothing more. This is something way over our heads."

"What makes you so sure? She told you something else you forgot to mention?"

"No." I shook my head. "She didn't tell me anything else, but her reaction to my question, then the questions *she* asked... doesn't that kinda say it all?"

Brandon was silent a moment, then nodded. "Call Nyx. *Now.* We need to give him some kind of heads up. If he hasn't already been got."

"What part of *this is over our heads* did you not hear?" I asked. "If he wanted our help with this shit, he should've dropped a hint when I asked his ass over and over is this something we need to be concerned about?"

"He's inked. We're supposed to watch his back."

I huffed. "Seriously? This shit is exactly why he never should've *been* inked! We've got enough problems without whatever this rose and thorn shit is!"

"*Grow up,*" Brandon snapped, shaking his head. "The nigga has a past, *so what?!* I know you're trying to live up to what your pops did for the club – he kept an eye on everybody, all that – *I get it.* But we're off that right now; we *have* to be."

"Based on *what*?"

"*The Fall,*" he countered, turning to glare at me as we pulled up to a stoplight. "I don't know who our enemies are right now, and we can't just let that ride. It's been too much fucking time, and we're out here looking pussy because we haven't made anybody pay for that shit!"

"We can't answer that call without a goddamn structure in place, Brandon! You act like we've done nothing when we've been building... *rebuilding*. What do you think we've been doing all day?"

"This *front office* shit is business, Tati. Yeah, it's important, I get it, but if we lose sight of the fact that somebody is gonna pay for trying to take us out—"

"I haven't lost sight of *shit*."

"Then you should understand exactly why a motherfucker like Nyx is inked. 'Cause that's exactly the type of muscle we need. Or what, you wanna take *Kev* to the front lines?" he asked.

"Fuck you!" I laughed, shaking my head.

There was silence between us for a moment, and then...

"Call Nyx," Brandon told me again, and I groaned about it, but... I called.

No answer.

I called Keira.

She had seen him earlier, talking to some chick she'd never seen in the bar before, but then she got called away for something. When she went back, he was gone.

No one had seen him since then.

Nobody knew where he was.

Not that he was *usually* easy to pin down, but this felt different.

Maybe because I knew what I'd done.

Had I... gotten him killed?

No.

*No.*

That was ridiculous.

That was some... thriller movie bullshit.

But still...

When Kev tried to talk his way over to my place for the second night in a row, I shut it down, wanting to be alone with my thoughts instead of getting poked and prodded.

No matter how good a little *poking* may have felt.

If nothing else, it would have been a good distraction from the problem I was having now, in my bed, which was not being able to relax. Even after popping melatonin, even with white noise in my ears, I was way too unsettled.

*You fucked up, kid.*

I could hear my father's voice in my head clear as day, offering a truth I didn't *want* to hear. My suspicions about Onyx had gotten him in some kind of trouble, with dangerous people. I wasn't wrong to be wary of him and his motives, but my reckless "investigation" had put a target on his back.

And for *that?*

I was dead ass wrong.

My eyes popped open and I stared up at the ceiling, debating the value of getting Kingston involved. He was a pretty direct line to Alicia—the only connection we had to her, really. I didn't *want* to go that route, no, but...

He was inked.

And that shit meant something.

Meant everythi—*what was that?*

I pulled my earbuds out and sat up straight, grabbing my phone to navigate to the app that would show me the feed from all the security cameras. It was the middle of the night, and I wasn't expecting anybody, but I could swear I heard knocking at my door.

Brandon was pissed at me, Keira was probably sleep, and so was Maite. If this was Kev, thinking he could change my mind... I was cussing his ass out via the mic; 'cause I wasn't opening my damn door.

Except... I didn't see anybody.

Weird.

*Was I hearing things?*

I didn't *think* there was any way I could have imagined a sound so vivid and loud, so I tapped into the section that would show me any recorded "events". Anything that had set off the motion detectors or certain sound sensors would be logged.

My eyes narrowed at my screen. There was definitely an "event" from a moment ago, but on the video clip, there was clearly nobody there at the door.

I frowned.

Maybe it was some wild animal or something?

I shook it off, dropped my phone beside me and closed my eyes again, trying again to force myself to relax.

*Shit.*

There the sound was again.

This time I got right up, grabbing my gun from the nightstand before I headed for my front door in the dark, checking the camera feeds on my phone again on my way. There was *still* no one there, and still nothing that would explain something like this. Just before I rounded the corner to my front door, the knock sounded again, clear as day. And yet... nothing on the camera.

*What if the camera is hacked?*

The thought stopped me in my tracks.

What if I was being shown a pre-recorded loop or something, and there actually *was* someone there? With my back to the wall, gun raised, I shot a text to Teo. He was the tech whiz around here and had installed my security system in the first place.

My next move was to call Brandon. If someone *was* here, if this *was* an attack...

*Shit.*

A loud thump made me abandon the idea of a call—I needed to defend myself, *now*. If I was going out, it *wouldn't* be quietly.

I turned the safety off on my gun, made sure I had a bullet in the chamber... and opened my front door, ready for whatever was on the other side.

Nothing, still.

*What the fuck?*

"Expecting someone?"

I turned my weapon towards the source of the voice, finger on the trigger. Before I could squeeze, the gun was snatched from my hand, and the next thing I knew, I was pinned against my front door, my hands twisted behind my back, my face pressed against the cold metal.

"Hey, sweetheart," Onyx murmured in my ear, sending a deep prickle of something fear-adjacent over my skin as I wrestled against him. He was heavy, too sturdy for my efforts to get away to do anything more than make me lose my breath. "You wanted to know what I do, right?" he asked. "You wanted to know what the thorns meant?"

I sucked in air for my distressed lungs to answer. "That you break into defenseless women's homes to rape and kill them?" I guessed, still struggling in vain against his hold.

"Calling yourself *defenseless* is a stretch of massive proportions, sweetheart." He chuckled; his breath warm against my skin before he very suddenly released his hold. "And I'm not here to do either one of those things to you."

"How the *fuck* did you get in my house?!" I asked, rounding on him, fists raised. "And I'm not your damn sweetheart. Is this funny to you?"

"Not at all." He shrugged, leaning against my foyer table. "It's very serious. I've never raped anybody personally, but killing? Maiming? Interrogation? Torture? I'm your guy. You wanted your answer, so there it is."

My heart was still racing as my eyes narrowed, my brain working overtime to process his words. "So you're... what? CIA gone wrong or something?"

"If I was CIA, I would just kill you for blowing my cover." He laughed.

"It's not a joke!" Pure frustration fueled my actions as I launched myself at him, fists swinging. I managed to clock him against the side of the head, but it was a glancing blow that didn't affect him as he easily pushed me away.

"Stop." He chuckled, which only pissed me off more. "I'm *not* joking.

You've been digging into shit you had no business digging in, and it could have gotten your ass in trouble. *Real* trouble."

"Real trouble with *who*? With *who?!*" I repeated, following as he turned and took it upon himself to go deeper into my damn house, stopping in my kitchen. "And you still haven't answered how the fuck you got in here!"

"The same way I would have gotten in anywhere. A very special set of skills," he said, taking the liberty of opening my fridge and picking a box of Chinese takeout. I watched, stunned, as he didn't even bother with a fork; he just opened it and started eating my noodles with his fingers.

"You're an *animal*," I huffed, even as I made sure to keep my distance. It wasn't lost on me that he'd confirmed all my worst suspicions, and now he was in my house.

Alone.

And nobody knew he was here.

"What are you doing here?" I asked, backing into the doorway in case I needed to take off running to get away from him.

He may have disarmed me once, but it wouldn't happen again.

He met my gaze, smirking at me as if he knew why I wasn't closer. "Making sure Alicia and her flunkies didn't kick your ass."

*So he definitely knows about that...*

I scoffed. "What were you going to do if they did?"

"Actually..." He stopped eating to look off in the distance, then shrugged. "I don't know. I *do* know nobody would have been happy about it." He shot me a grin, then stuck another pinch of noodles in his mouth.

He was incredibly nonchalant about the fact that he'd broken into my home, scared the shit out of me, and now he was just... eating my damn food.

I hated that the energy of it was so...

*Attractive.*

That was the word I didn't want to find—the truth I didn't want to accept about why his very existence bothered me so much.

Crossing my arms, I shook off the unwelcome feeling. "I was laying in here concerned that maybe I'd gotten you *killed*. Yet here you are, being a fucking menace."

He stared at me a moment, his dark eyes boring into mine, searching for something like always. Then he grinned, and it hit me like a jolt between the legs. "I think you like it."

Uncomfortable with how right he was, I shifted where I stood, glaring at him. "Why the hell would I enjoy having somebody constantly on my nerves?" I asked, halfway hoping he had an actual answer.

He dragged his teeth over his bottom lip, swiping a hand over his chin before he shrugged. "Because you're bored."

"Bored?" I drew my head back and chuckled. "When exactly would I find time to be *bored*, considering who I am, and what I do?"

He shook his head, and then over another mouthful of my noodles, said, "You misunderstand. I think you're bored in a very *particular* manner that I'm too much of a gentleman to specify."

"And I think that boredom draws you right *here*," he added, pointing at his chest with a wink that said it all, and...

*Shit.*

I huffed, refusing to let him think he was right, not easily, at least. "Are you *really* flipping this whole fucked-up visit into telling me you think I'm not getting fucked right?"

"I *know* you're not getting fucked right. Not if we're talking about *Kev*," he said, putting a very particular twang on Kev that almost made me laugh.

*Almost.*

"This is part of it, right?" I asked, frustration driving me to put my fear aside and stalk up to the counter as he continued digging into my food with his damn hands. "Your act? You charm people, you put on a show. The tattoos, the locs, the earring, the grill, the whole... *vibe*. Is that even real, or is this just a job for you? This is your costume? Me and Brandon marks?"

"I don't do that anymore," Onyx snapped, his whole demeanor switching as he barked out the words. "What you see is *me*. I'm never going back to that other shit—not as long as it's up to me," he added, a cryptic response that made me frown.

"What does *that* mean?"

He grunted and shook his head. "Nothing for you to worry about. Hey, what spot are these from?" he asked, gesturing at the noodles again. "These are good as hell."

"Nobody cares about those fucking *noodles*," I said, smacking them out of his hand, trying to send the container flying across the kitchen.

"Yo!" He reacted quickly, somehow catching the damn container, but his expression looked truly hurt. "I got drugged, kidnapped, and woke up in a windowless room because of you. I'm hungry, and instead of going to the buffet, I come check on *you*. And *this* is how you do?" He shook his head. "I knew your ass was mean, but this is *cold*."

Drugged?

Kidnapped?

A windowless room?

"You're serious?" I asked, and my anger drained in tandem with his answering nod. "Look…I'm sorry," I told him, in earnest. "I wasn't thinking about something like that happening to you, about anything happening to you. I just… I don't fucking know you, and you haven't exactly been forthcoming. I saw Alicia's tattoo, and I'd been working on putting two and two together, and I just…" I stopped, not even knowing what else I could say. What else there was *to* say.

"I've woken up in much worse situations." Onyx shrugged. "I can't blame you for being suspicious. In your position, you can't just trust whoever. You *shouldn't*."

I raised an eyebrow. "Including you?"

He shook his head. "Nah, I'm a man of my word. Blue wants the heads of the men who killed his father, and I told him I would help with that. That's exactly what I intend to do."

"He's not the only one who lost his father," I murmured, thinking out loud.

"He's not," Onyx agreed. "I know he's not the only one affected. I didn't mean it like that, to leave you out or anything."

I scoffed. "No, I wish I *had* been left out," I said, with a dry laugh. "It's a fucked-up crowd to be in."

He nodded. "I know how it feels."

I swallowed the lump in my throat as he met my gaze, searching, always searching. I didn't back down from it this time or look away… maybe not the smartest choice.

Once you gave in when somebody was looking at you like that, it was easy to get lost.

I shook my head, forcefully breaking the connection. "Is *this* even real?" I asked. "Or is it just what you do? This is part of it, right? Make me feel like you can relate to me, get me to trust you. Then you get under my skin, in my panties, in my head. And then what?"

Onyx blew out a sigh, then looked me right in the face. "It *is* what I do, honestly. But again—that's not why I'm here."

"Why *are* you here?"

"In Vegas, or in your house?"

"Both."

It was quiet, then he looked away from me, scratching his head. "I came to Vegas because I was looking for something," he said, finally putting the food down. "I spent most of my life at the mercy of somebody else, dipping in and out of characters that were nothing more than illusions. I was looking for something tangible. But I don't even know if that's within my grasp anymore."

I frowned. "Why wouldn't it be?"

"Things rarely seem to work in my favor," he replied, with a wry smile. "I'm feeling a little bit like I should quit while I'm ahead."

"What does that mean?"

"For you?"

"For the *Predators*."

"Nothing. I'll do what I said I would do."

His facial expression remained masterfully neutral, while he radiated this melancholy energy with an intensity that... I didn't know if you could fake that.

"What about you being here, in my house?" I asked, trying to shift the topic. "You already said you didn't come to kill me, so what is this?"

"I came because you *owe me*," he said, propping his hands on the counter and fixing me with this hungry ass stare. "My home... all my favorite spots to kick it... all of that is burnt because of you."

"They let you go."

"Yeah." He shrugged. "But I don't think I feel as safe as I used to. So I came to see what *your* spot was looking like. This is *nice*," he said, grabbing a paper towel to wipe his hands as he looked around in a very pointed manner. "I bet you've got a spare room."

My eyebrows shot up. "I know you don't think you're staying *here*?" I asked, in full disbelief because... "What part of *I don't fucking know you* wasn't clear?"

"Just for the night, Tati; you can spare a room for a *Predator*, right?"

"There are bunks at the clubhouse," I told him, shaking my head. "And it's not that far away."

"Yeah, but... I'm exhausted. Probably not very safe for me to be on my bike, honestly. I need to sleep off whatever the fuck I got injected with," he said over an exaggerated yawn. "I'm still feeling a bit loopy."

Damn.

He knew exactly how to prey on my guilt.

"Let me make a phone call," I said, not turning my back to him before I slipped my cell from the pocket of my sleep shorts.

"Fine by me." He shrugged. "I'm gonna see what you've got to drink."

*Of course he is.*

I unlocked my phone screen, considering my options for a moment before I called Brandon, knowing that was the best course of action. After a few rings, he answered, breathless, making me cringe as he said, "Guilt keeping you up?"

"In a manner of speaking," I replied, slipping out of the doorway as Onyx helped himself to my fridge. "Found your lost pet."

"For real?"

"Yeah, he showed up at my door and scared the shit outta me, on purpose. Turns out he's definitely a... mercenary, or whatever they call it."

"No shit, Tati."

"Don't start," I warned. "He's... insisting on using my guest room. They injected him with something, and he claims he can't ride. Even though he got here somehow."

"He's fucking with you."

"No shit, Brandon."

He chuckled. "I'm not sure what you want me to do about it?"

"I want you to get him out of here."

"You made this mess, Tati; you clean it up."

My mouth dropped. "So you're good with this stranger nigga in my house alone?"

"If you really thought you were in any kind of danger, this would be a very different phone call, wouldn't it?"

*Shit.*

He had a point there, but—

"Tati, I'm balls deep in my lady right now, I gotta go," Brandon grunted.

"Ugh. Goodbye," I whined, nose wrinkled as I hung up the phone.

I peeked around the door frame to find Onyx grinning at me.

"So!" he said, clapping his hands and rubbing them together. "Give me the tour."

## TATI

"A tour?" I asked, crossing my arms as I stepped back into the kitchen. "Your ass is *not* an invited guest that I'm about to show around."

His full lips spread into a wicked sort of smirk as he approached me, his height easily dwarfing mine, forcing me to look up.

"I'm looking around either way," he informed me, stepping around me into the hall. "You can either be in control of that or not. Choice is yours."

"Do they train you to be annoying at whatever black site you came from?" I asked, quickly moving to get in front of him. I couldn't have him roaming my house alone.

"Nah, that was charm school!" he called after me, and then he was right up on me, lingering way too close.

"What did you do to my security system?" I asked as we approached the front door. I was at least going to do the tour properly, from the front of the house and working back. "How did you make it sound like you were knocking, but there was nothing on the camera feed?"

Now that it had been pulled on me once, I'd never fall for the same trick again, but I still needed to know. Teo was likely somewhere doing the same thing as Brandon and hadn't yet responded to my text. He was going to have some explaining to do though.

Onyx shrugged. "You've got a good system, but it isn't infallible like you seem to think it is. I clocked all your cameras, and avoided triggering any on the way in. You didn't look at the inside door camera, 'cause you assumed your locks had kept me out. I knocked on the door from *inside*. Your system recognized the sound and still picked it up as an event."

I let out a huff. "That is terrifying."

"The world is a terrifying place," he said. "At least now you know."

I sighed, taking a mental list of shit to address with Teo. "So my system is bullshit. What kind of locks do I need?"

He chuckled. "It's *not* a bullshit system; it's pretty damn good, actually. Hardly anybody could get in here unnoticed like I did."

"Okay, so what kind of locks do I need to keep niggas like *you* out?" I asked, sucking my teeth when he grinned in response.

"You got a spare bunker somewhere?"

"Whatever, I'll just talk to my guy about it," I declared, and then moved on, walking him through a very quick, very annoyed, tour of my home.

"We'll skip this one," I said, bypassing the door to my workroom to continue on.

"Nah, nah. nah, *that's* got to be the most interesting room in the house if you don't want me in there," he said, grabbing the doorknob and pushing into the room anyway before I could catch him.

"Seriously?!" I screeched, launching into the room right behind him to hopefully get some quick control over the situation, and maybe steer him out before it turned awkward.

"Daaamn, Tatiana." He chuckled from in front of my wall of lighted display cases, where I kept the things that where the most... intricate. "You... are a naughty girl, aren't you?"

I crossed my arms over my chest, hoping to camouflage my hard nipples through the thin fabric of my shirt. "Shut up!" I huffed, "I'm not even into most of this stuff."

*This stuff* being a whole collection of items adorned with rose quartz embellishments, items of an adult nature.

Onyx pointed to a gorgeous, soft white, leather flogger in the middle of the display case—clearly a notable piece. I hadn't made that one, but I'd done the customizations—intricate rose quartz adornments inlaid on the handle.

It had taken weeks, and I loved it.

"So you're telling me you just look at it?" he asked, giving me skeptical eyebrows before his attention returned to the case. "You're a collector or something?"

"No, I make it," I explained. "Kinda. I didn't make that one, I customized it. Not that it's really any of your business; you're not even supposed to be in here."

"I am *way* too interested in this revelation for you to tell me it's not my business," Onyx said, turning to me. "Tell the truth—are you waiting on someone special to use it on you?"

"What makes you think I would want it used on *me*?"

His eyebrows shot up. "I should have guessed."

"Should have guessed *what*?"

He pulled his lip into his mouth. "*You* want to be the one to use it."

That sent instant heat to my face.

And my lack of an immediate response made him grin.

"I'm right, huh?" he asked, taking a step toward me, his hands tucked into his pockets. "You need a volunteer?"

I scoffed. "*Don't* tempt me."

Why did I say that?

*That* sent him swaggering up to me, getting even closer than he'd been when he was already *too* close before, and *God* he smelled good. Especially when he leaned in to ask, "So that *is* your thing then?"

I shook my head, taking a step back. "Again—it's not your business."

He grinned at me. "You don't have to be ashamed. We all have our kinks."

"I'm not *ashamed*," I snapped. "I've just nev—never mind," I said, pushing out a sigh as I tried to get ahold of myself. I wasn't an *act on impulse* kind of girl, and yet he had me feeling wild in the head, ready to just... *spill.*

Not good.

"Never *what*?" he insisted, closing the distance again. "Come on, you've learned more about me than ninety-nine percent of people tonight. I'd like to think we can talk to each other."

"Not about this," I denied. "Let's—*hey!*"

He'd grabbed my hand, yanking to pull me right up against him. The heat from his body seemed to sink right through my clothes as he looked me dead in the face. Those entrancing dusky eyes locked to mine and he put my hand to his throat. "Go ahead," he murmured. "See how it feels."

My hand flexed, squeezing against his throat.

Reflexively.

That was all.

Right?

My eyes went wide at the same time as his. He grinned, completely amused by this. I, on the other hand, was mortified.

I snatched away from him, shaking my head. "This is too much," I told him, backing away. "I'll show you the spare room, and then first thing in the morning you've got to go."

"Don't be like that." He chuckled, approaching to grab my hand again. "I'm fucking around with you."

"We don't have that kind of relationship, where you get to do that."

"You showed me your toys, you told me about your kink, and then the neck squeeze…" he groaned, making me clench my thighs as heat rushed through me again. "I feel like we're on the verge of a beautiful connection here, Tati."

"*Ugh!*" I snatched my hand away and headed out the door, down the hall as he laughed. "You, guest room, *now.*"

"Tati!" he called after me, and when I didn't feel him following, I turned in his direction.

"Are you waiting on something?"

"No." He shook his head, dragging his thumb over his bottom lip. "Just admiring how comfortable you look right now. Were you already in bed?"

I glanced down at myself, remembering that I *was* just in bike shorts and an oversized t-shirt—no lifting, no smoothing, no tummy control, hell… no underwear.

Obviously.

I lifted my head high, refusing to be embarrassed about my body, or what it was currently covered with. "I'm in *my* house," I said. "I will get as comfortable as I want."

He put his hand to his chest. "*Please,*" he pleaded. "Don't mistake what I said as a complaint, or criticism. I'm admiring the fuck outta the view," he confessed, the lust in his stare supplementing his words.

I propped my hands on my hips. "*Why* are you flirting so hard with me?"

He shrugged. "I'm feeding off the energy *you're* giving *me*. Ask yourself why *you're* flirting so hard."

My lip curled. "Nobody is flirting with you, Onyx."

"I beg to differ. You invited me in here with you barely dressed. You fed me. *Choked* me."

"Oh fuck off!" I said and then *immediately* wished I hadn't when he grinned, victorious.

He started closing the distance between us, giving off all the nonchalance in the world as he sauntered up to me. "What's wrong, Tati? Am I making you mad? Making you want to grab some stuff from your room in there?"

Arms crossed, eyes narrowed, I met his gaze. "I'm *not* going to fuck you," I declared.

To myself, more than him.

I was *not* going to fuck this man.

But...

"You want to," he said, still smirking as he leaned in, getting at eye level with me to whisper, "Don't you?"

I swallowed.

*Hard.*

"The guest room is the door at the end right there," I said, pointing past him.

"I'm down whenever you're down."

"There are towels and everything in the connected bathroom."

"I'm into whatever you're into."

"I can't help you on the toothbrush, so if you're still here when I get up, keep your shitty breath to yourself."

"No ass stuff though," he said, undeterred by my attempts to not engage him in *that* line of conversation. "I'm very secure in my masculinity, so it's not that—it's just not in line with my interests you know? But if you want *me* to put it in—"

"Get the fuck out of my face!" I snapped, finally, and he laughed, tossing his hands up as he backed away.

"I'm sorry," he said, and I rolled my eyes.

"No you're not."

He smiled.

A more dazzling sight than it really had any right to be.

"I'm not," he admitted. "Good night."

I was finally able to heave a sigh of relief as he turned toward the door I'd pointed him to.

*Good damn night.*

This whole encounter had me all...

*Flustered.*

Instead of lingering in the hall, I went back to the entrance of my house, this time in search of my damn gun. I found it placed neatly on the foyer table where Onyx had to have left it after he'd disarmed me like it was nothing.

Probably a good thing because, through the course of that whole infuriating conversation, if I'd still been armed, I may have shot him just to shut him the hell up.

With a heavy breath, I moved on, going back to my room. I hesitated for just a moment with my hand on the lock, because... was there even a point?

If he wanted to get in here, he'd already made it clear that he could.

And as Brandon had already forced me to admit... I didn't think I was in any jeopardy here.

Which was nuts, considering how much of a shift that was from my previous feelings about the man. *He* was absolutely still a dangerous man, but that didn't mean he would do any harm to *me*.

The only thing at risk here was the emptiness of my pussy, honestly.

I turned the lock.

If nothing else, having to unlock it to get out would give *me* something to think about.

My phone lit up in my hand, pulling my attention, and I frowned when I looked at the screen. I had several missed calls, all from Kev. It had been in my pocket, outside my sight line which meant outside my attention.

I rolled my eyes, not *really* wanting to make a habit of answering his calls in the middle of the night. We didn't need to set that kind of precedent, but since he'd called multiple times... it was probably best to see what was going on.

"Where have you been?" he asked as soon as the video call connected and I frowned.

"I'm going to give you a chance to correct yourself," I warned, already annoyed.

"My bad," he said, lifting a hand at the screen. "But I've been calling and you're not answering—I got worried."

I nodded. "I understand that, but it's the middle of the night. Why not just assume I'm asleep?"

"You're right. My inability to sleep isn't yours."

Now that he mentioned it... I could clearly see the tiredness in his eyes, which meant *he* should be sleeping himself. "What's going on? Why can't you sleep?"

"I was up working on the books for a client, and then... my thoughts wandered. Can't get my mind off this treasurer job," he admitted. "I know, you're not supposed to play favorites, but... you at least talked me up to Blue about it, right?"

I sighed. "Brandon and I have talked about it. He hasn't made the final decision yet."

"Okay... is it at least looking good for me, or...?"

"He will let you know what he decides, but I'll be honest with you; Gavin's father did this job. And he was killed in service to the club. Both of those things hold a *lot* of weight."

"But it's not the end all, right?"

"Right," I agreed, even though really... his chances were very, very low. "Like I said, Brandon will let you know."

"Okay. Okay," he repeated, sounding way more relieved than he had any reason to be. "Hey, if you weren't asleep, why didn't you answer the phone?"

"Well, because this is *my* phone. I'll answer it or not, if and when I *want* to," I explained with a grin. "The other reason is that I was handling *Predator* business."

"This late? I don't know if I like that," he told me, brow furrowed at the screen.

I frowned. "Excuse me?"

"You being up in the middle of the night, talking shop, in dangerous shit..."

"Um... I appreciate the concern, but it's... *not* your concern," I reminded him. "Maybe you and I need to cool off a bit. I feel like the lines are getting a bit blurred."

"Hold up," he said, eyes wide, suddenly more awake. "You're ready to call it a wrap because I was worried about you?"

"It's not exactly that," I told him, shaking my head. "The lines are not as sharp as they used to be, and I've got too much going on to be wrapped up in any confusion. We're sleeping together, and that's all. You don't get to question anything I do—especially for my club."

"I'm not *questioning*, I'm—"

"It's late," I spoke up, interrupting him. "I don't have the energy for this."

He pushed out a sigh and nodded. "Fine. Goodnight."

"Goodnight."

I ended the call before he could say shit else to me and I was tempted to block his ass too, for good measure.

I wasn't sure *why* his words had just irked me so much, but...*ugh.*

I blew out a sigh as my phone buzzed again, this time with a follow-up from Brandon.

***The killer is a much better look for you – Presidente.***

I rolled my eyes.

He barely knew Onyx and was on *this* type of propaganda?

What the fuck was I missing?

He was always on me about being too hard on people—it was a quality I'd inherited from my father, and I knew it could be a little much sometimes.

Brandon wasn't typically loose with his allegiance though. Between the two of us, yes, I was the one more ready and willing to question somebody's loyalty, while he was more even keeled.

Not *trusting* though.

Not with the *Predators*, not in this manner, not to this degree.

So what was it about this dude he saw that I didn't?

*Who knows?*

My eyelids were too heavy to dwell on it.

I closed my eyes, finally letting the excitement of the day float away, hoping sleep would find me easily.

It didn't.

Instead, I found myself listening in the dark for any evidence that I wasn't in my house alone. Anything tangible to blunt the insanity of the realization that I could just... *feel him.*

His scent was still in my nose, the heat of his gaze still burned into my skin, and it was making me feel more than a little ridiculous. Even in that very first moment, with my hands pinned behind me, the weight of his body trapping me against the door, making it hard to breathe, I was...

*Aroused.*

And now, still.

*Shit.*

Not giving myself a chance to think about it too hard, I reached into my bedside drawer for my vibrator.

Eyes closed, I pressed it between my legs, finding the sensitive mound of my clit. I turned myself over, face into my pillow, and I was back at the front door, damn near suffocating. Only this time, in my imagination, his hands were busy doing much more pleasurable things than keeping me pinned, pinching my nipples, playing between my legs.

My thighs clamped tight as my mouth opened in a muffled moan. I gasped into my pillow as the orgasm hit me harder than expected, faster than expected. Flipping over, I sucked in deep lungfuls of air as my stomach clenched in response to the steady stimulation, until I couldn't take it anymore.

I was numb between the legs, head buzzing with post-orgasm euphoria when I finally pressed the button to switch it off.

I pushed out a deep sigh as my eyes drifted closed again, knowing that *this time*, I wouldn't have any trouble drifting off, now that the last of my energy was sufficiently drained.

I'd consider the implications of my *own* comfort with having Onyx in my house overnight another time.

# Chapter Nine

## NYX



Music to my ears.

Literally.

I woke up to the sound of Tati blasting music I wanted to assume was about Kev, considering the way the artist was singing about some dude being *just anotha nigga on the hit list.*

I hadn't been hit yet, so it wasn't me.

Not that I wouldn't have gladly *been* that nigga last night, kinda shameful considering how easily she could've gotten me killed if Alicia's sentiment toward me hadn't been friendly.

I didn't know if it was a testament to how fine Tati was or how weak I'd become.

Either way, I couldn't deny it.

At least not in my head.

I peeled myself out of the nice ass sheets on Tati's guest room bed, getting all my morning scratching out of the way as I headed for the toilet. I was mid-stream when a basket on the counter made me smirk.

*Toothbrush and toothpaste.*

Brand new.

It could've already been there for any unexpected guest, forgotten.

Or maybe she'd outright lied.

There was also the possibility that, with me still dealing with the aftermath of being injected with a sedative, that she'd snuck it in without me noticing last night.

That prospect was more than a little alarming.

I was *not* the type of nigga people were usually able to sneak up on.

I also wasn't the type of nigga that usually got drugged though either, so there was that.

Shaking my head, I turned on the shower and climbed in, groaning in relief over the steady blast of hot water. I could at least leave this room clean, but there was nothing I could do about my stale clothes.

Not that Tati cared.

Musically, she'd moved on to rap now, and although I couldn't see or hear her, I could imagine she was belting *I don't give a fuck about you or anything that you do* right along with Big Sean at the top of her lungs.

*Ol' boy must have really made her mad.*

What did it say about me that the visual of a mad Tati was... *shit.*

The last thing I needed to be thinking about with my dick out.

For all the teasing I'd done to get under her skin, I knew better than to cross that line. It would only blur a situation that was already more complicated than it needed to be.

I finished my shower and got myself dressed, brushing my teeth and all that before I did my best to put the room back like I'd found it. Finally, I ventured out of the guest room, following the path we'd taken late last night to get back to her kitchen. That's where I found her, looking good as fuck, and just as... *comfortable* as she'd been last night.

Not the word I'd wanted to use, but the one that wouldn't get me kicked out.

*Fuckable* was more accurate.

Not to be crude, but if a man couldn't be candid with *himself,* who the hell could he be honest with? So much of my life had been devoted to embodying characters that I relished opportunities to give in to the thoughts that were truly, thoroughly mine.

And as of now, Tatiana Tate consumed those thoughts.

With the music up loud, and that *very special skill set* I'd teased her about, she hadn't heard me approach, so I was able to just observe.

She was...beautiful.

Objectively.

Not an opinion, but a fact.

Her deep brown skin was flawless, only marred by the occasional ink. High cheekbones, full lips, big brown eyes... She just looked so damn *soft,* so pleasing to touch. All that velvety skin was poured over the kind of curves that made it tough to remember—although I was my own man now, I still had a personal mission.

A mission that meant Tati should be off limits, even though every damn day made me question that a little further.

*Look at her.*

Even the way she pushed a handful of her long braids over her shoulder, then seemingly changed her mind to pull them up into a knot was sexy. What was *that* about? And that energy she carried with her, like she wasn't scared of shit *because* she wasn't scared of shit. She walked around like she was the boss of everything because she *was*. Second only to Blue, who had all the respect in the world for her.

That shit was beyond attractive.

Intoxicating, if you got too close to that magnetic fire she put off.

She was just so fucking comfortable in her own skin, and hell... I wanted to be comfortable in her skin too.

"Do you think I don't know you're standing there?" she asked, not looking up from where she'd been staring at the screen of her laptop.

*So she knows how to be watched, too.*

"As a matter of fact, I *did* think you didn't know I was here," I said, finally breaching the doorway into the kitchen. "You seemed like you were vibing with your music. I didn't want to kill it."

Her hands went to the computer, tapping a key that made the music suddenly switch off. "If that was really the case, you would have just left. But instead I have to look at you."

I sauntered up to the counter, leaning down across from her. "Now we *both* know looking at me is a privilege, don't we?"

"Here we go," she muttered, rolling her eyes as she turned her attention back to her screen. "Brandon is on his way over. So if you're reconsidering killing me for knowing your secret, make it quick."

"You don't know my secret." I laughed, moving around the kitchen in search of breakfast. I could smell it and saw the empty plate next to her computer. If Blue was coming, she probably hadn't made it only for herself.

"It's in the oven," she said, her tone full of attitude after she'd watched me peek around. "And what do you mean, I don't know your secret? You told me last night—you used to be a spy, an assassin, whatever. Just as I thought."

"And whatever you were, whatever it is you used to do, Alicia is connected too," she added, smirking.

"All that is true," I agreed, opening the oven to find a pan stacked with sausages, pancakes, and hashbrowns.

What I *didn't* say was that what she knew was the polite part. Hired guns, abductions, counter-espionage—most people had been exposed enough via TV and movies that it was easy for them to swallow.

But that stuff was only a fraction; the parts people could actually stomach.

"Don't get too excited about the food," she told me, as I started piling stuff on a plate. "It was all frozen. I get it from a girl who does precooked meals as a little business to pay for school. She's inked."

I frowned, looking up. "One of the *Predators* does frozen home cooked meals as a business? I thought being a *Predator was* the business."

"You thought wrong." She shrugged. "We can hire some people, yes. But everybody isn't into everything we do. Some people just join for the community. The majority of *Predators* are actually ninety-nine percenters."

I raised an eyebrow. "A ninety-nine percenter. What is that?"

"Ninety-nine percent of people who are interested in bikes, are just that —interested in bikes. They aren't about the... *Sons of Anarchy* type stuff. They just like to see it on TV."

I grinned. "And you are?"

"It's what I was born into," she answered. "I have the stomach for it, so I get it done."

"Interesting."

She frowned at me, but didn't say anything else for a few moments, so I took it as an opportunity to help myself to my plate. I paid no mind to her staring as I ate, but I could feel the questions radiating off her. So it was no surprise when she finally spoke up.

"Will you still be around after we finish with the *Marauders*?"

I shrugged, and then over a mouthful of pancake asked, "Why?"

"Because I want to know," she snapped, giving me a stern look that probably left most people shook.

I felt it in my groin, and started to tell her, but decided on a different route of teasing instead. "*Why* do you want to know? Don't want to waste your time if I won't be here next year?"

"Christmas lyrics? Really?" She rolled her eyes. "Anyway—we're getting into legal cannabis, as you saw at the dispensary. It's very lucrative, but potentially... no less dangerous than regular weed. We're going to need security, at the dispensary and on our courier teams."

I shook my head. "I'm not a corner boy, sweetheart."

She sighed. "I'm not talking about you being a corner boy, but you're right; you're *not*. You do too much. The cops would see *you* a mile away."

"Tell yourself whatever you need to." I chuckled. "Y'all got armored trucks and all that?"

"We will. Especially since we're looking into potentially doing our own growing."

My eyebrows shot up. "Oh shit, so not just distribution?"

"Not if I have anything in it," she replied, smirking. "I don't like leaving money on the table. I want it all."

She started to say something else, but her phone rang, and when she looked at it her face lit up.

"Excuse me," she said, already standing as she tapped the button on the screen and put the device to her ear. "Hey, Mama!" she chirped. "What's going on?"

Obviously, I watched her walk away like it was must-see TV, until I couldn't anymore, and then went back to my previous engagement.

Why wouldn't I, with the way her ass was moving in those shorts?

Yes, I had other things to be concerned about—like what my life would look like now that I was on Alicia's radar. I recognized the oversight in impulsively showing up in Vegas now. I should have done a lot more investigation.

But once I knew what I knew, I couldn't *not* know it, couldn't not act on it.

I was too late to work out the original plan, so this thing with the *Marauders*, well... it would have to do.

My thoughts were interrupted by a notification chiming on Tati's computer. It would have been easy to ignore, but it kept going off, so I moved around to where she'd been sitting to stop it, quickly realizing it was a video call from some type of private messenger.

I looked at the name, smirking when I realized it was Kev. I peeked around to see if Tati was anywhere in the immediate vicinity, and then parked myself right in front of the camera to answer it.

I immediately wished I'd had a camera set up to record his reaction.

Shock, then sadness, then *rage* before he was finally able to sputter, "What the fuck are you doing in her house?"

I shrugged. "Not much my man, I'm chilling. How you doing this morning?"

"Put Tati on the damn call," he demanded, crossing his arms.

Looking silly as fuck.

"About that," I said, peeking around for her again. "I think she's gonna have to call you back bruh, she's... occupied."

"What?"

I raised an eyebrow. "Busy. It means she's *busy*."

"Doing what?" he questioned, just before his eyes went wide with some sort of realization that made him add, "Did you... spend the night there?"

The look on his face – the *hurt* on his face – came very close to making me feel bad enough not to fuck with him.

But I hated niggas like him; lowkey slimy, charming enough to snake their way into shit they didn't deserve.

Like... Tati's bed.

"I did," I answered him, honestly, knowing what he probably thought I meant.

Was it fucked up?

Yes.

But it was worth it, watching his expression change.

"She let you fuck her?" he asked, in a low whisper that I could only assume was meant to be intimidating.

"Bro, come on. I would *never* tell a lady's business in that manner, it's a betrayal of privacy," I answered, digging the knife in.

He glowered at me, mad as fuck. "Just answer the question!" he pressed, with a little extra bass that made me raise my eyebrows.

"I understand you're emotional right now my dude," I replied, trying not to laugh. "But you don't get to demand shit from *me*. And I damn sure ain't about to tell you her business."

"So... yes. She let you fuck her."

I just stared at the camera.

And then, I grinned. "Tell me something—what *exactly* are you gonna do about it if I *did* fuck her?" I asked, not giving a shit if the question pissed him off.

I didn't like his damn tone.

And I'd already wondered why somebody with his bitch boy energy was able to pull a *Tati* in the first place, and now... my confusion was even more pronounced.

"You don't want to test me," he warned, serious as fuck, which was... hilarious.

So I laughed.

"I actually do," I assured him. "Tell you what, next time we run into each other at *Bottoms,* we'll talk about it then, okay?" I said, and I didn't know if he'd realized his mistake or what, but he was real quick on the *end call* button then.

*Bitch.*

"I see I made a mistake when I didn't tell you not to touch anything," Tati said a few moments later, when she stepped through the entrance to her kitchen and found me sitting at her computer. "What do you think you're doing?"

"Just trying to stay up on the business," I told her, shrugging as I moved out of her way.

She glared at the screen, then glared at me. "You think I don't see that *call ended* screen right there? Who were you talking to?"

"Nobody. Better known as Kev."

She groaned. "I wish Brandon would go ahead and put that man out of his misery."

"What do you mean?" I asked, going back to my plate.

"He's trying to get the treasury position in the club."

"I thought Ghost was on that?"

She nodded, eyes wide. "Exactly. But... Kev wants it, so until he hears a firm *no*, I guess he thinks he's going to... shit, I don't know what he thinks he's going to do. And I hope he doesn't expect to come whining to me about it after."

I chuckled, opening cabinets until I found a glass, then moved to her refrigerator. "Good pussy will make a man do stranger things."

"You don't know anything about my pussy, or how supposedly good it is," she retorted, her back to me as I glanced up, taking in a longing stare at her ass.

*It's definitely good.*

Kev wouldn't have been on the verge of tears about the possibility of me sampling it otherwise.

"Where the fuck y'all at?" I heard, in tandem with Tati's front door opening announced by her security system, a little feature I'd had to disable for my entry the night before.

"In the kitchen!" she called out to Blue, who appeared in the doorway a few moments later.

"Your ass is never ready to go when I get here," was the first thing Blue said to Tati, who sucked her teeth.

"You say that as if I'm not typically coming to get you, or like we really be having places to be early in the morning all the time like this. Get off my back, dude," she snapped at him, with a raised middle finger for emphasis.

"Damn," Blue said, putting a hand to his chest before he moved in to wrap his arms around Tati's shoulders as she struggled against him.

"*Stop*," she fussed as he forcibly planted a kiss on her cheek before letting her go.

"Don't be acting like you don't love me in front of company," he told her, moving in my direction now with his fist outstretched. I tapped it with mine as Tati let out another disgusted sound.

"I'll let y'all continue with your little bromance while I go put some clothes on."

Blue busied himself with breakfast while I, once again, busied myself watching Tati walk away. And then, I asked the question that had been burning on my mind.

"Ay... I mean no disrespect to you or her, but how the hell are you not..."

He looked up at me, eyebrow raised. "Not what?"

I scoffed. "Tati. She's bad as *fuck*. You telling me you don't see that?"

Blue chuckled and shook his head. "Nah, Tati is beautiful, but that's my sister pretty much. In every way except blood. I know how other people see her, and logically I understand it, but... I don't see her like *that*. Though clearly you do."

"Like I said man, no disrespect intended."

"None taken." He shrugged. "Why do you think I ain't come drag your ass outta here last night? I'd rather see her with somebody that can hold it down, over this shit she's been on lately. She needs somebody solid. She's not one of these docile chicks; it ain't gonna be easy with my sister. So... you can't be a bitch about it."

"Noted." I chuckled. "But... what are you even saying to me right now bruh? You think *I'm* the somebody solid...?"

Blue sat down at the counter with his plate. "You telling me you're not?"

"Nah, I'm just saying... I'm a little surprised at how easily you've welcomed me into the fold like this."

*What the fuck are you doing?*

Speaking my mind like this could easily backfire, and plant suspicions in his mind that weren't there, but... shit, I had to know.

"You don't strike me as the type of dude to be willy-nilly with confidence in other niggas," I continued. "So the way I see it, there's two possibilities. You *don't* actually trust me, and this is some kind of trap. Or you *do*, and it's because you know something I don't."

He nodded, thinking about it for a moment before he spoke. "You know how I said Tatiana was my sister in every way except blood?"

"Yeah."

"It's that way because our *fathers* were brothers in every way except blood. Thick as thieves. They fought together, played together... died together. And in the meantime, they raised me and Tati together; our birthdays are only weeks apart. They had a bond, like two sides of the same coin. And they instilled that in me and Tati. Talked about it all the time, this idea of people being kindred spirits with you, people you would just meet for the first time, sometimes even just *seeing* them, and just *knowing* those were your people. He had this idea," Blue explained, "that it was five people, that made like... a fist. A mighty fist. You, and then there was four other people on this planet, four other kindred spirits that once you connected with those people, there wasn't shit that could touch you. I mean... besides a bullet. Other than that though?" He chuckled. "Unstoppable. So, I got me, my mama of course. Tati. My girl, Nessa. And then... the empty place because of my father's death."

He looked right at me after that, and I crossed my arms.

"You're deadass?"

He nodded. "Deadass. I mean, don't get me wrong I ain't saying it's some usual kind of shit, I'm just saying that my father's lessons have never led me wrong. *Ever*. Kind of wish you could've met him. You're *exactly* the kind of wild nigga he would have liked a lot."

I blew out a sigh. "I think I would have liked to meet him too."

Still tucking into his food, Blue asked, "What kind of relationship you have with your pops?"

I shrugged. "Never knew him. And my mother gave me away when I was..." I scoffed, shaking my head. "Old enough to know I was being given away."

"So what, you were adopted? Foster care? Something like that?"

"Yeah. Something like that," I said, thinking about how calling *The Garden foster care* was a stretch of the mightiest proportions.

Even the worst neglect would've been better than what I'd faced at the hands of the Belrose family.

Blue shook his head. "You ain't got to be cool about the shit with me, man. I know there's some shit with you and the tattoo. Ace, and all of them killer-looking bitches she rolls with." He laughed. "I see the shit. I just like being alive, so I don't be asking questions. What is it, some secret society shit or something?"

"I think you know I can't say too much," I said, even though... at this point, was that even the truth? *The Garden* didn't exist anymore, so whose secrets was I keeping anymore?

Other than my former peers?

Nobody that deserved it, for damn sure.

"Ay, honestly I appreciate that you have a code you live by," Blue said, pulling me from my thoughts. "That shit is important. As long as you understand that *I* have a code I live by too. I'm bringing you in on this shit based on a gut feeling, but if it goes left?" He tossed his hands up. "I'ma do what I gotta do. I know, you're John Wick in this bitch." He chuckled. "And I respect that, but I ain't no slouch myself. And don't let Tati be nearby. She ain't a killer, but don't push her. She knows what to do."

I lifted an eyebrow. "Which is?"

"Aim for the head and empty the clip."

I nodded. "Can't argue with that."

"Can't argue with what?" Tati said, breezing into the kitchen looking somehow *even better* now that she was dressed, in slim fit jeans and a gauzy yellow cropped shirt that showed off a teasing sliver of soft skin and a pierced belly button. If that wasn't enough, it hung off her shoulders too, barely containing her titties.

"Well damn, you coming like that today, huh?" Blue asked, chuckling.

"Well, when you need to be on somebody's good side in a meeting, you've got to come correct."

"Okay, I feel like I'm missing something," I spoke up, interested in what the hell kind of meeting *that* outfit was coming correct for.

Blue chuckled. "We're supposed to be going to go see the *Renegados*. We need to know what side they're going to fall on in this thing. I feel like we can make a comfortable guess, but I don't want to make any assumptions. I want an ally. And Manuel Rojas – their president – has a thing for Tati."

"He sure does." Tati laughed, flipping her braids over shoulder. "All the boys do. I told you, Jake Lincoln wants to make mixed babies with me, talking about a damn alliance, I ain't dumb."

I pulled my head back. "That white boy I almost fucked up?"

Tati nodded. "Mmmhmm. I think that's why Blue wants me at this meeting, give Manuel something to look at."

"You're a damn mess," Blue told her. "*If anybody else* called you what *he* calls you, you'd be ready to fight," he said.

"They don't say it like he does," she insisted, grabbing her laptop to pack away. "*Seductora de chocolate*," she purred, sticking her tongue out. "*Grande!*" she added, rolling the *r* before she laughed.

"Big sexy chocolate," Blue laughed. "That's a turn on for you?"

"I ain't say all of that, it's just that little reverence he be putting on it, while he looks like he does." Tati giggled. "I like hearing it!"

"You just make sure you don't like it too much. Don't give his ass *any* steam," Blue warned.

"I'm good, first of all. And he's not trying nothing in front of you."

"I won't be there," Blue told her and her eyes went wide. "Something came up and Mama needs me to go to an appointment with her."

"What's wrong with Randy?" Tati asked, and Blue shook his head. "Not a damn thing. She's getting some dental work, and they've got to put her under anesthesia. She swears she don't want nobody but me there with her, so... I know you got it, but I don't want you out there with the homies alone. Why don't you take—"

"Maite," Tati spoke up, before Blue could say my name—the obvious journey he was taking, since he'd looked right at me. "Keira is covering the bar for me today, getting some training in."

A smirk spread over his face, and he shook his head. "Nah. Sketch ain't gonna do shit but add fuel to the fire. Take Ghost. Or Ozzy."

Tati scoffed. "I can't take neither of them to the *Renegados—that* shit is a problem waiting to happen. Maite and I can handle ourselves just fine, *Dad.*"

He blew out a sigh. "Fine, but I need your ass texting me with updates every five minutes. Fuck it, every three. And if I text you—"

"Text back, and you mean *immediately*," Tati teased, mushing the side of his head in a way I was pretty sure only she and maybe his mama could get away with.

"Hey, why don't I tag along?" I spoke up anyway, even though she'd obviously been trying to avoid that. "I should be getting to know these people too, right?"

"No," Tati said, hitting me with a stink face. "I don't need a babysitter, and if I *did* need a babysitter, it damn sure wouldn't be you."

"Y'all are something else." Blue laughed. "But nah, Nyx, I got something else I want to put you on, Mr. James Bond. A little reconnaissance mission."

I crossed my arms, listening. "Okay."

"So, we've been getting some light intelligence reports about the *Marauders*, and what they're up to, all of that," he said, "But I need something a little more... robust. I want more. I want it all. And I feel like you can get that."

"Not a problem," I assured. "I'll see what I can see, and report back."

"Good shit." He nodded. "So everybody's got their marching orders, right?"

"Right," Tati agreed.

I stared at her for another moment, really not a fan of whoever the fuck Manuel Rojas was, his damn nickname for her, or whatever he had going on, but I had a position to play.

So...

"Right."

# *Chapter Ten*

## TATI

"Now why'd you have to bring me into this?" Maite asked, fidgeting with her top from the passenger seat of the car. I'd barely pulled off from picking her up, and already, she was complaining.

I hit her with a side eye. For somebody who didn't want to be brought into this, she was sure as hell doing a lot primping in the visor mirror. "Now you know damn well your baby Trinidad is going to be over there."

"She's got a man."

I laughed at *that* shit. "That sure as hell didn't keep you from knocking la jefa down what... like a month ago?"

"Did you just call her a heifer?" Maite asked, eyes wide. "Why she gotta be all that?"

"*No*, la jefa, like, the boss, since she's... never mind," I laughed. "'Cause I think you're playing purposely dense."

"I'm not playing. I don't know anything, I haven't seen anything," she said, using a careful finger to wipe away a tiny lipstick smudge. "I look okay?"

"Why do you care? You trying to get bagged?"

"Maybe so, everybody else is."

I huffed. "Not everybody, babe," I told her, shaking my head. "I think I'm over it with Kev."

"Finally?"

"*Finally?* Damn." I laughed. "Was it like that?"

"You were the only person who couldn't see it, hon, that nigga is so corny."

I sighed. "No, I could definitely see it; that was a feature, not a bug."

Maite leaned forward, eyes narrowed as she frowned at me. "Now what now?"

"I said what I said." I shrugged. "I'm not trying to be serious with anyone, so *why* would I be fucking somebody who gives *settle down* vibes? That's how you end up catching feelings, and get your damn feelings *hurt*," I explained. "What sense would it make, being laid up with somebody I enjoy? Fuck around and have me telling that nigga I wanna have his babies."

She poked her lip out, eyes up to the roof of the car as she bobbed her head in a slow nod. "You know..."

"Salient point, is it *not*?" I laughed.

"I mean... if that's how you wanna get down..."

I sucked my teeth. "You could've been knocking down the bachelorette party bitches that just wanna 'be adventurous' for a night, but who do you do instead? *Fucking* Trinidad. Married and emotionally unavailable."

"Hold up, why am I getting dragged?!"

"It's not a dragging, just an observation."

"*Observe* some business of your own, like ol' boy from the other night."

My eyes were *very* focused on the road. "Who?"

"Bitch you know who," she scoffed. "You're off Kev's dick, *please* tell me you're getting on that one. I don't even *like* men and that nigga might could talk me into something."

Mouth open, I turned to Maite. "Are you talking about Onyx? He's fine like that to you?"

She curled her face up at me. "To me and *everybody*, girl! It's not even solely looks, he's just... *it*. Whatever the male equivalent of a bad bitch is— that's him. Could you imagine? Getting your hands tangled up in those locs? And girl, the earring? I would lick that shit."

"Maite!"

"*What*? He looks *clean*... but very dirty, probably. It's part of the sex appeal! Tell me you haven't thought about it."

I shifted in my seat, glaring out the window at the road. "Thought about *what*?"

"*Licking him*," Maite exclaimed, staring a hole in the side of my head, trying to get a response. "His teeth. His biceps. His *ink*. The curve he *undoubtedly* has, on his *undoubtedly* heavy dick. Have you seen how he walks?"

"I thought you didn't like men?"

"I don't," she agreed. "But that's not a man; he's *that nigga*. Tell me I'm lying."

Instead of answering, I sighed.

"So yes then?!" Maite screeched.

"Girl, fuck off."

"*So yes!*"

I rolled my eyes as Maite cackled in the passenger seat over my misfortune.

The way I'd fallen asleep with Onyx on the brain was bad enough without her dragging everything I was trying to forget right to the forefront of my mind. None of the filthy things I'd dreamed about were actually going to happen, and I didn't want that shit marinating in my thoughts.

Waking up to him still in my house made things a little awkward.

I'd managed to play it off well enough and talk my way out of being in his presence for an extended period today.

The *last* thing I needed was Maite encouraging my unsolicited attraction.

"This conversation is leaning very heterosexual," I groaned to her, disappointed. "Again, *I thought you liked bitches*. I thought you liked *me*."

"You won't give me any pussy, so this is your punishment." She laughed.

"You want it right now? Would that make this stop?"

She sucked her teeth. "Girl you know *damn* well you not doing nothing, stop playing."

"You right. 'Cause you only got eyes for one woman anyway," I teased, reaching over to poke her leg.

"*She has a man,*" Maite whined, batting my hand away.

"Mmmhmmm." I laughed. "That don't mean you can't look at her," I assured as I navigated my car up to the gates at the Rojas compound. "And it ain't gonna keep her from looking at you. You look good."

Sketch smirked. "Not too much?"

"Do you believe in such things?"

Maite was one of the most interesting people I knew. The day we met; she'd made it clear to me that she liked pussy—her words. She was a pretty bitch—her words. And, she had a variety of dicks she could bring with her to turn me out—her words as well.

She *was* a pretty bitch and I was flattered by the offer.

Certainty about my sexuality aside, I needed her skills as a tattoo artist, and couldn't risk mixing *that* business with pleasure though. The *Predators* needed someone new to do their ink, and my father had tasked me with finding them. The OG that had been doing it was, well... getting older. We needed someone to takeover.

I could *not* be fucking that person.

Maite batted her eyelashes at the guard manning the gate as we pulled up, stopping briefly to state our business before we were allowed through.

They knew us.

I tossed up my hand in a wave as we moved on, into what I referred to as the concrete oasis.

I hated the Rojas compound.

Why would they build out a bunch of concrete in the middle of the dry ass desert, like it wasn't hot enough out here? But it wasn't really my business —if they liked it, I loved it. The money they'd started getting after the Santiago cartel went down had done them well, and they'd spared no expense to be gaudy.

Honestly, it was the kind of money the *Predators* could be bringing in if we wanted to sell coke, run pills and all of that too. But *that* game hadn't been kind to us. It was a wonder our fathers hadn't died in prison, on charges from that shit. Daniel Whitfield and his lawyers had made the shit go away, with the understanding that *Predators* were off that. It was profitable, but too fucking dicey.

We couldn't risk it.

If nothing else, our divestment from those "industries" made it easier to be at peace with groups that could easily be our rivals instead, like the *Renegados*. Our relationship with them today was a continuation of bonds built by our fathers.

With the threat of an attack always looming, we couldn't afford to let them wither.

It was why I was here, looking ready for anything except business as we pulled up to the grand, stucco-covered front entrance to the main house. The large double doors opened and their leader, Manuel Rojas, came swaggering down the stairs.

He was younger than our fathers, but older than us, hitting a mark some-where right between old enough to feel like he was wiser than we were, but too young for us to take his "wisdom" too seriously.

Not that we thought he was a joke.

That would be a silly, dangerous thing to believe; behind the handsome, overgrown playboy demeanor was a shrewd leader. Five years ago, the *Renegados* weren't even a blip on the map.

Now?

They rivaled the *Predators* in membership and dwarfed us in income.

It was important that we never gave him the impression he was our superior, but equally vital to never forget he was capable of becoming our worst adversary.

The necessary balance here was... delicate.

"Tatiana," Manuel called out, as soon as one of his men had opened the car door to help me out. "*Mi seductora de chocolate*, how are you?" he greeted, making me blush as he pressed a quick kiss to each of my cheeks.

I wasn't kidding.

Manuel was charming and fine and he sounded good as hell saying that corny shit to me.

I *loved* it.

"And who is *this* lovely being?" Manuel asked, eyeing Maite as one of his people helped her out from the car too.

"This is Maite—she is the artist who does all the *Predator* ink for us, and also a good friend of mine," I told him, laughing as she made a big show of letting him kiss her hand.

"Such *exquisite* women, getting into such bloody business," he said, looking between us and shaking his head, as if it were a pity.

Because to him, it was.

He'd never been shy about letting us know he thought it was improper for women to be so involved in club business beyond looking good on a bike. And I'd never been shy about making sure he understood that I didn't give a fuck what he thought.

Today was a bit sensitive though, so I pressed my lips together, opting to simply let it go. There was already a chance this meeting would end on an awkward note.

I just nodded, motioning for Maite to come along as they took us into the house, leading us to Manuel's office. Before I could say anything at all actually, he spoke up again, to offer more fuel to that statement.

"This is all ugly stuff, mi amor," he said, shaking his head as he opened the office doors to welcome us inside. "This no place for women like you."

I turned in the doorway, hanging a little too close to him as I smiled. "Now what would Trinidad think about you calling me that?" I asked, flirting, but reminding him I knew exactly what this was.

And what it *wasn't* going to be.

Manuel smirked, unperturbed by my aggression when he took a step closer, his eyes lingering on my breasts before he said, "Maybe we should call her in, to make a point. She needs to see that she is not the only beautiful woman who has my attention."

My mouth dropped open, faking shock. "See that's how bitches wind up getting killed. It's me, *I'm* bitches," I warned him, shaking my head. "Don't you tell that woman that, I don't need her out for my head," I told him, leaning fully into it even while knowing Trinidad didn't give a shit.

Not when she had Maite dicking her down; the whole reason it had been so easy to get her to come along.

She stood next to us now, absorbing the whole exchange before Manuel took us further into the room, offering us seats. Before we could take them though, Trinidad herself was at the doorway to the office, halfway out of breath, and there was only one person in this room *she* had eyes for.

It couldn't be more obvious—to me, at least. Manuel went to his wife, snaking a hand through her thick waves of hair as he pulled her close. Maybe he was too used to her indifference because he didn't seem to notice the pure heat exchange happening between the two women.

She submitted to being kissed by him, but couldn't step away fast enough, getting as close to Maite as she could without raising suspicion.

"I'm Trinidad," she said, offering a hand to Maite, who smirked as she took it.

"Maite, nice to meet you."

Clearly, they hadn't spoken ahead of this.

The *what the hell are you doing here* was apparent in Trinidad's eyes before she forced herself to look at me. "Tatiana. How are you?" she asked, slipping her hand away from Maite to greet me with a hug. "I'm sure Manuel has forgotten his manners, getting straight to business, not giving me a chance to meet and greet our guests. Do you need anything? Something to eat? Something to drink?"

"They're fine!" Manuel grunted at Trinidad, who made a quick point of putting some distance between us.

*Huh.*

Maybe Manuel wasn't as oblivious as I thought.

I forced a smile on my face as I reached over to pinch Maite, warning her to fix her damn face—her expression had done something crazy when Manuel spoke.

"You're always *such* a gracious host, Trin, but no thank you, we're fine," I told her, trying to pull this tension together before it had a chance to go left. "We can actually keep this brief, Manuel," I told him. "We just wanted to offer you the respect and courtesy of talking to you about a certain... issue... in person."

He held up a hand, then looked to his wife. "Leave us. And close the damned door."

Beside me, Maite shifted, and I pinched her again, trying to get her to fix her damn face as Trinidad slipped out the door. Once she was gone, we finally took our seats in front of Manuel's desk.

"Pardon the interruption," he grunted, shaking his head. "Tell me, what is this issue the *Predators* have sent women to discuss with me?"

This time, Maite pinched *me*.

I quickly schooled my expression into something more neutral than I felt about his little jab, in favor of getting straight to business. "The *Marauders*," I said, folding my hands together in my lap. "You know what they did."

"Do I?" he asked, eyebrows raised as he feigned ignorance.

"You know what they're incriminated in, a fucking massacre," I said, rolling my eyes when he cringed.

"Mi amor, *language*—"

"Oh fuck off, Manuel," I replied, over the faux politeness. "Let's get to business. Somebody is going to answer for the slaughter of our members, and all fingers point to their club. Am I wrong?"

Manuel sat back in his chair, arms crossed, and shook his head. "No."

"Okay then. As far as *we're* concerned, there's only one acceptable answer. Blood for blood. That's what we live by, all of us," I said, making it plain. *Reminding* him. "We just want to make sure that in doing that, we're not stepping on *your* toes."

Manuel frowned, sitting up. "Do you think we are their hired help or something?" he asked, coming with unnecessary aggression.

I wouldn't play into it, so I shook my head. "Of course not. But you *are* their supplier. If we take them down, it's a potential disruption to your business."

Manuel's chin lifted. "I had not thought about that."

Yes he had.

If we caused an issue in their supply chain, they would show up at our door without question, expecting some sort of restitution. He was counting on us not considering that shit, so he would have a reason to have a problem.

I wasn't fucking stupid.

Before I could continue the conversation, Manuel spoke up again. "If you embark down this path, you are not talking about snuffing them *completely* out, right?" he asked. "Blood for blood is just the head of the man responsible, not an entire organization."

"Well..." I inhaled a deep breath, considering it. We hadn't made any decisions like that quite yet because we needed everything in a certain order before we moved at all. "I think we have to just cross that bridge when we come to it," I told him, meeting his gaze without backing down.

After I said that, Manuel stared at me for a long moment before he nodded. "I'm sure we can fill in any gaps in distribution that might occur. Especially if we could potentially move product with the *Predators*—"

"*Not* on the table," I said, immediately shutting the idea down.

"I don't think we can leave anything off the table at this point," he countered coolly.

"We most certainly can," I offered right back, in an equally impassive tone. "*Predators* no longer deal in extralegal activity of any type, outside of single-event exceptions for official club business. Our hands will not touch your product," I said, making myself *absolutely* clear. "Is that going to be a problem for you?"

His eyes narrowed; thick black brows furrowed together. "What if it is?"

I smiled. "Well, that would be a shame, considering how long our families have been allied with each other."

I pointed to the *Santa Muerte* statuette in a place of prominence on his desk.

"My father gave you that, right? As a sort of coronation gift, after the *Predators* helped you turn Santiago Cartel territory into Rojas territory. We helped you secure the prominence you have now," I reminded him, making sure my breasts were on a nice display as I leaned across his desk. "Manny," I breathed, purposely softening my voice. "Let's not make this something it doesn't have to be. *Predators* will *not* touch your product, period. Not up for debate. But...we might be able to offer you a little room in our territory. As an olive branch."

I didn't *want* to offer him shit, but since he was being difficult...

"I'm listening," he said, even though his eyes were firmly planted on my cleavage.

"We won't run your people off the strip," I offered, sitting back. "But you keep them away from *Reverie* and *The Drake*."

"Away from *your people*," he correctly surmised and I grinned.

"Exactly."

Weed and recreational shit was one thing, but the other clubs dealt in the *real,* life-ruining, no turning back type of drugs. Addicts and other interested parties would get it in Vegas one way or another, but I wasn't about to agree to offering up Black people on a fucking platter as his permanent customers.

He sat back too, thinking about it for a moment before he nodded. "The high-end customers at the casinos will more than make up for what the *Marauders* can't do anymore," he agreed.

"Only for a year. And only if it comes to that," I added. "If the *Marauders* regroup—they keep selling for you. Everything continues as normal."

"I'd rather have more of an insurance."

"And I'd rather not have to have this conversation at all. But here we are." I shrugged.

Momentary anger flashed in Manuel's dark eyes, but then he smirked. "Well. I see. This is why Blue sent you," he said. "He knows I would have a hard time staying angry with someone so beautiful."

I smiled. "You're very sweet. Blue would have attended himself, but he had a family issue come up. He sends his regrets."

"I doubt that."

"Doubt what you must, Manny," I said, maintaining my eye contact with him. "But he respects your character enough that he sent *two* beautiful women to deliver this news, knowing they were safe in your presence. I'd think you recognized it as a testament of his trust."

"Of course," was his dry reply. "In any case, I think we've occupied enough of each other's time today, no?"

A grin spread across my lips as I stood. "Is this your way of kicking us out?"

"Absolutely not," he assured, as he stood as well, already walking to the door. "I have another meeting shortly and need to prepare. But please, feel free to stay as long as you'd like. I'm sure Trin would appreciate some guests for lunch," he offered.

"Thank you, but no," I told him, *fast,* to keep Maite from accepting that invite. "We should be on our way."

I gave her a *look* to keep her mouth closed as Manuel's people led us out of the house. It wasn't until after we were back in the car, and I'd turned on the device Teo gave me to check for any sort of bugs, that I signaled for her to speak.

"So, I *hate* that guy," she exclaimed, fussing all the way down the driveway as I navigated back to the main road. I let her go off until we were away from the compound, then tapped a few buttons on my console to call Brandon.

"Is Manny going to be a problem?" he asked, with no preamble.

I blew out a sigh, thinking through the details of the conversation before I answered. "Probably. Yeah."

# Chapter Eleven

## TATI

TATI

"We're going to have to do something about the Lady OGs," Brandon said quietly, prompting me to look up from where I'd been tucking into my plate.

It was much later in the day now – night, actually – and I was at my mother's house, where Brandon and his mom had popped up so Randy – Brandon's mother – could show Mama something.

"What makes you say that?" I asked him, keeping my face completely serious, even though I already knew the funny ass answer.

He scoffed, instantly catching on to the fact that I was about to fuck with him, muttering something under his breath about "*goddamn tooth gems*".

*Tooth gems!*

That was the "dental procedure" Randy had dragged Brandon to the dentist with her for, and honestly… I thought it was the funniest shit in the world. Her little bit of anesthesia had worn off now, but not enough for her to drive, so she'd made him bring her by to show off.

"It *looks good*," I insisted, because it did, and she was so happy with it.

I didn't personally understand the appeal of the tiny diamonds embedded in her teeth now, but it was certainly quite blingy and pretty. I already had a feeling I'd be getting dragged to the dentist next, to hold *my* mama's hand while she got hers done.

"You're such a hater," I told Brandon, nudging his shoulder while our mothers chattered away across the garden about the things they had coming up.

He frowned at me. *"I'm* a hater? They're wildin! The new bikes they got, the hair, now *tooth gems*?" He looked over at where they were standing, then leaned into me a bit more. "You know she's talking about a fucking tummy tuck? A *tummy tuck*! What she need that for?"

"If you're jealous that your mom wants to be a badder bitch than you, just say that," I teased, making his frown go even deeper. "Seriously, I don't understand what the problem is. They're grieving and getting through it the best way they know how. They need something to do."

"They could be part of the club!"

I shook my head. "It's too painful, Brandon. It's barely been a year since *The Fall*, and... their wishes were clear. The death of our fathers meant *we* took over, so no manner of poking, or prodding, or trying to get them to change their minds is gonna work. This is their retirement. And if they want to use their time and money getting nipped, tucked, lifted, buying bundles, I'm not about to hate on it. They've been through a lot."

He sighed. "I'm just saying... who they trying to look good for?"

That made me raise my eyebrows.

Suddenly... I understood his real issue a bit more.

I put an arm around his neck, leaning into him. "She's not trying to get over your dad already. You know that, right?" I asked. "Not in the way you're thinking. If she *was,* she'd be well within her rights, but I don't think it's that."

"Then what is it?"

"Those niggas were *so* touchy feely with them, so free with the compliments and affection... but they don't have that anymore. They're just trying to feel good about themselves on their own. All the little insecurities they were constantly reassured about, their husbands aren't here to quiet the noise anymore," I explained. "We can't be pissy about them doing what they need to do to be okay. Nobody is being pissy with us for this whole war we're starting 'cause our daddies died, so we can shut the hell up about Randy's tummy tuck, Carmen's butt lift, whatever the hell they want to do."

"Butt lift?!" Blue groaned. "Ah, hell."

"Is that really all you heard nigga?"

*"No,"* he insisted. "I'm just saying—"

"Nothing. As long as they are being safe, we are going to let these girls do whatever the hell they want. Okay?" I asked, and he shook his head as he glanced at his phone.

"Man, whatever."

"I know it's whatever." I laughed. "Don't be a hater."

He smirked at me. "Nah, *you* don't be a hater," he countered.

"What does that even mean?" I frowned. "What are you talking about?"

"You'll see," he insisted. "Ay, have you heard from Kev today? I had a call with him earlier."

I cringed, grabbing my glass of water for a swig. "Uh-oh. *The* call?"

He nodded. "Yeah. I went ahead and let him know we were going with Ghost, but I tried to break it to him easy. Told him we would set up a time to maybe talk about him consulting on some private investments or something, but he wasn't really trying to hear it. I expected him to show up at *Bottoms* later so I could talk to him in person, but he never showed."

"Aww," I said, pouting for a second on his behalf. "I haven't talked to him, but Dove shot me a text earlier, asking if something was going on. I don't know if he's still there or not, but he was drinking away his feelings earlier at *Allure* with his favorite girl."

Brandon shook his head. "See, this is why I don't want you fooling with that nigga. Why is he at *Allure* in Sanaa's face dealing with his disappointment instead of talking to you? What kinda shit is that?"

"Uh-uh." I laughed. "He did the right thing; 'cause *I* don't want him crying to me about it. Go talk to the bitch you pay to care."

"That's cold, Tati!"

I shrugged. "I'm not trying to be cold, I just... had already warned him as much as I could. I made it clear to him that it was a long shot, which should've already been obvious, if we're being honest here. Of *course* the position was going to Ghost."

"Well yeah, but still, that's *your* homie," Brandon teased.

"*You* approved his ink," I countered, and he pushed out a sigh.

"Only one I question, every damn day."

I looked up as the doorbell rang over the garden speaker. My eyes went to my mom first, who looked just as surprised, and then to Brandon, who didn't at all.

"What did you do?" I asked, a quiet sinking feeling settling into my chest as he stood.

"Ms. Carmen!" he called, grinning at me before he turned to my mother. "I hope you don't mind. One of my guys needed to give me a report in person, so I told him it was okay to swing by."

"I don't want no wild hoodlums in my house!" She laughed.

"I already got you, me and Tati are going to go talk to him outside."

"*We are*?" I whined, but I knew there wasn't really much I could do and I already knew exactly who "his guy" was that needed to show up at my mother's house for a report. Onyx had spent the day with Teo doing reconnaissance, and whatever he had to say... I wanted to know.

Now.

"*Shit,*" I cursed as I hefted myself out of my chair. "You make me so sick."

"Why you mad at me?" Brandon asked, laughing, as he led the way back through the house to the front door.

I stopped to glare at him. "'Cause I can't believe you got this nigga at my mama's house."

"You don't even know who it is," he claimed, looking goofy. "I said one of the guys."

I sucked my teeth. "Don't play with me," I told him, then took the last few steps to the front and flung the door open to, sure enough, find Onyx on the other side.

*Shit.*

Maybe I should have taken a moment to mentally prepare.

He was draped in my mama's doorway looking fresh from my wildest dreams in a long-sleeved tee that was made *just* for those biceps of his. He was looking down at his phone, so his locs had fallen in front of his face. He pushed them back in reaction to the open door.

"Your meeting must have gone well? You appear to be in one piece still," he said, with a slow perusal of my body that made goosebumps spread over my skin.

The good kind.

Well... depending.

"Why the fuck wouldn't I be?" I asked, frustrated by my body's treacherous reaction to his gaze.

He lifted his chin, giving me a grin that left me feeling even *more* murderous than I already did. "Why so hostile, Tati?"

*Because I was sick of his damn face, that's why.*

"Does your guest want to come inside?" my mama asked from somewhere behind us. "I was just playing about him not being welcome, let that young man come in and get a plate."

"He's fine," I countered with a little more snap then I intended with my mama, so I turned to her and apologized.

She gave me a look —an annoying, knowing look—that I couldn't say anything about. "Brandon, baby your mom wants you to come look at these blocks I put down in my garden so you'll know which ones to go get her."

"*Goddamnit*," Brandon muttered, but then immediately put on the right attitude for my mother. "I'm coming, Ms. Carmen," he told her. "Nyx, kick it with Tati for a second, let me handle this."

"Yes, go be a good son before you lose her," I teased him, earning a middle finger as he strolled off.

"It's good that he takes care of his mom the way he does," Onyx said pulling my attention to him.

Grudgingly.

"Yeah." I nodded, stepping outside to keep him out of my mother's house. I didn't need her making conversation – and plans for my fucking future – with him. "Any man that wouldn't, I'd have to question his character."

He looked away from me, scratching his chin. "I can see why you'd say that, but don't you think that's the type of thing that should be taken on a case-by-case basis? Everybody's mother doesn't deserve that."

Something about that statement made me narrow my eyes—not because it bothered me or even that I disagreed. It just made me wonder.

I met his gaze, trying to figure it out, but the intensity of his eyes was too potent, as usual. I had to look away.

"That's not what you're here for, right?" I asked, shifting the subject back to more pressing matters. "You have an update for us?"

He nodded. "Teo put all the data on the private server too, but we got some good shit. I put him on some shit I was familiar with from... prior employment. So we were able to do some digging with a few extra tools y'all didn't have access to."

"Like what?"

"I might have to kill you if I told you that," he said, wagging his eyebrows. "Seriously though—no need to worry about it. The point is, we got all the location information, bank accounts, all that. And after spending a couple hours digging through text messages we scraped from the cell provider, we've got some...supposed... names."

I drew my head back. "*Supposed* names? What does that mean?"

"It means..." He shook his head, pushing out a deep breath. "There might be more to this than we thought."

"In what way?"

He sighed. "So LVPD claims they have intel confirming *Marauder* involvement, right? But we didn't see anything about it *from* any of them. No planning, no codes, none of that. But afterward, there's chaos, while they're trying to figure out what happened. They're denying any involvement."

I rolled my eyes. "Of course they are."

"To their own people?" he said, which...

Okay.

That was a little weird.

If it was a sanctioned attack, certainly there would have been some type of communication about it. Even if the actual strike was planned in person, they would have conveyed to the other members to stay out of the area, to lay low, *something.*

"I'm not sure if what we *think* happened is what *actually* happened," Onyx continued. "It seems like the *Marauders* have had a lot of confusion going on since it went down, which is the exact opposite of what you'd think. Taking out the leaders of a club like the *Predators*? That's big shit. Legacy-making shit. But instead it's chaos. They're trying to figure out who could have possibly been wearing their colors."

I blew out a sigh. "So... stop talking around the point and just say it plain. What do you think is going on?"

"I think this shit was a setup." He shrugged. "I don't think it was the *Marauders.*"

"Okay... talk me through it."

"Think about it, who benefits from dissension between the clubs, gangs, whatever you want to call it?" he asked, hands up. "Whose interest is it in to start a war between two of them? And not recklessly, calculated, 'cause it can't be between the two most powerful, that might be too obvious. But if you pit them against each other, one by one, and make it personal... Not turf wars, but something way deeper than that..." He pushed his hands in front of him, implying that the rest was an obvious conclusion.

I didn't disagree.

I just couldn't wrap my head around it.

"Keep talking," I said, crossing my arms like it was going to help me think.

Onyx shrugged. "I don't think the *Marauders* are tough enough, *smart* enough, to start a fight like this. They might hate our Black asses, but the *Predators* are twice their size, we're allies with the people who supply their recreational and financial lifelines... Really, we could take them out by having the *Renegados* cut them off. But, because it's personal, doing that would be too easy. You look like a bitch if you don't shut it down. So it's blood for blood—"

"Because it has to be," I finished for him. "It's blood for blood 'cause if it's not, somebody else is going to try us. And when *they* try us, they're probably going to come harder."

"Exactly," Onyx agreed. "And the motherfuckers that try you—"

"Will be the *Renegados*," I murmured, shaking my head.

His eyebrow went up. "So you already know?"

"It would be idiotic not to."

"I'm glad you know," he said. "What do we do about it?"

"We move forward as usual," I said, peering past him into the dark as a light rain started up. "We keep doing what we're doing. We get the intel; we prepare for war. With the right person."

Before either of us could say anything else, Blue was back at the door, and for some reason, so was my mom.

"Hey baby, Brandon said y'all were about to all head out, so I want to give you this, and one for this handsome young man too," she said, holding up two overfilled paper shopping bags of food.

One for me, one for him.

I rolled my eyes.

"Thank you ma'am, they were working me like a dog. Nobody ever wants to feed me right," Onyx said, immediately turning on the freaking charm for my mother.

I rolled my eyes at that too and got myself pinched on the inner elbow for it.

*Hard*.

"Ouch, mama!" I whined, pouting at her.

She raised a finger at me, shaking it in my direction as she spoke. "Don't you be rude... I know your daddy taught you, you always make sure your people are taken care of."

"Yeah, Tati, I want to be taken care of," Onyx said and Brandon started cackling like a fucking hyena.

"I'm going home," I said, giving my mother a quick, salty peck on the cheek because there was no way I was leaving without kissing my mama. "Tell Ms. Randy I said goodbye, whenever she comes up from your garden for air."

"I will, baby. You go on and get home," she told me. "It already started raining, and it's supposed to storm bad. I don't like all that flash flooding. You call me as soon as you get settled, you hear me?"

"Yes ma'am, I will call you like I always do," I told her, ducking back in the house just long enough to grab my keys and purse. "I'll see you later," I told Brandon.

I said nothing to Onyx, although as soon as I was in my car I regretted it, because that made it *so obvious* he was under my skin.

*Why is he so freaking under my skin?*

I shook it off.

It was late and had been a long day. I needed to go ahead and get myself home.

At my house, I locked my doors behind me and got my alarm set, then poured myself a big ass glass of wine to drink while I got the food she'd sent with me stowed away. I was just getting wrapped up – and pouring a second glass of wine – when my doorbell rang.

"*This better not be his ass,*" I muttered as I pulled up the cameras on my phone.

I sighed when I realized it was Kev on the other end of my camera—not Onyx, which was where my mind went first, leaning all against my front entryway like he owned the place.

"You've had people worried about you," I told him over the speaker. "You okay?"

"No... I'm not," he said and I stood up a little straighter when I heard the obvious slurring in his words.

"Are you *drunk*?" I asked. "Did you drive over here like this?"

"Yeah," he answered, looking forlorn as he gazed up at the camera. "I didn't know where else to go."

"Home, Kev; you should have gone home to sleep this off and get yourself together."

"I need to see you. Talk to you."

I shook my head, even though he couldn't see me. "You haven't called though. You just showed up, *after* spending half the night at *Allure*. Why not go to Sanaa's house, talk to her?"

"She's not you," he declared, breaking into sudden sobs. "So I went... I waited for you at *Bottoms*, but you didn't show up tonight."

"Because I've been busy... taking care of *Predator* business, and then I had dinner with my mom. I'm tired, Kev... you should get home. Use the app to order a ride."

As *soon* as I said that I heard the roll of thunder from the storm my mother must've been talking about. Vegas was typically dry, but when it rained, it came down like a bitch, and *suddenly*. In what seemed like the next instant, thick sheets of rain started pouring down from the sky.

*Ugh.*

"You can come inside to wait, okay?" I told him, using my phone to unlock the door. I met him in the foyer, hands on my hips. "Why in the world would you drive over here when you've been drinking?"

He looked so damn pitiful coming through the door that I really did feel bad for him. I knew how much he wanted that position, but I *also* knew Brandon had been as objective as possible in making the decision.

Still.

From Kev's point of view, that probably didn't make it less frustrating.

"I've just been... shit, trying to make sense of it," he said, pushing out a sigh as he put his back to the wall, eyes pointed to the ceiling. "I get it, Ghost has been inked longer, and his father had the position first, but... damn. I really thought it was going to be me. I thought you were going to make it happen for me."

My eyes narrowed. "I told you from the beginning that it wasn't my decision, it was Brandon's. It wasn't up to me, and honestly, even it was... I can't say the decision wouldn't have been the same."

His gaze came to me, defeated. "Damn. I... guess I should thank you for your honesty?"

"No," I replied. "I just don't want to lie to you. You probably would've been a good choice too, but Gavin was simply the better candidate for the *Predators*."

I wasn't sure if my clarification made it better or worse, but I was trying to be nice.

Blame the liquor.

I really should've let him just sit outside and hoped for the best, but I didn't want to be *mean* to him.

I just definitely, definitely wasn't fucking him anymore.

This was pitiful.

"You know I'm heading out of town—private island, all expenses paid. Got some stuff to set up for a client. You should come with me."

I shook my head, laughing. "Let me guess, somewhere with no extradition treaty? You have a tax shelter to set up?"

He smirked. "I can't confirm or deny. But seriously... come with me."

"I can't do that. You *know* I can't," I told him. Jetting off to a private island *did* sound like a nice escape, but his complete lack of grace in accepting not getting the treasurer position... didn't make my pussy wet.

At all.

"You should look at it like... a reset," I told him. "Go get your mind right, unwind, and then come back better, you know?"

Kev nodded over my words, then blinked, surprised, as he took in my appearance. "You dressed like that for dinner with your mother?" he asked, stepping way too close, way too fast. I could smell the liquor emanating from him and immediately pushed him off.

"I had *Predator* business earlier and didn't change," I explained, taking a few steps back. "Go ahead and grab your phone; order that ride, remember?" I asked, as my own phone started ringing.

*Shit.*

I was supposed to call my mother.

"I gotta answer this. *Order the ride*," I said, leaving him in the foyer as a loud crack of thunder rumbled through the house. "Hey Mama, sorry," I told her as soon as I had the phone up to my ear. "But in my defense, I'm not actually settled yet; I got distracted."

"Hopefully with that *fine* young man that was flirting with you at my door," she teased, and I rolled my eyes.

"Please don't start."

"Don't start what? Asking you why you hadn't introduced me to him before? Well that's okay, you can tell me all about him *now*."

"Oh my *God*." I laughed, picking up the glass of wine I'd poured earlier. "There's nothing to tell. Onyx is the new guy. Brandon had him come by to give us some info. That's it."

She sucked her teeth. "Mmmhmm. I know that ain't it, but I'm gonna let you slide for now."

"Only because you don't like being on the phone when it's raining, girl." I chuckled. "I'm sure I'll have to get you off my back about this later."

"Long as you know. Love you. Bye."

"Love you too, Mama," I said, lifting my glass to finish it off once she'd hung up the phone.

"So Onyx had dinner with your mother too?"

"*Shit*," I sputtered, damn near choking on a mouthful of wine from the shock of hearing Kev's voice from right behind me. Coughing to clear my throat, I turned to face him, nose curled in annoyance. "What are you talking about?"

With his face crumpled like he was on the verge of tears; Kev shook his head. "You said you went for dinner with your mother, dressed liked you wanted to be slutted out," he said, stepping toward me, too close again. "Did you dress like that for him?"

"I dress like this all the time. It's what got *your* attention, remember?" I snapped, setting my glass down on the counter. "So no, I didn't dress like this for *him.*"

"But you did fuck him?" he questioned, right in my face.

"Okay, this is getting crazy; maybe you *should* just wait outside. I'm sure the porch is protection enough from the rain, and if not, maybe it'll sober you up some."

He shook his head again. "Just answer the question, *did you fuck him*? Is this why I didn't get that position? 'Cause he's my replacement?"

"Kev, get out of my house," I said, carefully, quietly, trying to keep my composure.

"*Did you fuck him?!*" Kev bellowed, making me shrink back, but he'd already snatched me by the wrists and dragged me against him. I tried to snatch away from his grasp, but that only seemed to make him squeeze tighter.

"Motherfucker let me go, *right now*," I screamed, trying in vain to wrestle out of his grip.

"Or what?!" he growled at me. "What the fuck is *anybody* going to do?"

I aimed a knee at his groin, tried to, but he dodged it, slamming me against the wall behind me. Colors exploded in front of my eyes as my head bounced off the hard surface and I realized very suddenly that...

Nobody was going to do anything.

There was nobody here to help me.

"*Did you fuck him?*" he asked as he slammed me against the wall again, and even though I didn't even know exactly who he was referring to anymore, I shook my head, struggling to even keep upright.

"No. *No,*" I groaned because it was the truth and because I wasn't stupid. I wasn't about to antagonize him. Not that it mattered.

"Good," he said grinning right in my face as he put a hand around my neck, and squeezed, dragging my half limp body away from the wall, out of the kitchen.

To my bedroom.

# *Chapter Twelve*

## NYX



"So you think *Rojas* could be the real culprit behind this?" Blue asked from the other side of the pool table, no trace of amusement in his face. After Tati left her mother's house, we'd taken off too, with me trailing him so we could talk about what Teo and I had found.

Now we were at the clubhouse; a meeting place that worked out well for me, since once this was done, I could find an empty bedroom here and pass out. I really hadn't had time to fully process my run-in with Alicia yet and couldn't say with any confidence that I truly understood her angle.

There were too many possibilities in the air for me to sleep anywhere with nobody watching my back.

To answer Blue's question, I shook my head. "Nah, I don't want to have you looking at the *Renegados* sideways without cause, so we'll get more information before we make that kind of assessment. I'm just saying... it's possible."

"Heard you," he said, frowning when his phone started ringing. He gestured for me to give him a second as he slid the device from his pocket.

Once he'd looked at the screen, that frown softened as he answered. "Tati, you know it's way past your old lady bedtime," he joked with her like he usually did. But then, suddenly his expression shifted to one of profound concern. "Tati, what's wrong?" he asked, straightening from the slouched position he'd been in and dropping his stick on the table. "Talk to me. Stop playing."

I glanced at Teo, then Ozzy across the room in front of the TV, wondering if they might know what was going on. Both shrugged, so my eyes went back to Blue, watching his face go through a lot of changes.

"You're serious?" As he listened to whatever was being relayed, he scrubbed a hand over his chin before his expression landed on something I could only describe as homicidal. "I'm coming," he said, and then pulled the phone away from his ear for a moment like he was putting it in his pocket before pulling it back to his ear. "Do you need me to stay on the phone?" he asked. "You sure? You're *sure*? Okay. I'll be right there."

His arms dropped to his sides after the call had presumably ended, and he just stood there for a moment, eyes closed, fists clenched.

Only for a moment, though.

"We gotta go," he said, pointing to me even though he was already halfway across the room, and I was already right behind him.

"What's going on?" I asked but didn't get an answer for that.

"Ozzy, spread the word, we're on lockdown. I need everybody accounted for, including the OGs—you understand?"

"Yessir," he nodded, already putting his bottle down and grabbing the remote.

"Teo, find Ghost for me. I need him on high alert, and get Retta up too, in case we need the armory," Blue said, doling out more instructions. "And uh… Keira. Call her and tell her to meet me at Tati's in an hour. You got that?"

"Consider it done," Teo assured, and then Blue looked at me.

"Let's go."

Instead of his car, which he'd used earlier because he was chauffeuring his mom around, he went straight for his bike—it would be faster. I hopped on mine and followed him, paying no mind to the pouring rain as we traveled the now-familiar path to Tati's house.

*What the fuck was going on?*

It had to be serious for Blue to institute a lockdown, mobilizing weapons and shit. My first thought was my worst thought – *Predators* vs the former *Garden* – and if *that* was it…

*Shit.*

My allegiance would fall with the *Predators* until there was no one left to backup. I didn't even have to think about it very hard. But… there was really no question of who would win that mashup; the *Predators* had numbers and brute force, but *Roses* and *Thorns* were bred killers, who you wouldn't know were coming until they'd already had a knife to your throat.

But there was no reason – no *good* reason – for a clash like that to ever happen.

At least none that I could think of.

As far as I could tell, Alicia and her orphaned soldiers had been in Vegas for years; the *Predators* had been here longer. Throughout that time, they'd peacefully coexisted.

The only apparent change was my presence.

But we were approaching the last turn onto Tati's street, so I'd have to think through those implications another time. *Now* was the time to figure out what the fuck was going on.

The house was completely dark when we pulled up, and I couldn't tell if that was a good sign or not. Blue still wasn't saying shit, and I stopped asking, since it was clear I wasn't going to get an answer. I followed him up the driveway and into her house, which he had a key for, closing and locking the door behind him.

The security system wasn't armed.

I pulled the gun from my waist and moved in front of Blue, ready and willing to put a hole or six in anybody who wasn't supposed to be there.

"Tati?" he called out, and my head whipped around, trying to glare his ass into silence. I had to remember though; he wasn't trained for shit like this the way I was.

Still, when there wasn't an answer, it concerned me too. I rounded the corner into her kitchen first since that was the most open space of her home. It had only taken a few minutes in her space on my first visit to understand that she thrived on cleanliness and wasn't an *I'll get to it later* kinda person.

The nearly empty wine glass on her counter, illuminated by the moonlight coming in through the windows made my stomach flip.

When I glanced back at Blue, he was looking at the same thing, and his expression let me know my reaction to it wasn't off the mark. It was clear that Tati wasn't here or in the great room area though, so I shifted my focus back to finding her.

Ominous energy permeated the air as we headed out of the kitchen and up the hall. I stopped cold when a dark spot on the floor got my attention. With my foot, I poked at it, tightness blooming in my chest when it streaked into a familiar substance.

Blood.

I could tell, even in the dark.

Splattered across the sleek hardwood floors, probably seeping in to create a stain leading to one of the doors. Blue and I exchanged a look before we headed there, to the room I knew was Tati's bedroom.

At the door, I stopped and listened, finally finding a sound in the bleak silence that saturated the house.

Running water.

The shower.

*Fuck.*

"Wait here," Brandon told me, as he pushed the door open into the room. It was dark there too, but dim light spilled from a doorway across the room.

I nodded, agreeing to his instruction, but my stomach was turning in knots as he disappeared into the adjoining bathroom. Anxiety kept me from staying still, driving me to pace the blood-streaked floor for several moments before I couldn't take it anymore.

I took my ass right back to her front door, to the security panel that was there. After a few taps on the screen, I was looking at the previous footage from the security camera pointed at her front door, going back hours.

Rage flooded my nerves when I saw Kev stumbling up to the door.

I played the first clip, taking in the whole conversation, disgusted at how fucking pathetic this dude was. She'd only let him in because of the damn storm.

Because she wasn't heartless.

She couldn't send him out into that rain with a clear conscience, and that compassion was what his bitch ass had preyed on.

I hated the length of time between the clip of her telling him to come inside and wait for a ride – one he'd probably never even ordered – and the next one. Nearly an hour later, it caught him on the way out—limping as he made his way down the front steps. When he glanced back, there was a full shot of his face that gave me a tiny bit of satisfaction. He was scratched and bloodied up, which meant that, at the very least, Tati had managed to get some licks in too.

But he'd walked out of here.

I'd much rather have had to rush over here to help Blue get rid of a body.

Instead... I knew exactly what that running shower meant.

I stopped what I was doing, swallowing hard to fortify my nerves before I switched to the other front door camera, the internal camera, which would show me a view of the entryway and hall.

The one I'd counted on her not checking when *I'd* broken in to scare her just about twenty-four hours before. I watched, just getting angrier and angrier as the screen showed their initial interaction, then him following her into the kitchen.

Not even ten minutes later, they were back on the screen, with her fighting against him as he dragged her down the hall to the bedroom.

The blood splatter hadn't happened until he came back out.

She had to have gouged him with something that made a pretty good wound, but... *fuck.* I couldn't even let my mind go to how he'd probably made her pay for *that.*

I turned the screen off, my head swimming with a nauseating blend of fury and worry as I strode purposefully back down the hall.

I knew what I needed to do.

Finding a little closet next to Tati's laundry room full of clean linens, I gathered what I needed to replace whatever was there. Back in her bedroom, the shower was still going, and I could hear Blue's voice, hear the coaxing, soothing in his tone as he talked to her.

Entirely too fucking familiar.

I blocked it out as I stripped the bed, trying not to focus too much on the bloody state of the sheets. I bypassed the laundry room and tossed all that shit in the kitchen, near the garbage. Whatever was going to be done with it could be decided later.

With a roll of paper towels and a can of Lysol, I sanitized the mattress and let it air out for a bit before I took my time making up her bed with the fresh linens.

On the off chance that she even wanted to be in this room.

Once that was done, I shifted my attention to the floors, trying to get everything back to as close to a "normal" state as I could.

I was finishing up when the shower turned off, finally.

I grabbed the shit I'd been using to clean and made sure it was out of the way, hesitating in the door frame. I didn't know if it was better to be out of sight or exactly where she could see me, so she wouldn't have another question in her mind, another thing to be concerned about.

It wasn't until they'd both appeared at the bathroom doorway that I realized I'd been holding my breath.

*I'm gonna fucking kill him.*

That was the *first* thought in my head when my gaze landed on Tati, her pretty face bruised and swollen, her eyes glossy and full of distress. She was wrapped tight in a robe, and Blue was helping her walk, a little detail that made my fists itch with a fresh wave of anger.

She looked at the bed, confused at first, but then understanding washed through as she looked at me, making an easy deduction.

"Thank you," she said; her voice hoarse as she spoke, with none of the usual dynamism I'd grown accustomed to from her, like she was... *broken.*

He'd taken her fucking energy.

Somehow, *that* was what pissed me off the most, of everything in front of me.

All I could offer was a nod because this whole thing was... too much.

Too recognizable.

I moved out of the doorway, leaving Blue and Tati to have whatever conversation they needed to have on their own as he helped her into the bed. I waited, in my own mental battle against the skeletons in my closet for him to give me some sort of instructions.

If I followed my own instincts right now... this night was going to get bloody, quick, and I couldn't give in to that. 'Cause once I did, if there were no boundaries, no restrictions... I wasn't sure I'd come back from it.

Not with everything I was keeping suppressed.

A few moments later, Blue came out to find me. "It was Kev. No police," was the first thing out of his mouth.

"Obviously." I nodded my agreement.

With Tati being who she was, even if the *Predators weren't* involved in any type of illegal activity anymore, the police weren't going to take this shit seriously. They could barely be counted on to take it seriously even when the victim was "upstanding". The Black vice president of a local motorcycle club they didn't want to exist would go straight to the bottom of their list of priorities.

*If* they didn't invent some supposed crime for *her* to be guilty of, just to drive the knife in.

Not only that, but I could tell from the look on Blue's face—whatever the police would have done, even in the best-case scenario, it wasn't fucking enough.

I agreed.

"I'm going to stay here with her, and Keira is on the way. We might end up taking her to a hotel, or the clubhouse, or one of our places... I don't know. But she said she's fine for now."

She wasn't fine.

She just didn't have the energy to make a decision.

It wasn't my place to say that, though.

"What I need from you," he started, but I shook my head.

He didn't even have to say it.

"Consider his ass delivered," I told him. "I saw the security cameras."

Blue blinked, and shook his head, probably clearing away whatever visual that brought to mind. "Hold nothing back. Use any and every resource, every connection."

"Understood."

Putting his hands to my shoulders, Blue looked me right in the eyes. "I want him whole."

I raised my eyebrows, confused. "After what this motherfucker did?"

Blue shook his head. "Let me rephrase that," he offered, dropping his hands. "I want him *alive*. Whatever happens after that is for Tati to decide."

I nodded, understanding. "Did she say anything?" I asked. "Not that she needs to. Like I said, he's all over the cameras."

"Which I don't understand," Blue said, crossing his arms and leaning back against the wall. "Does he think we won't come for him?"

I sighed. "I've been wondering the same thing. He was drunk when he got over here, and I don't think it was planned, but... you would think he knew better than to give in to some shit like this. And if he knows better but still did it anyway, he has to believe he's going to be shielded from the consequences."

Blue nodded. "Yeah. We need to find out who his financial clients are, probably some corrupt politician or something. *Fuck*. I can't believe I didn't —" He stopped, shaking his head as he tried to calm whatever was happening in his mind.

He pushed off from the wall, swiping a hand over his head. "Her pops... he died in the hospital, not on the scene. I talked to him," Blue explained. "I promised him, that I wouldn't let anything happen to her. I've been talking to Ozzy about security—*hired* security. I hadn't brought it up to Tati yet 'cause I knew she wasn't gonna like it, but with the shit we're doing... we can't just be out here with nobody on our back. I thought we had time."

I nodded.

They *did* need real security, especially now that they were dipping into the drug business—legal or not. I'd even considered bringing it up to them myself, but had held off, not wanting anything in the way of what I needed to do first.

"This shit isn't your fault," I told him.

"It's Kev's fault," Blue agreed. "He did what he did. There're no excuses for that, and he's gonna get his. But if I'd done what I *knew* I should've done.

Then *this?* Wouldn't have happened to my fucking *sister*. She's... how am I gonna explain this to Carmen?"

He scrubbed a hand over his face, staring at nothing for a moment before he shook his head. "I'm gonna go back in here and see what she needs. Whatever fucking secret society black ops shit you gotta do, get it done. I want my hand around his neck in the next twenty-four hours."

I shook my head. "It won't take that long."

"You were right to contact me."

"I don't need your validation. I know I was right to call," I countered, then immediately tamped down my misplaced frustration. The shrewdness of the decision hadn't made it any easier to be sitting across from Alicia again, when I still hadn't processed my feelings from the last "run in".

But at least this time I was fully lucid.

When I'd left Tati's house and hadn't found Kev at any of the first obvious places —his house, *Bottoms Up*, his mother's house, *Club Allure*, or his office, I'd made the call to Alicia.

It probably wouldn't have taken more than a few hours to find him on my own, but I didn't want to spend a few hours doing that—I wanted his ass *now*. With everything at her disposal, Alicia could make that happen.

I didn't have the patience to allow my pride to keep me from asking for her help.

Especially when I considered what had, so far, been left unsaid.

"This shit is my fault," I told her, speaking aloud the thought that had been plaguing my mind since the door of Tati's bedroom. I'd come to Alicia's estate and had spent the last hour waiting for an update from the team she put on it.

Plenty of idle time for my mind to run wild.

When Alicia just lifted an eyebrow, but didn't say anything, I expounded on my words.

"I antagonized him this morning. I knew he wasn't shit, and I poked at him, egged him on. I think that... I think it put fuel on whatever fucked up fire he had going on."

"You're serious?" Alicia asked, frowning at me.

She'd been sitting with me the whole time, mostly in silence, but the occasional question had come up.

"I am."

She huffed, shaking her head. "Nyx, you are entirely too smart to *truly* believe that man assaulted Tati because he was pissed off at you."

"Look at the timing," I argued. "I fucked with his head, threatened him this morning, and then tonight... this is what it is."

From her seat across from me, Alicia narrowed her gaze. "So in the course of a day, a normal, *not* rapist just decided to become one because *you* pissed him off? That might be the most self-centered bullshit I've ever heard."

My eyebrow shot up. "What?"

"This *isn't* about you Nyx, although I understand why you might be confused," she said. "What *he* did is what *he* did, and that doesn't have anything to do with you."

She stood from where she sat, coming to sit beside me and squeeze my shoulder. "We're going to find him. And when we do, he is going to have exactly the kind of night he deserves. So let's keep the focus where it belongs. Starting with... how is Tati?"

I shook my head. "About like you would expect. Last time I spoke to Blue, she was refusing to go to the doctor to get checked out."

"I'll get in contact with Blue, see if I can send Loren over there," Alicia mused.

I raised an eyebrow. "Should I know who that is?"

Alicia grinned. "You will. She's a good friend—my daughter's mom."

"Your *daughter*?" I asked, confused.

"My partner, Cree, he has a child with her," she explained.

"And you and her friends?"

"Yes, we are."

I shook my head. "And everybody is just... good? It's not messy?"

"It is leaps and bounds less messy than a lot of situations that should be very simple," she said, shrugging. "Everybody is happy, and healthy, and I've got no complaints. *I'm* happy."

"That's possible?" I asked, genuinely. We weren't exactly poster children for what anybody could consider a normal life. Our chances of gaining – and maintaining – the usual markers of "happiness" were next to none, as far as *I* knew.

Alicia sighed. "Even with all the fucked-up stuff between...Yeah. It is. Even for you. And Tati will be okay, too. She has all the resources, all the support—"

"That's not exactly a guarantee, is it?" I interrupted. "It was never okay for my mother, and... look how that went."

I knew that wasn't a fair comparison; it wasn't one to one.

My mother may have had money at her disposal, but any sort of community, any sort of care... she had none.

We'd both suffered for it.

"I'm so sorry for what happened to you," Alicia said, and this time when her hand came to my shoulder, it lingered. "None of it was okay. If it makes you feel any better... you weren't the only one I couldn't protect. In case you were ever thinking it was just you," she told me, and I shook my head.

"I know that shit wasn't your fault," I admitted. "It's not like any of us were given many choices of our own. That's what they put a failsafe on us for, right?" I chuckled, trying to find some humor in a situation that wasn't at all funny.

"But we're free now," she reminded me, with obvious strain in her tone. "I know it's a hard transition. It was hard for all of us, but... my transition was slow. Probably the easiest of everybody. The toughest part was once the memories started coming back, you know? The stuff they'd tamped way down deep, buried but not destroyed. I can't imagine how difficult that is for you too."

"My shit was never buried," I told her, with a dry smile. "I was never given the privilege."

Alicia sucked in a breath. "Are you serious?"

"Yeah. But I'm good."

"No, you're not," Alicia countered. Her hands came to my chin, turning me to face her. I wanted to hate it, but... I didn't. "You've been out there by yourself, but you don't have to be alone. We're here for you, Nyx...for real."

I shrugged her off, shaking my head. "I'm good by myself."

"Then what did you come to Vegas for?" she questioned. "And where have you been since *The Garden* went down?"

The second inquiry was a little easier to answer.

Only a little.

"Drifting," I said, offering another shrug. "Country to country, city to city, continent to continent. Exploring. Just... *being*. It's not like I had anywhere to be, anywhere to go. Not like I had a real home."

"But you *do*," Alicia countered. "And don't roll your eyes, at me, I'm serious. I know it didn't feel like it when you were out there by yourself—or when I left. But Nyx, you have people who give a shit about you. Me, Isaiah, Blue, Tati, the other *Predators* since you share their ink."

I shook my head. "They don't even know me like that yet."

"And yet they've welcomed you," she said. "Who did Blue take to Tati's house with him tonight? Who did he send to go find the person who hurt his sister? *You.* There's no question in my mind—he didn't do that lightly. He did it because he trusts you."

I scoffed. "He shouldn't."

"Why not?"

I chuckled. "Because it's not smart."

"Maybe not, but it's human. You get to know people, you get vulnerable with them, you get comfortable with them. That's how relationships go."

"So what, you're a guru now?" I asked, laughing, and she shook her head.

"No, not a guru, but I do know a little bit, from experience. You don't have to be alone anymore. You have family, as fucked up as we may be. You've got us."

I didn't get a chance to refute that and... I wasn't even sure I wanted to

Honestly, this was too much happening at once, too much of a mental overload, too much anger and emotion swirling at once.

I didn't even know what I was doing right now.

The knock at the door brought clarity.

I looked up just as another familiar face walked in, mostly serious. But there was a hint of a grin as he raised his chin to salute me. "Look at this pretty motherfucker," Isaiah said, stepping in with his hand outstretched to shake mine for the first time in a long ass time.

He and I had fought like hellions as kids, but as we got older, we were paired together. We worked well as a unit for the same reason we clashed—we were both angry, wild motherfuckers. That connection and familiarity with each other had bred friendship, right on the cusp of what could have been considered brotherhood.

Which meant it had to get stamped out.

They put him on protection duty, at *The Garden*, and sent me off to lose whatever humanity I had left.

"Nah," I told him, laughing as I easily shook his hand. It was crazy to instantly still feel that same familiar connection. "That's you, nigga."

"Oh please," Alicia interjected. "You are two sides of the same pretty boy ass coin," she said. "Nyx just has more hair. Isaiah, do you have something for us?"

"I do, actually," he said, holding up the tablet he'd walked in with. "An hour from now, Kevondre Woodson has a private flight, chartered out of the *Hamilton Luxury Transport* airfield."

I scoffed. "He can't be serious? Hamilton, as in Nessa Hamilton, Blue's girlfriend? Is he trying to be funny?"

"Nah," Isaiah said. "It's a shitty countermeasure. And it's exactly what caught him up. He has two flight plans, that one and another with a different private carrier. He didn't use his name on the other one, but all the details are the same. It's him. The *HLT* reservation is supposed to be a decoy."

Alicia nodded. "Yes. But it's weird that he isn't already gone. I would think he would be in more of a hurry."

Isaiah spoke up. "These flight plans were made yesterday. He already knew he was leaving, so... maybe that made him bold enough to carry out the assault, thinking his getaway was already in the works."

"When did he make the plans?" I asked.

"It was pretty late at night."

Okay.

So before he had his call with me.

That offered the tiniest bit of reprieve from my guilt. My antagonizing him definitely hadn't helped, but it seemed like he already had some plan of action ready to go.

"What was his end game with this?" Alicia mused. "Why did he even leave her alive, after what he did? He had to know the *Predators* weren't going to let this rest, so what more would he have had to lose, when he was already about to leave?"

It was a fucked-up thing to consider, but we had to.

Why *had* he left her alive? It wasn't as if killing her crossed some special line after the shit he'd already done, so what was it?

"Do you know if he drugged her?" Alicia asked, making me frown.

"I don't think so, but I'm not sure. What makes you ask?"

"It would just make a little more sense. If she was incapacitated and couldn't call anyone, it would've given him time to make his getaway, without killing anybody."

Isaiah nodded. "I'm guessing he left because he needed to get his shit in order before he got on the flight?"

"We don't have to do all the speculation," I spoke up, shaking my head as I stood "We can just get the answers directly from the bitch himself."

THERE WAS nothing I hated more than a man who preyed on women.

That wasn't a particularly unpopular opinion by any means—they were societally unacceptable in general, but experience had given me a *specific* distaste.

A personal disdain.

That was why it was no hardship for me to sit fully immersed in the dark shadows of a mostly empty airfield, waiting on Kev to show up.

Actually, it was damn near a gift.

It gave me plenty of time to think.

*What if he doesn't show up?*

Huh.

I hadn't really considered that.

The intel was good, and we were rarely wrong about our deductions when it came to things like this.

One of us?

Maybe.

But *all* of us coming to the same incorrect conclusion, that Kev would be here?

It just wasn't very likely.

But still—*what if?*

I grinned to myself, thinking about it. If he didn't show up here, when I found whatever hole he was hiding in, I was going to make him hurt even worse for inconveniencing me.

*That was* what if.

Unbidden, the visual of Tati's bruised, battered face came to my mind. Before I could shake it off, it had already morphed into my mother. I closed my eyes, trying and failing not to allow myself to be lapped over with a wave of memories, pulling me under.

Memories from before I'd been turned into what I was now.

Back then, I couldn't do anything about the predators—the wolves who didn't even bother disguising themselves as sheep. I couldn't even reach the high cabinets in the kitchen without help. All I could offer was... triage.

The unfortunate aftercare of abuse, tasks no one should have to contend with, but *especially* not a fucking child.

A sound in the distance made me drag myself out of the pit of those thoughts.

I was only waiting for a few more minutes before Kev showed up, rushing in with a bag slung over his shoulder. His scratches and shit were cleaned up now, and he was limping, but he still somehow had a smug ass expression on his face.

I hated this motherfucker, and in this moment, he was reminding me of another motherfucker I hated – the one who'd committed the original sin that fucked everything up – but I couldn't access. Not just him either, all the others.

But they weren't here.

Kev was.

So... I was about to take it all out on him.

"Headed somewhere?" I called out from my place in the shadows, and like the bitch he was, Kev jumped hard as fuck, high as fuck. If I was a betting man, I'd wager he'd pissed his pants a little.

"You stay back! I'm armed!" he called out, trying to put a little extra bass in his voice as his eyes darted around, trying to see where I was. I remained in the shadows, stalking, moving to a new position so I could fuck with his senses.

Then I stepped out into the light, my hands steady as I aimed. "Me too."

The shot rang loud in the empty space, echoing off the walls as Kev dropped. He clutched his leg, writhing back and forth as he screamed in pain.

"Did you fucking *shoot* me?!"

I laughed as I crossed the wide space, heading for him. "You are not very bright, are you? You heard the gunshot, I'm sure you feel that fucking bullet in your shin. But... *did I shoot you*?" I chuckled. "Did I, Kev? You tell me."

I crouched down near him, just looking as he continued to twist in pain.

"Help! *Help*!" he screamed and I just shook my head as he started trying to crawl away from me.

"Not sure what good you think *that's* going to do," I said. "Nobody is coming to fucking help you."

I'd already made sure of that, sliding any staff I'd encountered a wad of cash to go home to their families without seeing anything.

"You know what I think?" I asked as I stood, closing the distance he'd put between us. Once I reached him, I kicked him hard, right where I'd shot him.

His injured screams were music to my fucking ears.

"Shut the fuck up," I demanded, aiming my gun right between his eyes. He flinched, covering his head with his arms as he started crying.

*Disgusting.*

"I think you bet on that exact thing with Tati; that nobody was there to save her," I said, crouching in front of him. "I don't think this was... a crime of passion, or whatever the fuck. I think you wanted her alone, no one to help, nobody who could come to her defense. I'm here for her retaliation though, bitch. And I'm thinking real hard about sending you back to anybody who cares about you in bite-sized pieces."

"I've got a kid! A baby on the way! *Please*," he sobbed, and I snarled.

"*You better not be talking about Tati.*"

"No!" he yelped. "Not... not Ta—"

"Don't you fucking say her name," I growled, pressing the gun right between his eyebrows as he blubbered.

"No. It's one of the dancers. At *Allure*. She just... she just told me, and... *please,*" he pleaded.

"Don't beg me for shit—*especially* not your miserable life. Not having you around would be doing that child and its mother a favor. As a matter of fact..." I sighed, then walked a few steps away and shot him again, in the hand this time.

I waited until he'd stopped screaming to start talking again. "If I put a bullet through your head right now... It would be the best gift anyone ever gave a child."

"Please! I can do better. I can be better, I swear." He kept up his pitiful petitioning, and I shook my head.

"Your begging doesn't mean shit to me. As a matter of fact—it's negative points. 'Cause I've got a question..." I bent down, pressing the barrel of the gun right under his chin this time. "Did Tati beg you?" I asked. "After she was considerate enough to let you in her fucking house, did she *beg you* not to do what you did?"

He looked away, trembling in pain.

I shoved the gun against his throat. "*Answer me!*"

"Y-ye-yes," he managed to choke out, and it took everything in me not to put a bullet in his head right then.

*Only* because my instructions were to deliver him alive did I take a step back, trying to reel myself in.

"But you did it anyway," I said, repulsed by his blubbering face. "So explain to me why the fuck you think you deserve more grace than you gave her? *Huh!?*" I kicked him again, then walked away, putting some distance between us before I did worse.

All that crying and whining and begging, but nothing to say for himself.

*Piece of shit.*

"No answer? Right. You can't answer. Don't even fucking try it," I said, watching, bored, as he managed to shakily pull a gun from his waistband. I didn't even move as he aimed it erratically in my direction and pulled the trigger.

The bullet hit the wall a solid six feet away from me.

I sauntered up as he struggled to aim again, bending to easily take it right from his fingers. "Do you know what an apex predator is?" I asked. "Let me define it for you. An apex predator is the top of the food chain in their respective ecologies. Sharks dominate the water, lions dominate the Sahara, men dominate humanity. You've heard of this, right?"

When he nodded, I scoffed.

"Yeah, I bet you have. I bet you think you're some sort of *alpha male*, high-value man, right? That *bullshit*. The shit men like you, who shouldn't even breathe the same air as women like Tati, believe. But let me tell you something, you are the *bottom* of the fucking barrel. You and people like you, who abuse women, kids, people weaker than you—you are the dirt under the feet of men like me."

I stood up, putting a boot to his head, and pressing down, ignoring his screams. "I could kill you, and not even flinch about it. I *want* to kill you. But I won't."

"Thank you! Thank—"

"Don't thank me," I growled at him, grinding my foot into his scalp. "Other people are questioning why you didn't just kill Tati when you did what you did to her. They think it makes no sense. But I understand you, Kev." I laughed, mushing his head in with my foot, causing another pained groan before I moved away. "You wanted her to live with it. So I want you to live with *this*. We're not going to give you to Tati today. You see, she's probably still processing, you know?"

I crossed my arms, nodding.

"We're going to *wait*." I grinned. "Because what *I* think is going to happen, is that there is going to come a point – I don't know when, but it's going to come – when she isn't going to feel afraid, or lost, or hurt, or confused by what you did anymore. She is going to get *very, very, very, very,* fucking angry. And *that's* when we're going to give you to her." I laughed. "You're going to live with *that*. While you wait."

"I'm not going to live with shit, you shot me!" he exclaimed. "And you're standing here letting me bleed out!"

"Stop whining like a fucking baby; you're not going to bleed out," I told him. "This is why I like to use small caliber weapons. In the right places, they don't do lethal damage," I explained. "And I am going to shoot you in all those places, until my clip is empty. You'll live. But man... you will *suffer*."

I smiled, crouching in front of him again, enjoying the pure terror on his face.

"I've gotta admit, I *love* this journey for you, Kev."

# *Chapter Thirteen*

## TATI

Tali taught me how to step outside of myself.

It was a technique she'd employed when she was in pain and she was often in pain—mentally, physically, emotionally. She had plenty of reasons to want to step outside of herself, to take her mind somewhere else, somewhere where the pain didn't exist.

We hid it from my parents, the way she would poke me with a needle to induce the pain I was practicing getting away from. I didn't have anything to escape otherwise, not the way she did. It was probably why she'd never thought to warn me, that while you could escape it in the moment... afterward, your body still remembered.

The ache, the terror, the chaos, the outrage ... it was burned into you, just lying dormant.

Or maybe it was just me.

Maybe she hadn't known.

Tali wasn't tuning out a violent assault—not from outside her body at least. She was her own aggressor and she could never get away from herself. My assailant wasn't present, except for the immutable traces lingering in my peripheral.

Not vivid, at least.

Thank God for blunted edges.

"Are you okay?"

I blinked, realizing Maite was there in my living room with me, standing next to where I'd parked myself on the couch.

There were two pills in her hand, and I took them without asking what they were before I swallowed, chasing them with a deep gulp of water from the glass she offered with her other hand.

No, I wasn't fucking okay.

How could I be?

Still, I nodded, glancing away as I fortified the lie. "Yeah. I'm fine."

"You know it's okay if you're *not* though, right?" she asked, her pretty face pulled into a deep, contemplative expression that made me smile.

Bless her, for trying.

"I don't want to *not* be okay, so I'm going to fake it instead."

She frowned, taking a seat next to me. "I really don't think it works like that."

"It works however I say it does," I declared, not caring how insane it probably sounded. "Does the swelling look any better now?"

Maite looked at me, really examining instead of just telling me what I wanted to hear. "Some. Just a little, but... you still look like you've been in a cage fight."

I smirked.

I was okay with that comparison because I may as well have.

It had been three days, or maybe five, or maybe a week since I let Kev into my house to wait out the storm. I hadn't at first, but I did remember that now.

Remembered talking to my mother.

Him overhearing and attacking me.

Dragging me to my bedroom.

Until I couldn't, I'd fought his ass with everything in me, punching, scratching, biting, gouging him with a pen from my bedside table, whatever I could until he'd thrown me down on the floor and knocked my lights out.

The next time I'd opened my eyes, he was on top of me.

*Inside me.*

Grunting and moving, muttering awful shit to me while intermingled sweat and blood dripped off him, onto me, and I, only half cogent, begged him to stop.

He didn't.

That was when I went to go be with Tali in my mind.

"You definitely look a *lot* better though," Maite reiterated and I nodded.

"Good. A few more days and some good concealer, then I need to be able to get back out there. There's still business to tend to."

"I'm pretty sure between Brandon and Keira, and the others, they've got it under control."

I scoffed. "*Keira* is not the vice president of this club."

Maite frowned, reaching out to lace her fingers through mine. "Tati, *nobody* expects you to jump right back into it. It's okay to not—"

"I don't need it to be *okay* to not do shit!" I snapped, snatching my hand from her. "I need it to be okay *to*. I get it, everybody wants me to know it's fine to be soft and vulnerable, and whatever the fuck else, but *I don't want to*," I explained, trying to blink back sudden tears. "I don't want to hide and take a break, I want to... go back in time and not open my damn door. That's what I want. That's what *I need*."

She raised her hands. "I didn't mean any harm."

"I know." I shook my head, pulling myself up from the couch. "I'm sorry. I'm... gonna go lay down."

When I got to my room, I looked at the bed, remembering what had happened after Kev had dragged me up from the floor.

Then I went and got in my shower. It was terrible for my skin, I knew that, but it was like I couldn't get clean enough, couldn't get the smell of his cologne off me, couldn't rid myself of the feeling of him.

Under the sprayer, I let the hot water soak through my braids and pour over me until I couldn't stand it, and then I grabbed my body sponge to actually wash.

To *scrub*.

I tried to settle into it—the steam, the rush of sound, the smell of the eucalyptus bundle I'd had Brandon refresh for me. Tried to relax and let the anxiety of what had happened drift away.

But nothing trumped the reality that my own hands felt strange on my skin.

My thoughts about sexual assault had typically been constrained to the limits of what I could do to protect myself from becoming a victim. Shit I shouldn't have to think about – a burden I shouldn't have to bear – but this world was what it was, and that was the unfortunate reality.

I never thought about... the aftermath.

It never occurred to me how, in the wake of being assailed, I wouldn't feel like *myself*.

It...*hurt*.

I was one of those women gladly obsessed with every inch of herself—my dark skin, full lips, "negro nose", my soft belly, rolls, cellulite, all the things I was supposed to hate.

I didn't.

I *loved* it.

I wasn't afraid of my nudity, didn't shy away from it in the mirror. I knew exactly where to touch myself—and did, often. So much that it was damn near part of my routine, a hormone rush that helped get my mind right, ready to face the day.

But this time when I moved my hands over my body in the shower... there was a disconnect. The familiarity was gone and my palms felt foreign. I slipped a hand between my legs, looking for the exact right place. I'd read enough articles in the last few days, enough stories from survivors to know that for a lot of women, *this* was triggering.

Their hands felt like their assailants, brought back flashes of their attack.

For me...

I just felt... nothing.

*Nothing.*

And as bad as I knew the alternative could be, I couldn't help wondering if this – the nothing – was maybe somehow worse.

It was enough to make me irate.

"*You're being ridiculous,*" I told myself, and then rinsed off and left the shower, wrapping myself in my most comfortable robe.

I'd cleaned my room countless times since the assault, and my mother had, and so had Keira and Maite, but I still felt like I could smell him. Maybe I'd just never noticed the way that bastard had permeated the energy in here, even before he had resorted to... *this.*

I'd gone about my affair with him all wrong. He never should have been allowed in my space, never should've been able to get so close. I was so wary of Onyx, meanwhile the snake in the grass was right in front of me, in plain fucking sight.

I... couldn't believe how stupid I was.

Blowing out a sigh, I looked at my bed again.

Tried to tell myself his presence had been removed with the soiled sheets we'd burned in the backyard.

My mother wanted me to come stay with her.

Brandon wanted me to come stay with him.

They weren't the only ones who thought it was too much for me to still be in the space where my assault had happened. Keira and Maite were just waiting on the smallest shred of a sign and they'd be packing my shit.

But this was *my* space.

And being expected to leave it felt like I was being forced to make a concession, felt like giving him something *more* without permission. I loved my house, loved the way I'd decorated, loved the memories I'd had built here.

This was my safe haven, my sanctuary.

Why did he get to take that away too?

*Everything is fucked.*

I knew Onyx had found the motherfucker, that he was locked away somewhere, rotting in a windowless room. I hadn't been able to bring myself to actually do anything with that information.

I understood why they hadn't just killed him, but I almost wished they had.

This was something I didn't want to think about—I didn't *want* to be a killer.

It was one thing to be willing to defend myself in the moment, to assert the kind of dominance that created a bubble of protection around us.

I could do that without a second thought.

Calculating it was something else.

Vividly, I remembered our fathers sitting us down to tell us how they'd come to choose the name *The Predators* for the club. It was never supposed to be a warning to anybody else—it was a reminder to *us*.

Of human nature.

It was a reminder of humanity's failings, moral and otherwise.

We were predators and had to decide how to navigate that responsibility. The leader of the pack did what was necessary to take care of the rest, he worked for his community. This was common among predators in the wild. They didn't kill just because, they didn't eat when they weren't hungry. They didn't stalk and terrorize for *fun*.

For gratification.

Human predators were the ones that preyed on the vulnerable just because they could.

And *that* was something our fathers never wanted us to be; the type of predator we didn't take our cues from.

I pushed thoughts of Kev exactly where they belonged—out of the forefront of my mind.

I got in my bed and grabbed my favorite toy from my bedside drawer. Not because I was aroused or even wanted to be.

I was just chasing the same thing I'd been chasing in the shower.

*Anything.*

But nothing came.

Including me.

Usually, all it took was a quick couple moments with this thing pressed to my clit and I was perfectly content, ready to pass out asleep. This time, no matter what angle, no matter what speed, no matter what pressure, I couldn't find *the* feeling.

I hadn't *been* able to find the feeling, and it was that – the not being able to – that was driving me fucking insane. I just wanted my body to feel like my body, my skin to feel like my skin, and it wasn't happening.

So I put on some clothes and went to my workroom instead.

Maybe I could finish something in here since I couldn't finish anywhere else.

*Terrible joke*, I reprimanded myself in my head.

But I had to find humor somewhere.

I shook my head and tried to focus on the crystal in front of me. A large piece I'd been working on—a carving of a rose, a bigger version of the one Tali had made me all those years ago. Once I finished it, I wanted to take it to her graveside to show her, but my progress on it was slow.

I wanted it to be perfect.

I could only work on it when I was in certain moods and I already knew today wasn't one. Still, that was the piece I picked up, sitting at my bench with it clutched in my hands, making no move to do anything.

*If Tali was still here, how would she react to all this?*

What would be her way of offering comfort?

I smiled.

She'd probably have me at *Bottoms* getting drunk or something, but really... when I thought about it, if Tali was here, I probably wouldn't even have been dealing with Kev. And if Tali was here, Brandon would *really* be my brother.

I shook my head, thinking about how deeply the two of them had been in love. Brandon had been so damn paranoid about my father finding out, only to discover when it was too late that he'd always known. He'd just been waiting on them to say something.

It'd hurt Brandon when she died—helplessness consumed him, along with the baseless belief that he could have done something.

I'd felt all that too.

It was *why* I'd been moving the way I did. Tali's death hurt so bad that it didn't make sense to add *more* people I could potentially lose to my heart. Keeping a healthy distance was just so much safer.

Until it wasn't.

"Knock knock."

I looked up from the rose carving I wasn't actually working on to see Onyx at my workroom door. A bit of a surprise, considering I hadn't seen him since the night he left my house after changing the sheets for me.

"Hey," I said, putting the rose down. "What's wrong? Did something happen?"

His eyebrows went up. "Something has to have happened for me to come through?"

I shrugged. "You haven't, so..."

He chuckled a little. "No, Tati. Nothing happened, I've just been a bit busy," he said. "Filling in the gaps."

"You mean taking my place."

"No." He immediately shook his head. "I could never do that. Nobody can. It's okay for you to rely on your chain of command, damn. Everything shouldn't be on just the two of you."

I nodded.

He was right.

Although for obvious reasons our fathers had been the most significant loss for us, specifically, the whole club had taken a hit. It was a move that would have completely killed the *Predators* as a club if they hadn't already prepared me and Brandon for it.

We were busy grieving and managing the club and maybe having a war and building a whole business... and rebuilding the chain of command had been another welcome distraction from it all.

But it was still tough.

"So what are you doing here?" I asked, and he stepped through the door, holding up a bag of food. "Maite called me, said you really wanted Thai food. She asked if I could bring it."

My mouth dropped open for a moment, confused, but then I shook my head. "I didn't tell her I wanted food. And even if I did, I wouldn't have asked *you* to bring it. Thai is my favorite though, aside from my mother's cooking. Which is probably why she did this."

He nodded. "I get it. Have the most handsome nigga she knows bring you your favorite food, seems like guaranteed mood booster, right?" he said and I laughed.

"Something like that."

"Okay well... I hear you; you didn't ask for it, but... are you hungry?"

I frowned, thinking about it.

I *should* be, considering I hadn't eaten anything today, unless me picking at the breakfast Keira had dropped off earlier counted. Another side effect I guess, of being so disconnected.

"I could eat," I agreed. "*Should* eat."

"Come on then," he said, leaving the room with the bags instead of just handing them over, heading toward my kitchen as I followed.

"Um, I can feed myself," I told him.

"Good, grab a plate," he said, giving me a confused look. "You handle yours, and I'll handle mine."

I wrinkled my nose. "Yours? So you stopped to get me food and grabbed yourself something too?

"That a problem?" he asked. "I been working, I've gotta eat."

"Onyx, all you *do* is eat. It's always about food with you. *Every time I see* you, you're eating." I laughed. "Like it's just your damn favorite thing to do."

He caught my gaze, smirking as he put the bag down on the counter. "As a matter of fact, eating *is* my favorite thing to do, Tati," he told me, with a little wink that...

*Oh.*

Okay.

The *anything* I was looking for earlier?

There it was.

Right between my legs.

*Something.*

But instead the mischief I'd normally see from Onyx, his amusement was quickly replaced with regret, eyes wide. "Oh shit, I'm sorry. You probably don't—"

"No! *No*," I insisted. "Please be normal with me. Everybody's tiptoeing around me, always asking if I'm okay. But how could I be when everybody is treating me like I'm not?"

"Fair enough," he nodded. "But are you doing everything that's necessary for you to be okay? 'Cause I've got to be honest with you—everybody is kind of feeding off your energy here."

"How would you know? You haven't even been around."

He drew his head back. "Tati, you act like you don't want me around on *regular* days. So I fell back, not trying to be another nigga in your face after what you just went through with ol' dude. Why *wouldn't* I find somewhere else to be?"

I shrugged, not really knowing how to answer that because he was right. I did treat him like he got on my nerves because he *did* get on my nerves. But him not being around, for some reason, wasn't really acceptable either.

*Why?*

"You were always in my face before," I said, pulling the top off of my container of food. "The only thing that changed is me getting assaulted. Are you not attracted to me anymore because of that?"

*Shit.*

I didn't think through those words before they started coming out of my mouth, but it seemed like as shocking as they were to me, they were for him too.

*Had I really had that in the back of my mind?*

His eyes were wide before he shook his head leaning onto the counter as he responded.

"Look, I was trying to be respectful by giving you space, holding back on my... *let me rub on your booty* energy," he said, biting his lip for a second before he continued. "But I hear you when you say that's not what you want. So come here, let me feel it."

"Shut up." I laughed, holding up a hand. "I'm *not* saying that."

"Aren't you though?" he asked, making much more sense than I wanted him to. "Maybe you *don't* want me touching you, I'm not saying you do. But what I'm hearing is that you need to know I still *want* to touch you, right?"

I stuck a forkful of food in my mouth so I wouldn't have to answer, but since Onyx just looked at me, waiting, I finally conceded with a nod. "Yes."

"Okay." He laughed. "So like I said, come here."

I scoffed. "I know it sounds so stupid," I said. "And I don't even know why I'm talking about this with you. Where did Maite go?"

"She was on the phone and stepped out. But why wouldn't you talk about this with me? I seem like a bad person to talk to or something?"

"I'm not saying that," I denied. "I'm just saying... how much can you really relate? I mean, *look at you*," I said. "You're not going home and feeling like your space isn't really yours anymore, scared of what someone might decide to just walk in and do. And I bet your whole *show me that you can break into my house* prank doesn't seem as funny anymore now, does it?"

"You're right about that," he agreed, then swallowed the food in his mouth before he kept talking. "But if you'll recall, I came here that night because I wasn't feeling very secure about the safety of my own space. I'm *not* saying it made it right to scare you, but I *am* saying that it's not really accurate that I can't relate. Not on that one."

"Okay, I'll give you that," I said. "But again, look at you. Who's making you do anything you don't want to do? Who's forcing themselves on you? *Inside you?*" I asked, quickly clearing my throat in hopes of disguising the sudden emotion that had built in my throat.

Onyx put his fork down, staring at me for a moment before he spoke.

I was expecting to hear *you know what, you're right.*

The line instead that came out of his mouth was, "Actually, you're still wrong."

When I opened my mouth to contradict him, he shook his head. "No, I said what I said, you're still wrong. I know you think you know what I'm all about, but you don't. And I'm too over the shit to keep it anything but a buck right now, and I think you'd appreciate it more if I did anyway. So let's just get into it."

My eyes were wide the whole time he was speaking, completely caught off guard by his words. "What do you mean?"

"What I mean is that, even though I'm not even bound by the same rules and expectations as I was before, all somebody has to do is play a certain song – one I don't even know, so I can't avoid – and I'm the goddamn Manchurian candidate. That's—"

"I know what it is," I interrupted, waving his explanation off.

I'd seen the movie.

"But how is something like that even...? Who...? *Why*...?" I stammered, not even able to fully articulate my confusion.

"Fucked up reasons and fucked up reasons *only*." He shrugged. "Me, and everybody like me, we were... programmed, for lack of a better way to put it. Forced to do shit we otherwise never would. And there wasn't *shit* you could do about it; you just have to live with it after."

"That's awful."

"Yeah, it is. And I'm..." He chuckled, shaking his head as he pushed his food away from him. "I'm not even sure it's the worst thing."

"What could be worse?" I asked.

"The training," he immediately answered. "To be what I was, you had to be exceptionally well-trained and I'm not just talking about fighting. You had to be able to hold a conversation with anybody in any room, blend into any lifestyle. You had to be charming, fascinating, seductive. And you had to be able to follow through. Create an experience for your mark."

When he didn't finish, I straight up asked him, "What does *that* mean?"

"It means exactly what you think it means, Tati." He confirmed my worst suspicions, shaking his head. "I know you don't want it to mean that, but it does. And training doesn't suddenly start when you're eighteen, it starts with *puberty*. And then they wonder why you're so fucking angry and try to tamp it down," he muttered, shaking his head. "I was a special case, because of a specific dislike the person who ran the place had for my mother. What they couldn't take out on her, they took it out on me. So... my 'childhood' was pretty fun."

"Onyx..."

"Don't be *sorry*," he interrupted, somehow already knowing what I was about to say. "You don't have to be sorry; it wasn't you. But just know if you're ever over here feeling like you're by yourself... you're not. And this isn't any of that *somebody had it worse* type shit, and it's not about *me*. I'm just..." He pushed out a sigh. "Like I said... you're not alone."

For a long moment I was quiet, and then, "Is that how you thought to change the sheets? And clean? Because of what happened to you?"

He shook his head. "Nah. Because of what I saw happen to my mother. I was the one who took care of her after it happened. I helped her clean up. She was... scared and all that in the moment, but she handled it in her own way I guess. She seemed fine. But I actually think that shit triggered her 'cause then she got *way* worse."

The tears I was trying to hold back stung my eyes, but I blinked them back, not wanting to make it any more of an awkward moment. "Do you mean she... hurt you?"

"Physically?" He shrugged.

He was always fucking shrugging, trying to play everything off, make it seem like no big deal.

But it was.

"Nah not really," he continued. "Everything with her was psychological. Mental."

I pushed out a sigh. "I know you said not to tell you I'm sorry—"

"So don't."

"But I am," I said, moving to wrap him in my arms before he could protest, pulling him against me in a hug. "I don't care if you're a grown, scary motherfucker now, you weren't then. And that shouldn't have happened to you."

"I appreciate that." He chuckled, pulling back enough to look me in the face. That intensity was back, like he was looking into my soul, and I hated it. But I didn't shy away, not even when he asked, "Do you feel better?"

Instead of giving a shallow answer, I really considered it, thinking about it before I responded. "I think maybe a little. Not because of what you've told me, but just... getting some of it out."

"Good."

I kept my eyes locked with his, and asked, "Do you?"

"Nah." He laughed. "But my shit is cauterized at this point. I'm not sweating it anymore, because what good would it do? Anyway, have you thought about moving?"

I frowned over his sudden change of subject and shook my head. "No, not really," I told him, and then explained my reasoning for staying.

"I thought you said you wanted to be okay though?" was his response once I was done, and I raised an eyebrow.

"What?"

"You said you *just want to be okay*, and yet you're staying here when you don't feel safe...because you want to prove a point. Because you want to make the space be something it's not anymore, based on what it was before."

"Who asked you all that?" I asked, sucking my teeth.

He laughed. "Nobody, but I'm saying. We're putting it all out there, so let's put it out there. Staying here as some way to avoid letting Kev 'win' is silly. That shit is *silly*, Tati," he repeated. "If it doesn't feel good for you, what's the damn point? He's in a basement somewhere, rotting until *you* decide what happens to him. So you look at this situation, and you're telling me that moving somewhere that makes you feel happy and safe, that feels like *he* won?"

"Again—*who asked you*?" I said, mushing his shoulder since I was still right up on him.

"Nobody." He chuckled, grabbing my hand. "I'm just telling you what I see. And from what I see, you don't have to prove anything. To anyone," he added, looking up at me.

"Up" wasn't exactly correct. He was seated, and I was standing, but still, he was at *just* the perfect alignment for me to only have to lean in a bit to kiss him if I wanted to.

Which... for some inexplicable reason, was *exactly* what I wanted. I didn't know which to blame—my body or my mind. I just knew that feeling I'd been chasing through countless showers, and in my bed not that long ago... there it was.

So easily sparked by his presence.

The very same urge whose absence had me wondering if I was losing my mind, *there it was*. I couldn't... *not* give in to it. I'd been trying too hard grasp this feeling—I *couldn't* fight it.

Wouldn't.

So... I didn't.

I stepped between his legs and kissed him, and he let me, and... *God.* The pressure of my lips against his was *such* a sweet relief. I couldn't explain it if I tried, but it was like a cool drink on a hot day—refreshing and soothing, and damn near holy. His fingers dug into my waist, pulling me in closer as I put my hands to his face, deepening the kiss.

*My* kiss.

And he let it be, despite both of us knowing he could easily shift the dynamic. I greedily moved my tongue in his mouth, lapping against his as he kissed me back.

Did he taste like the amalgamation of spices from the spicy food?

Yes, but I didn't care, not in the slightest. I was way too focused on the fact that I wasn't *broken,* not as much as I'd thought. I *could* feel something, and it was everything I hadn't known I needed.

Arousal poured out of me, driving the passion of the kiss, and making me sink against his body, and soaking my panties, and making me dizzy.

"*Shit,*" I breathed, finally pulling back after we'd been kissing long enough that I needed a breath. "What was that about?" I asked, with my face still right up against his and he raised his eyebrows at me.

"What you asking me for? That's all you, sweetheart."

"My name isn't sweetheart."

He smirked, suddenly pulling away from me. "Isn't it, though?" he asked, then grabbed the lid for his food to put it on as he slipped out of his seat.

"What are you doing?" I asked, putting a hand to my tingling lips, not knowing if it was the spices or something else causing the sensation.

"I'm getting out of here before your ass gets me in trouble," he answered, and honestly...

I didn't have a rebuttal.

He *did* need to leave.

Before there was... trouble.

"Hey, are you leaving already?" Maite asked, suddenly breezing in.

"Yep!" was his only response as Onyx skirted past her with his food.

She turned to me, eyes curious as she asked, "Um... did I miss something?"

# Chapter Fourteen

## NYX

It wasn't sleep that eluded me.

Nah, sleep came easily, almost every night.

What I couldn't seem to grasp was... *peace*.

The tradeoff for sleep that came easily, was that it came with nightmares. But not the stuff that was forgotten as soon as you sat up, stuff you could easily brush off and never think of again because it wasn't real.

Mine were the kind that haunted you with your eyes wide open... reminders of a past that wouldn't let me go.

There was no way around it, and nobody I could talk to about it. Painfully few people would even understand, and among those... they had their own shit to contend with.

And it wasn't as if I was a stranger to toughing it out on my own.

I pulled myself from the bed at the clubhouse, swiping a hand over my forehead to dry the sweat I'd woken up in.

That simple action on the way to the bathroom gave me an idea—I needed more of that.

*More sweat.*

I got my shit together and then checked in with Ozias, so someone would know where I was. And then I held my feet to the fire of an invitation that had been causing me pathetically undue apprehension since I'd received it.

I went to Isaiah's basketball court.

Not that it was *his*, specifically, it was just at the community center where he worked when he wasn't on task for Alicia. The night he'd assisted with finding Kev, he'd pulled me aside, insisting that we needed to catch up.

For obvious reasons... I was hesitant.

I wanted nothing more than to put my past behind me; it was my whole reason for being in Vegas in the first place. Rebuilding my connection to people who were emblematic of the trauma I'd faced—*literally* the stuff of my nightmares...

It didn't seem wise.

*I should get as far as I can, as fast as I can, in any direction. Anywhere but here.*

That feeling rankled at me but didn't weaken my resolve.

I wasn't going anywhere until it was over, and it wasn't over, so... I had to fucking deal.

I had to cope.

So I set about the task of completely wringing myself out on the court, to the point that there wouldn't be energy left at the end of the night for my brain to divert to dreaming.

"Ay man, you gone shoot the ball or not?! I gotta get my ass home!"

*Oh, shit.*

My thoughts had me distracted.

I launched the ball from my hands, laughing at Isaiah's reaction to me scoring that final point when it slid easily through the net.

"Don't be salty, *you* said shoot it. If you'd let me think about it a little longer, I might have psyched myself out," I told him, running to grab the rebound.

It had actually been a long ass time since I'd played, so the first few games were basically massacres. But once I got my bearings, I was keeping him on his toes.

"I *let you* have this one, gotta make you feel like a winner somehow," Isaiah cracked. "Gotta keep your confidence intact, so you come back out."

Clearly I recognized the hint – the extension of another invitation – but as much willpower as it had taken to come out *this* time? I couldn't make that kind of guarantee.

Instead, I focused on the other part of his words.

"What you trying to say?" I asked, stopping to face him. "I can't take a loss without being a bitch about it?"

Isaiah drew his head back, lips twisted in disbelief. "You say that shit like it's new information. You never could take a loss; your ass was always ready to throw hands when you didn't win."

I immediately opened my mouth to argue the point, but then thought about it for a second and...

*Shit.*

He wasn't wrong.

As a kid in *The Garden*, I was wild, sensitive, and *hated* losing, to an irrational degree. I'd just already lost so much – had so much *taken* from me – that when it happened in a casual context, where I had the illusion of a modicum of control?

It was a problem for me, so I was making it one for everybody, ready to throw hands with any and everyone.

I was gone win *something*.

But...

"I've changed," I spoke up, shooting another basket even though we weren't playing anymore. When it bounced off the rim instead of sliding smoothly through the hoop, the usual disappointment gave me a little flinch, *nothing* compared to the internal rage I would've felt about missing a shot all those years ago.

"Haven't we all?" Isaiah responded to my declaration, grabbing the rebound before I could get to it. I didn't chase him down for it, just gave him room to make a couple shots of his own.

*He* had changed for sure.

Hell, *change* was putting it lightly; he'd gone through a whole damn metamorphosis.

The nigga was married and had a damn *baby*.

The last shit I would've ever expected.

"So you ended up with Alicia's baby sister," I said, bringing my thoughts into the open as he made his way back down the court to where I was. "That's wild."

He shrugged. "It's not that wild. That's where they put me in *The Garden* after they separated us, you know? She was a big deal."

"Yeah, so was I." I chuckled. "Only instead of giving me a productive detail, they sent me off in the wilderness like an animal."

He started toward the bench, gesturing for me to follow, and I did. "In her defense, she wasn't nearly as violent as we were," he said, then took a long swig from a water bottle. "You know what's crazy? When I think about it, everybody I started connecting with... I always got separated from. They did it to everybody it seemed like, they didn't like us getting close. But over the last few years...everybody's coming back."

"Don't get too used to it," I told him, using the towel he tossed me to wipe the sweat from my face. "I don't plan on hanging around long. *Can't* hang around long."

"Why?" he asked, dropping to a seat on the bench. "You got somewhere better to be?"

*Fuck.*

Why did that question... sting?

Growing up with my mother, things had always been rather fraught, but in a fucked-up way... I *belonged* there. It was home.

Being abandoned at *The Garden* was my first lesson in not getting too comfortable with that word, and still... I'd gotten used to it. I had missions to accomplish, times when I was sent away. And when I was there it wasn't like there were goddamn warm hugs and cookies waiting.

And yet... it was where I was supposed to be.

I could take everything off, the gear, the character, the façade of invincibility, *everything*.

And I could just... *be*.

So to answer Isaiah's question... "Not really."

I didn't have anywhere *else* to be, no, but I also couldn't stay here. This thing with the *Predators* was getting way more complicated than it was ever supposed to. I'd come to Vegas for a very specific task, and with that out of reach, I should've moved on.

But I hadn't.

And now I kept finding myself drifting into thoughts of the club's vice president—her eyes, her energy, her body, her *mouth*. In more ways than one. The slick shit that came out of it, the intoxicating softness of those lips, and the damn *possibilities* I hadn't yet seen.

All of it, fucking dangerous.

None of it more alarming than the unfamiliar depths of emotion she inspired, with little to no warning of the shift.

If she said there was an enemy, cool, I was prepared for war.

If anybody did her harm, I was taking it back in flesh.

If she smiled... I wanted to be the one who put it there.

*Dangerous.*

And not just for me, for her, too. These waters weren't just uncharted, they were... alien. I could step into a role and be what the situation called for, but... it would be just that.

A role.

And Tati deserved better than a damn performance.

"You ever worry you're fucking up her life?" I asked Isaiah, knowing I was going down a complicated road by even bringing the shit into conversation.

Fuck it though.

"Who? Dacia?" he asked, instantly perking up when referring to the former *Rose* who was now his wife.

I'd seen her before, but never met her, and as with everything in *The Garden*, I was wondering now if that was on purpose. There were so many of us there, and yet so many ways we hadn't crossed paths.

It was too coincidental to not be by design.

But what *was* the purpose?

To wreak distrust?

To make us loners?

If that was the case... shit. It kinda seemed like all the training, the trauma, had created the *opposite* effect. Now that we weren't part of that organization anymore, we were gravitating to each other more than ever, with nothing except our own lingering demons standing in the way of us banding together.

So fucking close, but so incredibly far.

I nodded, confirming my overly simplified articulation of a much bigger question—if he was concerned about the potential negative impact of his presence on Dacia's, and now, their child's life. It wasn't as if we were bred to be husband material, let alone for *fatherhood,* so it was a Russian roulette for us to step into it.

Isaiah's gaze dropped as he took another long guzzle from his water bottle, then nodded. "Yeah, I worry about it. All the damn time."

"What do you do about it?"

He shrugged. "I remind myself of my mission."

I raised an eyebrow. "Mission?"

"Yeah—my self-imposed objective. I *put* myself back in her life after we'd been separated. I made a conscious choice to step into this relationship. Nobody made me do that," he said, frowning at his hands. "So the idea of walking away from it... that's something I could never do to her. I made the commitment, and all I want in this life is to stand by it—I've got the chance for something I don't deserve and was *never* supposed to have. I can't fuck it up," he told me, shaking his head.

"But doesn't working with Alicia contradict that?" I asked, pointing out what was obvious to me, but... maybe not so much to him, since he was right there in it.

"Yeah, it would," he agreed. "That's why I *don't*. I'm connected to her because of history, and family, but I give it distance. Alicia called me because it was you. I helped with that Kev shit because it was *you*. Other than that? I'm just Coach Zay to the kids here." He chuckled. "I even got my tats covered 'cause I don't need any potential trouble."

"What do you mean, *potential trouble*?"

He leaned in to speak as a group came into the gym. "Think about it. I've got these kids at a game and somebody sees it. Somebody who knows what it means. Maybe they think something is gonna pop off, so they hit first, and now all of a sudden there's a shootout at a kids' basketball game. I don't need that. And neither do they."

I nodded, taking in his words as something I hadn't considered—mostly because a regular life wasn't something I'd considered. Yeah, there were *Predators* who had good corporate jobs, graduations to attend, cakes to bake, shit like that. And apparently some former *Roses* and *Thorns* were on that too.

But what *I* gravitated to was the gritty shit—maybe because it was all I'd known.

"Before I reconnected with Dacia, I was doing mercenary work," Isaiah continued. "It was... familiar. It's a relief to not have to be on that shit anymore, to just be me, figure out who the fuck that is, you know?"

"Yeah." I nodded. "But I gotta ask, why mercenary?"

"'Cause what else did I know? What better talent did I have?" He shrugged. "I'd been separated from Tamra—"

"Wait, do I know Tamra?"

He laughed, then scrubbed a hand over his mouth, trying to cover it. "Uhh...yeah. You know Tamra."

I frowned. "Why you say it like... oh. *Oh*. That's the one y'all sent to approach me at the bar?" I guessed, thinking back weeks ago to when they'd snatched me from *Bottoms*.

"Yeah." Isaiah chuckled. "She was my partner I guess; before the takedown. Which, speaking of takedowns—"

I sucked my teeth. "Nigga, you used that word specifically so you could bring this shit up, I ain't dumb."

"I definitely did but listen..." He laughed. "You should be proud of yourself. She said you went down hard and they had to pull out the *big* voltage on you."

Just the memory of it made me twitch. "Don't joke about that, I still feel a little electromagnetic *right now*."

Still cackling, he put a hand to his chest. "Been a *while* since somebody hit you with one of those, huh?"

"I don't miss it," I countered, rubbing my head as I remembered the *acclamation training* we'd had to go through in *The Garden*. In context, it was probably the least traumatic "training" we'd faced there, but that didn't make it an easy memory. Pepper spray, kicks to the nuts, taser, stabs, you name it, we'd been subjected to it so we would know what it felt like, and could, theoretically, shake it off.

"We knew Tamra would get your attention." Isaiah chuckled. "Thick, brown skin... you always had a type."

I nodded. "I can't dispute that. But I can say, the shit never would have gone very far."

"Right," he agreed. "Because you've only got eyes for Tatiana Tate," he said, with this look on his face like he knew *exactly* where I was coming from with that.

Shit.

Was it that obvious to others, or was it because he was one of the few people in the world who could claim to know me pretty well?

Not that it mattered.

I couldn't let myself settle into anything with her, knowing I needed to be bouncing at any moment. Instead, here I was hanging around being part of the team, only making the shit *more* complicated for when I inevitably regathered my common sense and left.

As if I'd thought the *Predators* up, my cell phone rang.

*Blue.*

"Give me a second," I told Isaiah and he nodded.

"I need to check in with Dacia anyway," he said, hopping up from the bench to make a call of his own while I answered mine.

"What happened? Everything good?" I spoke as soon as I had my device up to my ear.

On the other end of the line, Blue laughed. "Why do you always answer the phone like I'm about to tell you to suit up for war?"

"'Cause any call might be *that* one," I replied. "What's up?"

"How good are you at moving couches?"

I frowned. "Couches?"

"Yeah," he said. "Tati needs some people to help her get moved into her new place. We're still in the process of vetting everybody again, and I don't want a bunch of randoms around her yet, inked or not."

*New place?*

I hadn't heard shit about it until now, but it wasn't as if there was a newsletter about everything that went on with Tati. After that moment in her kitchen, I'd been keeping my distance, not wanting to lean into anything I shouldn't.

And *that* definitely qualified.

"Me either," I agreed with Blue. The kind of predator that Kev was had to be surgically weeded out or it would spread like a cancer.

"I knew we'd be on the same page. So you're coming through, right?"

*Shit.*

*So much for keeping my distance.*

"What time you need me?" I asked, knowing it would spark questions I didn't care to answer if I turned down the request. Blue and Tati were close like siblings, but I had no clue if she'd told him what had happened between us.

So far, my best guess was that she hadn't.

"Now, if Keira or Ozzy don't have you on something else," he said. "Or shit, I guess you do have a life outside our shit too, huh?"

I laughed, cause... not really.

I hadn't been around Tati, but I was fully enmeshed with the *Predators*, to the point that the *"vacant"* placard on the door of the tiny bedroom I'd semi-claimed at the bunkhouse had my name on it now.

Keira's doing, not mine.

Truthfully, I was worn out from being on the court all morning with Isaiah, which had been the goal in the first place, so I was too tired when I passed out tonight to experience the usual nightmares that morphed from my dreams.

I hadn't had the whole picture when I'd shown up to accept his invitation to *"come shoot around"*. I knew now though that this was his actual job, one he'd picked up with Ace's dude, Cree. It was a – cool as fuck – community center situation that put him in position to intervene for kids that were eerily similar to the kind of kids *we'd* been.

Young, wild, and in need of structure.

In need of somebody who gave a fuck.

"Nyx, you there?"

*Shit.*

"Yeah, sorry, I can come through," I answered, knowing I still had a bit of energy left in the reserves.

"Cool," Blue said. "Just come by Tati's."

"Bet."

Once we'd hung up, I looked over to where Isaiah was back and had started gathering his stuff.

"You got somewhere to be?" he asked and I nodded. "Good, now I don't feel bad for kicking your ass out of here." He laughed. "I need to go relieve my old lady—baby duty."

I grinned. "Would you ever have imagined saying some shit like that ten years ago?"

"Only in my most impossible daydreams," he said, extending a fist in my direction.

"It's a good look for you," I told him, standing so I could return the gesture.

"You could have the same," he proposed. I instantly shook my head, already walking away when I responded, "Nah, too close to science fiction."

A wife?

A family?

Just the thought was hilarious. Especially the idea that back then, I would've been able to fathom anything close to a "happy ending". But wasn't his fault that we were on wildly different pages where it came to the possibilities of shit like that.

Back then?

Living past the next day was the pipe dream for me.

I'd just stepped outside the community center, and was halfway to my bike, when a sleek black Benz whipped with into the spot beside it. I was on high alert, already reaching into the little drawstring bag I'd tossed my gear into until the window slid down, and a familiar face clad in oversized shades peeked out at me.

"Get in," Alicia called out. "I need to talk to you."

"I've got a cell phone; that's what most people use these days when they wanna talk."

Her head dropped back against her headrest, annoyed. "I like to talk in person," she said. "Can you get in? *Please?*"

I pushed out a heavy sigh and then glanced around, considering it a small price to pay for the fact that she was housing Kev's criminal ass at her compound until we were ready to deal with him. After a moment, I dropped the stubborn shit and took the short walk around to her passenger seat to climb in.

"How did you know where I was?" I asked as soon as the door was closed.

I already knew she wasn't going to give me a real answer, so it was no surprise when she just smirked.

"I always know where you are," she teased. "Now tell me, what do *you* know about *Jardin D'origine*?" she asked.

"Nothing," I shrugged. "Never heard of it."

"Yes you have," she said, shaking her head as she peered out the front window and waved to Isaiah as he passed, heading to his car. "You just didn't know the name. *Jardin D'origine* is the first garden program, headed up by Renard Belrose."

"Here we go with this motherfucker again," I groaned.

"Yes, here we go. I dug into him being stateside, trying to figure out why. He was looking into motorcycle clubs."

That made my shoulders tense.

I frowned but nodded. "If we think about how *The Garden* was connected to the Santiago cartel, whose territory was taken over by the *Renegados*, it makes sense."

Alicia shook her head. "It's deeper than that. I think he's taking advantage of the Santiago-Rojas connection to dig into the *Predators*. Rojas is the *Marauders'* supplier. Just before the ambush that took out the leaders of the *Predators*, the *Marauders* had an influx of new members. New members that are mysteriously nowhere to be found now."

With my elbow propped against the door, I propped my chin in my hand, processing her words. "Are you saying... you think it was *Thorns*?"

"I'm not ruling it out," she said. "We might need to talk to them. Their leader is retiring, and his son, Jake Lincoln, is taking over. You familiar?"

I nodded. "Thought I was going to have to kill him one day."

Alicia's eyes went wide. "Can you *not* be killing people willy-nilly? I thought we discussed this?"

"I said I *thought* about it."

"Uh-huh." She chuckled. "Anyway, I don't *think* it was *Thorns*, but they were definitely hired guns, one way or another. Remember us talking about how it seemed strange for the *Marauders* to do something like that, when Rojas is their supplier *and* ally to the *Predators*?"

"Yeah. It's seeming more and more like a setup of some kind."

"Exactly." She nodded. "Renard being here doesn't feel coincidental. Especially since he's not here alone."

"What?"

She pushed out a sigh before saying more. "He's got a couple *Thorns* with him. I can only assume they're... in the upside down or whatever the fuck you want to call it."

Now I understood what the heavy breathing was about. "He played their song."

"Yeah."

"That's not good."

"No shit," she quipped. "Not for anybody involved."

"What do we do?" I asked, after we'd sat in silence a few moments. "How do we find out what his end game is?"

"I don't know," she replied, staring out the front window again, but this time, she wasn't actually looking at anything. From the way her eyes moved, I could tell she was assessing the situation. "I'm not even sure what it *could* be. *The Garden* is tied to the Santiago cartel, they get taken down, and now Rojas is in charge. Maybe Renard didn't like that, maybe it's revenge. So he's counting on stirring up enough tension to get the *Predators* to take him out."

"It makes sense."

"It does, but... I don't know. I feel like I'm missing something," she mused, shaking her head. "There's a piece of this puzzle I need to figure out."

I pressed my thumb into the indentation under my bottom lip, scratching as I tried to figure out my next words. Finally, I just spoke. "Why does it matter to you?" I asked, meeting her gaze as she turned in my direction. "This motorcycle club shit, isn't it out of your purview?"

"Are you serious?" she asked, eyes narrowed.

"Yeah."

"Nyx... *I* took *The Garden* down, remember?" she said, tossing her hands up. "I destroyed the family business and put his brother in jail. He and Etienne may have had ideological differences, but they're cut from the same monstrous cloth. I have to believe that it's no coincidence that he's here. Yes, there's the Santiago cartel connection, all that, I know. But... again. It's very convenient."

She did have a point there.

I couldn't blame her for being on high alert; when dealing with the Belrose family, it was necessary.

"I'm going to figure out how to get closer to Renard," Alicia said, breaking a fresh wave of silence. "I've already got a couple irons in the fire. Including your old flame."

I raised an eyebrow. "*My* old flame?"

"Margeaux."

*Damn.*

I legitimately hadn't heard that name in the longest time.

"You know where Margeaux is?" I asked, trying not to let my genuine interest read as me being eager.

"She's in Europe," Alicia answered. "I sent somebody to get her."

I smirked, shaking my head. "I hope you sent somebody who knew what they were doing."

"Well I would have sent *you*, but you're a little occupied, aren't you? Can't have your old flame getting in the way of the new…"

I scoffed. "Don't start that."

"Oh, I already have," she teased, reaching over to grab my chin. "Are you going to go see Tati today?" she sang.

"As a matter of fact, I am. Gonna help her move into a new place."

"She's moving? Good. She needs fresh energy around her anyway. Has she said anything about Kev?"

"Nah, not to me. And Blue wants to let him stew anyway," I told her. "I think there's just so much going on, it's hard to know where to focus the energy."

"Is he antsy about acting on the *Marauders*?"

"Not at all." I shook my head. "Honestly, the opps are background noise right now," I explained. "They don't want to move on anything until Tati has had some time to come back to the action."

"Is everybody good with that?"

"I don't think they have a choice." I chuckled. "Blue says we're focused on the business shit, so that's just what it is."

"As it should be," Alicia agreed. "I should let you go, so you can get home and shower before you go to Tati's."

I frowned. "Why would I do that when I'm just going to go over there and sweat and move boxes around?"

Her mouth dropped open. "Nyx, I *forbid* you to go over there smelling like a gyro with extra onions. Do *not* do that to her."

"I don't smell like that." I frowned, sniffing my armpit to check.

She pressed her lips together, eyes wide. "You're right; I forgot the yogurt sauce. Get out of my car."

"Daaamn, that's how you do?" I laughed, opening the door.

"Yep, that's how I do. I'll be in touch," she called through the open window as she pulled off, leaving me with a lot of pondering of my own to do as I climbed on my bike.

To go back to the clubhouse and take a shower before I went to help Tati.

# *Chapter Fifteen*

## NYX

I WALKED IN ON AN ARGUMENT.

Actually, I couldn't tell if it was an argument, or more of a "heated exchange", but either way, Blue and Tati were going at each other in a way only brothers and sisters ever did.

Meaning it wasn't my fucking business.

I made myself busy with the boxes Keira pointed out to me between her own attempts to interject in their disagreement—input they *clearly* weren't interested in. I was happy to tune their asses out and act like the shit wasn't even happening until I heard Blue say, *"Goddamnit Tati, ain't nobody driving all those damn bikes to storage just so they can be close to you, and that's the end of the shit."*

*All those bikes?*

Clearly, there was something I'd missed.

"Hey," I said to Keira, who looked up from her tablet ready to spring into action. "How many bikes does she have?"

Keira's eyes went wide like I'd lost my mind, but then a grin spread over her face.

"Come on."

Tati and Blue had taken the loud shit deeper into the house somewhere, so it was an easy decision to follow Keira through a door in the hall that blended in with the textured wallpaper, one I hadn't been shown during my "tour".

"Watch your step," she told me, gesturing at the black hole in the wall. I hadn't fully taken a step before twin rows of light illuminated one after the other, creating an effect like one was being "lit" by the next to create a line of sparks.

That sudden luminosity revealed a pristine oversized garage. One end was occupied by a white Bentley convertible and a red Range Rover in a matte finish, but the space was dominated by bikes. There was a wide range of styles, from vintage to conceptual, each on its own rounded raised platform like in a showroom.

*Whew.*

I wasn't even really *into* bikes like that and even I knew this shit was impressive.

I stepped out onto the glossy floor, trying to figure out what to even look at first.

"Is she a collector?" I called over my shoulder to Keira, thinking she was still in the doorway behind me.

She was not.

When I didn't get an answer, it prompted me to turn around. Blue and Tati were standing in the door. Blue was glaring at me like I'd fucked up, and Tati was glaring at *him*, looking very smug.

"See? Even *he* gets it," she quipped, parking her hands on her hips. "How the *fuck* am I supposed to just choose a couple?!"

"Maybe start with the ones you actually *ride*?!" Blue huffed, stepping into the garage to gesture around him. There were a solid fourteen or fifteen bikes up on the elevated daises. "This is why I told you not to buy all this shit," he added, muttering *those* words as he moved to stand next to me. "Why are you encouraging this shit, bruh?"

My mouth opened, confused about how simply standing there was doing... anything. Before I could say anything though, Tati was already in his face.

"First of all, *fuck you*!" she said, jabbing a finger into his chest.

I didn't envy him being on the receiving end of whatever point she was trying to prove, but I liked that she was up and about like this.

And... I liked that she was cussing somebody out, honestly.

It felt more like *her*.

"Second of all, *this shit*? My daddy gifted me some of these, so watch your mouth, uh-kay? My Black Dahlia is not *shit*; it would dust any-fucking-thing in your garage. And yes, I'd like to put that to the test," she challenged, with this wicked sneer that *shouldn't* be turning me on, but...

"Tati, will you—"

"Thiiiird," she said, her tone dripping with sarcasm as she talked over him. "*This* is why you tried to talk me out of my collection? This exact situation? You're a fucking prophet now? You had it in your head, *Tati is gonna get assaulted and wanna move, so she shouldn't buy these bikes?* Really, nigga?!"

Blue groaned, mushing her in the face to get her away from him. "You know *damn well* I'm not saying this *exact*—"

"Okay so why the fuck you say it then?!" she challenged, smacking his hand away.

"Because the shit is impractical!"

Her mouth dropped open. "So is a *goddamn sex bench* you keep in a *goddamn sex room* for you to tie bitches up with, but you didn't let impracticality stop you when you were building *that* shit, did you?!"

"*Whoa,*" I said, eyes wide. This was officially, *firmly* in the realm of shit that wasn't my business now, and I wasn't sure they even remembered I was there.

"I use that shit, used it last night for your information, *that's* why I have the limp I lied and told you was from working out." Blue countered Tati's argument, ignoring me. "How often do you ride these fucking bikes?!"

"One—some of these are meant to be admired, not ridden. The ones that *can be ridden,* get ridden! Two—*too much* damn information! Lie to me next time, cause *ew.*"

He shrugged. "You brought it up."

"Hey, I'ma get back to those boxes," I called out, trying to get as far out of *this* mix as I could.

Both their heads swung in my direction, both their arms crossed, faces still pulled in the glares they'd been giving each other.

"Hey, see if she wants you to toss one of these *ornamental* bikes in a box for her," Blue quipped.

"*Ornamental*?!" Tati scoffed. "I'm sick of you!"

"Yeah, I'm sick of your ass too," he said, pulling out his phone, which had started chiming in his pocket. "Shut up, it's Nessa. Hey, gorgeous," he crooned into the phone, his tone completely shifting from the one he'd been using with Tati.

"Get the fuck outta my house!" Tati called after him as he headed back through the garage door. "Ask Nessa if you can have some pussy so you can stop acting like one!"

He turned around, flipping her off. "She gave it all to me already. Move your own shit!"

"I will!" Tati snapped, stomping after him. In the doorway, she turned to me with a smile like nothing had just happened. "There's a bunch of boxes in the kitchen."

I just looked at her. "Okay, but... y'all good?"

"Who?" she asked, looking genuinely confused as she thought about it, and then grinned. "Oh! Me and Brandon?" She waved me off, laughing as she stepped through the door with me following. "That's... Tuesday."

My eyebrows shot up. "Y'all fight like that a lot?"

"That wasn't a fight; we're making sure we still love each other," she explained, I think, and then stopped moving so suddenly that I almost walked into her. "You smell *really* good," she said, looking up to meet my gaze.

*Maybe Alicia was onto something.*

"Did you expect me not to? Do I usually stink?" I asked, frowning.

She laughed—started to laugh, then bit down on her lip to suppress it. "Honestly? I try not to notice how you smell."

My frown went a bit deeper. "Why?"

A little sigh pushed from her as she pressed her back to the wall behind her, eyes still locked with mine. "I... think you know why."

... yeah.

I could hazard a guess.

And if I played off that guess, it would be a prime moment for flirting; in other circumstances, I would. Two weeks ago? I would have.

Before the assault, before that kiss, before this... *shift.*

She couldn't have been more wrong about it when she was wondering if I wasn't attracted to her anymore; *that* turn of events wasn't even a possibility. But the off-the-cuff dalliance we may have been able to entertain before... that wasn't a prospect anymore—not that it ever should have been.

But that kiss... the kiss had me thinking things I really, *really* shouldn't.

Yet another sign I was getting a little too comfortable around here.

"What was all that about though, with you and Blue?" I asked, trying to switch the subject from this dangerous one.

She sighed. "My new spot only has space for maybe four bikes and one of the vehicles. Six if I leave behind one of the cars, which I'm kinda considering, since I only drive when it's raining anyway. But I don't want to leave *any* of my babies. I might be in an all-white mood one day, black on black the next. And then pink. I never know." She laughed. "So I don't want to pick."

I chuckled. "You know you're going to have to though, right."

"Yeah," she huffed, shaking her head as she started walking again. "I've already decided I'll just rotate them out. I'm not selling this place any time soon anyway."

I frowned. "Okay, so what's the argument about?"

"Nothing." Tati laughed. "I told you; it's just a Tuesday."

As if to highlight her point, when we rounded the corner, Blue was still there, carrying boxes out to the truck parked out front. Keira approached us with questions for Tati about what was left, which gave me the perfect opportunity to put some space between me and her.

"Ay, come help me with this," Blue called out to me from the living room, already positioned at one end of the couch.

I went straight into action, helping him lift the heavy furniture and carry it out to the truck where we slid it into the spot that had been left open for it. Afterwards, I started back into the house, but he stopped me, pulling me aside to ask a question I'd been dreading, but expecting.

"So what's going on with you and Tati?" he said, arms crossed as he waited for an answer.

One I... didn't really have, to be honest. "Does it... seem like something is going on between us?" I countered, making him chuckle.

"Don't do that shit, bruh." He sighed. "That's my sister, and you know better than anybody what she went through *two weeks* ago. You can be real with me, right? 'Cause otherwise—"

"It's not about being real or not," I interrupted, shaking my head. "There just ain't shit for me to say. Could there be something? Probably. But like you said, she's... in a tenuous space right now, and I'm not trying to complicate that. *Besides* the fact that I'm not really a *stay-in-one-place* kinda nigga, so—"

"So you're leaving?" he cut in to ask and I pushed out a breath before I nodded.

"I'll keep my word. I'll help you get at whoever is responsible for the shit with your father," I assured. "But after that... I gotta keep moving."

He bobbed his head. "What the fuck are you running from? Alicia and her people?"

"Nah, I'm good with them, I think. I'm not running from anything external, but if I stay still too long... I don't know. It might get too quiet up here," I told him, tapping my temple with a single finger.

He seemed to understand – and accept – that explanation, but still made it clear. "I'm gonna hate to see you go, especially in the wake of what Kev's bitch ass turned out to be. We don't let just anybody into this fold, and... shit. I need real niggas to balance the bullshit, you know?"

I chuckled. "Definitely a shortage these days, but you've got a solid roster."

"Not if I keep losing people cause they're scared to be somebody's damn boyfriend."

"Well damn." I laughed, putting a hand to my chest. "That's how it is?"

"It is." He shrugged. "It's how I see it."

"Do you have this man-to-man conversation with everybody Tati gets involved with?"

"Nah," he denied. "I never did with Kev; 'cause I never saw shit for him. Never saw shit for any of the niggas she entertained."

"So why the fuck are you pressing *me?*"

"'Cause I see some shit, obviously," he countered, looking at me like I was stupid for even wondering. "I hear what you're saying, but I also see the energy she has with you. I see how she looks at you, and how you look at her; you motherfuckers ain't fooling anybody," he said.

"You a fucking matchmaker or something, nigga? What *is* this?"

"It's me doing my part for my goddamn sister," he answered. "Look, this shit is y'all's business, and I'm not trying to insert myself. When I was with Talia, I had to talk to Tati, and later, her pops. Now, with Nessa, her brother-in-law got at me on her behalf, and I had to talk with her other siblings too. This is what we do when we're taking care of our own."

"I get that, but I just told you, it's not like that."

"And what I'm telling *you* is that I'll believe that when I see it, but in the meantime; let's be clear that when it comes to my sister, it's hands first questions later. Y'all are grown, so I ain't in the details and don't wanna be. But the malicious shit? That's DOA."

"Unnecessary message received," I told him, knowing he wouldn't let it go until he thought he'd gotten through to me.

And it wasn't that he hadn't, I just didn't need this shit.

"We'll see," Blue said as he walked off, fishing keys from his pocket. "Keira, come on, let's go drop this shit off!" he called into the house, and a few moments later, she came bustling out, with a box in her hands. She loaded it up, and they peeled off, leaving me alone with Tati again.

It was strangely quiet.

Music had been playing when I'd arrived, but maybe whatever device she'd been using was packed away now, being prepared for the journey.

I discovered her tucked away in her workroom, holding the same rose carving that had been in her hands the last time I'd found her there.

"You good?" I asked, not stepping fully into the room, since the energy felt... different. There were boxes in here, but nothing seemed to be moved from where it had always been. Somewhere between when I'd split off to help Blue with the couch and now, something for her had shifted.

She tried to be discreet in drying her face with the back of her hands, but when she looked up, her eyes were glossy, contradicting the front it seemed she wanted to put forth.

"This is part of why I don't wanna leave," she said, her voice thick with emotion as she looked around the room, fingering a tiny crystal rose on a chain around her neck. "When I wanna feel close to Tali, this is where I come."

I nodded because I understood, but at the same time... "This is just a room," I told her, stepping in. "Your memories are what pull you close to her, not any four walls."

"I know," she agreed. "It's just... it *feels* like I'm leaving her behind. She helped me pick this house. These shelves were in her room, some of these crystals... this was hers. Her thing. I just co-opted to feel close to her after she was gone."

"So bring it with you," I suggested. "What's the problem; you need help breaking them down for transport or something? I can—"

"Oh my God, *shut up*," she groaned and my eyes went wide, surprised. "I know how men think they need to shift to rescue mode every time a woman complains, but maybe... don't."

I held my hands up. "My bad. I just—"

"Wanted to fix it." She nodded, clearly already understanding. "But there's nothing to fix; I don't *want* anything fixed," she clarified. "Everybody wants me to be okay, to be '*good*'. But... I just want to feel."

She wasn't sad anymore; she was fucking *frustrated*.

Shit.

"Tell me how—tell me what you want me to do," I said, catching myself early enough to not ask how I could *help*, when she'd just made herself abundantly clear.

She stared at me for a second, then put the rose carving down on the table as she stood. "Brandon is gonna be pissed if I go anywhere alone. So can you take me somewhere?"

"Where do you need to go?" I asked. "And, we'd have to take one of your vehicles, I only have my bike."

A smile curved the corners of her lips.

"I'll give you the directions as we go. And your bike is fine."

I could've said no.

Could've offered to ride next to her or even just insisted that we drive.

I didn't do any of those though.

Five minutes later, we were flying down the highway, Tati's arms tight around my waist as we maneuvered. Her idea of giving me directions was a subtle nudge with whatever hand matched the direction she wanted me to turn.

I was a bit confused when her navigation led us to the clubhouse.

But then, we rode right past it, no indication to turn down the long road that led to *Predator* land. Instead, we kept going, further out than I'd been before, finally veering off just before I got a little concerned.

The sun was starting to dip as we pulled up to the cemetery.

She didn't give me an opportunity to question her motives before she was already off the bike, her stride purposeful. I kept a bit of distance as she stopped at her destination—a grandiose headstone in pristine white, directly next to a similar black one.

I didn't have to get close to know.

Instead, I gave her *more* space, while I looked around, quickly deducing that these were *Predator* burial grounds. My eyes scanned the other headstones, stopping with an unexpected hitch in my step when I ran across one identical to the black one Tati was standing near.

The former president of the *Predators, Jesse Garrett.*

Blue's father.

There were flowers dying at the base of it, still fresh enough that they had to be recently placed. Most likely, by Blue's mother, whose grief had been lingering longer, deeper than her son wanted for her.

I'd overheard the phone calls, stood in for meetings so he could tend to her, all that.

She must've been a good mother.

I found myself thinking so often in what I could observe of his engagement with her. I'd never met her, had made it a point not to, actually. Even the thought of it now made me shift, uncomfortable.

How fucked up was that?

That the potential nurturing energy of a woman who actually cared for her children was damn near a *trigger*.

I shook my head, wanting to pull myself away from the grave, but I couldn't. Blue's words from weeks ago, that ridiculous ass fist analogy, was playing in my head again.

*It's not ridiculous.*

It just made me uneasy.

I didn't get down with superstitions and the supernatural and all that, so the idea of some kind of *fate* or destiny or whatever, the idea that something beyond my control dictated who I was or where I belonged, who I should be connected to... it fucked with me.

Blame it on the mommy issues, I guess.

Her personal demons had driven her to name me – *brand me* – as she did, and she made sure the story of it – the meaning she gave it – was imprinted on me, impossible to forget. No matter how hard I'd tried to be what she needed, what she didn't have, *anything* except the beast she'd designated me... there was no getting around it.

The darkness was just... *in me.*

Waiting for any goodness I could devour.

She wasn't afraid of me because there wasn't any goodness in her to take, and on that... we didn't disagree. I'd loved my mother as much as any child could in those circumstances because she was all I had. And despite the privilege surrounding her, because of who she was... I was all she had too.

In her own way... she'd loved me too. But it was never, never a secret that she simultaneously reviled my existence, and knowing what I did about how that came to be... I couldn't blame her. She named me after a deliverer of nightmares because at the time of my birth, that was all I'd ever provided, from the moment of conception.

And then she laid every bit of groundwork for me to live up to the name.

Whether or not I'd wanted to, I had.

First out of anger, then obligation.

*Subjugation.*

For a long ass time, I didn't have a choice in the matter, so I'd leaned into it like a badge of honor. But I didn't want that anymore.

It didn't *have* to be that way.

Alicia had changed.

Isaiah had changed.

And a whole host of others.

They were fundamentally themselves still but stripped of the labels and expectations others had forced on them, free of *The Garden's* domination.

Just fucking *free.*

Alicia had talked about suppressed memories coming back, having to work through them to get to that place of freedom, which was the first checkpoint to... *happy.*

Maybe *that* was why I'd initially come to Vegas.

To look the architect of my nightmares in the face, so maybe I could move on from layer after layer of bullshit piled on me, since *birth*. Since *conception*.

It was too much muck for any one man to wade through, probably.

And Blue thought *I* belonged in his mythical fucking fist?

I scoffed, looking down at his father's grave, at those dying roses, to shake my head.

"*You should have left behind something better for your son*," I muttered, turning to walk away.

Tati was still poised in front of her lost loved ones, head down. I could hear her voice, too muffled by distance to make out the words, but I could tell it was a private conversation.

It was getting dark though and I wasn't exactly into spending the night among graves.

Even so… I waited for her to look up.

When she did, her eyes were glossy again. This time, she seemed much more at peace than she'd been in her work room.

I closed the distance between us, trying not to pay attention to how fucking pretty she looked with her braids pouring over her shoulders and that serene expression on her face.

It was a damn graveyard.

*Not* the place.

"You ready to head back?" I called to her. "Folks are probably worried about you."

"I let Blue know where I was," she answered. "But yeah. I'm ready."

She didn't have me take her back to her old place; we went to the new one, which was considerably closer to the clubhouse. Blue and Keira were already there, along with Ghost and Teo, unloading more and more of Tati's things.

I ignored the look Blue shot in my direction and tried to ignore the obvious space everybody was giving me and Tati. Instead of focusing on trying *not* to look like something was up, I just did what I would've otherwise.

Made myself useful.

"What made you decide to pull the trigger on this?" I asked, helping her unpack the boxes for her new kitchen. "Last week you were telling me you didn't want to leave."

"I was having trouble sleeping," she told me. "Among other things."

I stopped what I was doing, turning to where she was stacking plates in a cabinet. "Things like what? Nightmares? Hearing things?"

"Those too." She nodded, shifting to meet my gaze. "I was kinda hoping that being in a new space would help me... reconnect with myself."

"What do you mean?"

She sighed. "Have you ever felt like a stranger in your own body? Like you stepped out of yourself to cope, and now..."

"You can't get back," I murmured, nodding.

I hated that I could relate, but...

"That's been me, for the last two weeks," she revealed. "And I'm sick of it. Over it."

"Understandable, but that's not a lot of time."

She closed her eyes. "It's just so fucking frustrating. Everybody says to just give it time, but I don't *want* to give it time. I want to be whole. I know that's not realistic," she quickly added, holding up her hands. "But knowing that it's out of reach, I'll settle for something familiar at least. Like in the kitchen the other day."

"In the kitchen?" I asked, so wrapped up in listening that I was momentarily clueless until she smirked.

"When I kissed you."

*Oh.*

*Shit.*

*When did she walk over here?*

One moment, she was across the room, and the next, she was right in front of me, staring up to meet my gaze. "Was it that forgettable?"

She asked that question in a soft whisper, as she put a hand to my stomach.

"No," I answered immediately. "I haven't stopped thinking about it."

She smiled. "Good."

*Good?*

In that whisper, with those eyes, and that smile, and her hand slipping under my t-shirt... She was a fucking *monster.*

"Can I tell you something?" she asked, standing so close that the heat from her body was permeating my clothes.

"Yeah." I probably would've given an affirmative answer to *anything* she asked me when she was looking at me the way she was, touching me like she was, near enough to count her damn eyelashes if I wanted.

"I was gonna fuck you."

All the air left my lungs. "What?"

"You heard me."

I did.

But... *shit.*

My eyebrows went up. "That day in the kitchen?" I asked and she shook her head.

"No. Before that. I hadn't admitted it to myself yet, but the energy we had... the *chemistry* we had... that tension, and animosity, with no real reason? It only ever would've been solved without clothes," she said, her lips turning up into a little grin. "It was inevitable. I know exactly what I was gonna do to you."

"*Do to me.*" I chuckled, biting down on my lip. "So you weren't playing, you were gonna *fuck* me."

"Yeah." She laughed. "And now..." Her gaze dropped, the humor suddenly gone, replaced by this pained expression that made my chest feel tight. "Now it's like... I don't even know that girl anymore, the one who would do something like that so freely. So *happily*. I'm... shit." She blew out a sigh, abruptly stepping back. "I don't even know why I'm talking about this —you didn't come over here for this."

"I didn't, but we can talk about it," I told her, grabbing her hand to keep her from walking away.

"There's nothing to talk about. I don't have anything to say," she denied.

"Listen then," I said, already knowing I was about to fuck up. Her eyes were glossy with tears, again, probably more frustration than anything, and I couldn't blame her.

"This is stupid," she huffed. "To be bothered about such a thing—"

"It's not stupid," I cut her off. "Stop saying that. It bothers you because it was important – *is* important to you – to get this dick and I get it 'cause it's impeccable, so—"

"Oh, *God*." She laughed, covering her face with her free hand.

"Yeah, go ahead and practice saying that," I told her, making her laugh harder.

'Cause I couldn't fucking help it.

All I wanted was that smile.

"Listen," I said, grabbing her under the chin to lift her head. "It'll happen."

She sniffled as I wiped her face dry of the few tears that had escaped her attempts to fight them. "What makes you so sure?"

"Like you said." I nodded. "It's inevitable."

Destruction always was.

# *Chapter Sixteen*

## TATI

"— IS UP SEVEN PERCENT COMPARED TO LAST QUARTER, WHICH IS phenomenal; we're seeing the results of all the things you've been working to put in place," Keira said from beside me in the car, holding up her tablet to indicate the numbers, even though I was driving and couldn't really look at the screen.

Giving me a debrief I hadn't asked for.

For three weeks now, she'd been falling just short of outright refusal to keeping me in the loop, insisting everything was under control, and I could be comfortable focusing on my "healing", whatever that meant.

At this point, I was antsy.

I was trying to give Keira her space though, to thrive in the role.

She was notably young for the responsibility, only twenty-five. But she'd been Tali's friend, then became mine after Tali's passing, then got inked. She was smart as hell, organized as hell, and damn near family, so when Blue and I had to rebuild our chain of command it was an easy decision to place her in the secretary role.

It was approaching a year and there was never a moment I'd regretted it.

Especially when she did things like this, noticing that I was over my invol-untary sabbatical and not even waiting for me to ask for the update.

She just went with the flow.

"Kingston sent over the fact sheet for a bar he's looking at on the strip," she continued. "He wants to know if we'd be interested in part ownership. I went ahead and looked over the

DETAILS AND MADE a recommendation to Blue since there was a cutoff time on that one."

"And what was your recommendation?"

"I think it's a good investment," she answered, with an affirmative nod. "The Whitfields have a Midas touch, and all the right connections to insulate against most bullshit. Any partnership he offers us is going to be worth looking into."

"I agree. What else?"

"Well, speaking of him, I have an update on progress with the dispensary. We'll have to have the *Marauders* squared away first, but our suppliers are ready to fulfill an order at any time."

I nodded. "Good. And what about the growers?"

"Still pulling together land packages for us to review."

"Okay. I want you to make sure they understand that's not a priority; we have a lot of irons in the fire and a lot of cash going out. We should probably dam the flow a bit."

Keira's eyes went wide, lips parted in surprise, but she quickly covered with a smile and a nod. "Uhh... okay, definitely."

"Is something wrong?"

"No, not at all. I'm making the note now."

"*Hey,*" I said, putting a hand over her screen to stop her tapping away. "Look at me."

She hefted out a little sigh, then did as I'd asked, meeting my gaze briefly before I had to look at the road again. "Yes?"

"Is there a problem?" I asked, in a tone that made it clear I wasn't fucking playing. I *really* didn't take it with her often, but I was picking up some weird energy that I needed to understand.

*Now.*

"No." She sighed again. "I just... when I brought all this up to you, it was just an update, not an opening for you to start being the boss again."

I frowned. "Keira... I *am* the boss," I said. "We're not going to have a problem stepping back into our lanes, are we?"

"What? *No,*" she insisted. "You're misunderstanding what I mean." Keira reached over, covering one of my hands on the wheel. "Tati, I cannot *wait* to turn VP shit back over to the VP." She laughed. "But... I also don't want you stressed about work shit when you're supposed to be taking it easy."

"I love you for that, but... I'm sick of taking it easy," I replied, giving her hand a quick squeeze.

She nodded. "I know. I *know*. Which is why I was giving you the update, but you weren't supposed to take it as an opening. Not until you're ready to come back."

"And who decides when I'm ready to come back? You? Brandon?"

"No—*you do*. Tati, you say the word and I'll step back into my normal duties. But I'd really rather you give yourself at least a damn month to just... *be*."

"Sis, I've *been*." I laughed. "I've *been* enough for seven bitches and I'm sick of *being*. I need to get back to some sort of norm."

Keira blew out yet another sigh. "I hear you, but honestly? I'm worried about you, Tati. I know, everybody copes differently with something like what you went through, but I'm scared that you're just blocking it away, or suppressing it, or something instead of really dealing. Which I get, completely. I just don't want that to blow back on you and be worse than it would've been if you'd taken a different path."

"That's valid," I admitted. "Completely. But I'm not even... I don't know... it's not like I'm having nightmares about the assault, or like I'm scared of the dark, you know? I'm comfortable around the guys, all that. The typical reactions to something like this, for whatever reason, it's just... not what I'm feeling."

"Okay." She nodded. "So... talk to me. What *are* you feeling?"

"Vacant," I replied. "Like I'm just not *myself*. I just want to get back to me."

"That's why you want to get back to work? You think being back in your routine will help?"

"Partially," I agreed. "But it's deeper than just work. I... I haven't orgasmed in weeks," I revealed, getting the words out fast before I changed my mind about saying the shit aloud.

Keira twisted her face up at me, nose wrinkled and all. "Bitch... welcome to the club." She laughed. "I don't know what kind of schedule you were normally on, but the rest of us mortal women aren't exactly putting up numbers in that category."

"I'm talking about *self-pleasure*, too," I explained, laughing at her reaction. "I know most niggas can't find a clit without a detailed map of the topography, but I can't even get *myself* off. Which is... insane."

"*Oh*," she said, clearly understanding the issue now. "But... Isn't that really common, to have a hard time enjoying any type of sex? I mean... Tati... you're probably fucking... *traumatized*."

"Not probably, definitely," I concurred. "But that doesn't make me hate it any less. And it's not even just that I'm not enjoying it, it literally doesn't feel like *anything*. Like all my nerve endings just fucking froze or died. Except for when... never mind."

"No ma'am," Keira huffed. "You opened the line of conversation, don't clam up now; except what?"

I groaned, mentally kicking myself for the slip. But... fuck it.

"Except... when Onyx is around."

"Oh!" She sucked her teeth. "Girl, I thought you were about to say something surprising."

"*Wow.*" I laughed. "I'm just obvious as hell with it, huh?"

"I wouldn't say *obvious* as hell," she countered. "There's just not really any suppressing the chemistry with the two of you. Remember when he got inked? I was pretty sure one of you was gonna end up choked. To death or completion? Couldn't say for sure."

"*Keira!*" I gasped, gripping the steering wheel tight as I laughed.

"What? Y'all were giving big *fuck me like you hate me* energy is all I'm saying." She giggled. "And now it's... I don't know. More smoldering?"

"It's *something*," I agreed. "I kissed him."

"*What*?!" Keira shrieked. "*When*?!"

I sighed. "A couple weeks ago." I glanced over at her, already seeing the mental calculation happening in her head. "Yes, it was 'too soon'. No, I don't regret it. Yes, it was everything. No, I have not known peace since."

"*That's* why he was all antsy the day we moved you into your new place, isn't it?"

I frowned. "I don't remember him being antsy."

What I remembered was him taking the time to listen to me and not trying to force me to feel something I didn't.

What I remembered was the heat of him between my legs, the sturdiness of his back against my breasts, the clean scent of his locs as I pressed my face into them while he whipped us along the highway on his bike.

What I remembered was him telling me that us fucking was inevitable.

He'd made sure to stay away from me since then.

"Does Dove know I was coming to this meeting?" I asked, as I pulled into the parking lot at *Allure*. The new club had changed hands now and was officially ours, so there was a need to touch base with Dove, to make sure she had everything handled.

Keira raised an eyebrow at me. "Should I have let her know?" she asked, peeking out the window to wave to our escort, two lieutenants who'd ridden in front of and behind us, and were now parked on either side.

"No, not necessarily. I just haven't been here in a few weeks, haven't been the point person in a while, so—"

"Stop it," Keira scolded, gathering her bag to exit the car. "It's no different than any other meeting."

"Don't patronize me," I warned. "Are you sure all the bruising is gone? I feel like I still have a bit right here."

She pointed. "It's a shadow from the trees over there. You're playing."

"I'm not playing, I'm fucking nervous. Does everybody know what happened?"

"The details? Absolutely not. But I won't pretend there's no speculation. You're suddenly out of sight, club on lockdown, Kev MIA, everybody under scrutiny. The important thing though, is that everybody is on your side. We look to you like you're the fucking North Star."

I knew she was trying to be encouraging, but really it just made me even more nervous. Before all this, the leadership role wasn't *easy*, but I'd accepted it and excelled.

Now?

I barely knew who the fuck I was anymore.

I didn't need anybody looking to me.

Still, I pulled it together with a deep breath and got out of the car, head held high. If nothing else, I knew I *looked* good, so I drew on that to make my way inside the club with Keira right at my heels.

As soon as we'd crossed the threshold, I knew something was off.

A glance back at Keira confirmed she was feeling it too and she moved to step in front of me. She didn't pull her weapon, but she had her hand at the holster, ready. The woman working the hostess stand sent us straight back to Dove's office but didn't give any clues otherwise that something was amiss.

"I put out a beacon to our guys outside," Keira muttered over her shoulder as we approached the door. "They'll get the message out if needed. Or we can just turn around. I don't *think* we're in danger, but something is weird."

I shook my head. "Nah, let's see what's going on."

Keira nodded her compliance with my choice and raised a fist to rap at the door before she pushed it open. We found Dove sitting at her desk, no hiding the exasperation on her face as she glared at the person seated across from her.

Sanaa.

"*Where* is Kevondre!" she snapped, popping up as soon as she saw me in the doorway.

Before anybody could do anything, Keira had chopped her in the throat, putting an instant halt to her attempt to get in my face.

"Whoa, she's pregnant!" Dove exclaimed, standing to come around the desk and attend to Sanaa on the ground, coughing as she tried to catch her breath.

"Well if she wants to keep it, she should be a little more careful with her actions, shouldn't she?" Keira said, directing her words at Sanaa before she stepped over her, taking a seat at the desk. "Now, about those numbers we needed to discuss?"

I fought the urge to smirk, knowing Keira's actions had likely caught them all by surprise.

Not me.

Her aura of amiable competence matched who I knew her to be, but it didn't remotely tell the whole story. Keira was a fighter, had always been, really. Once I'd graduated high school and couldn't be the one around all the time for Tali's protection, Keira had picked up the reins and bridged the gap, even though she was younger.

When it came to the people she cared about – when it came to her *ink* – Keira didn't fuck around.

Now Sanaa knew.

"We uhh... have a different matter to deal with first I think," Dove said, eyes still wide with surprise over what Keira had done as she helped Sanaa up from the floor.

I crossed my arms. "What could possibly take priority over *Predator* business?"

"This *is Predator* business," Sanaa choked out, placing a protective hand over her non-existent belly as she glared at Keira. "I'm having one, after all," she added, looking directly at me. "Y'all call the *Predator* kids cubs all the time because the majority grow up and get inked."

I narrowed my eyes. "The current generation of *Predators* are still having kids right now. When *those* kids get inked, we can start calling it a pattern. And *you* are not inked anyway."

"But Kev is," she countered, finding the nerve to smirk. "So it'll be my baby's birthright, won't it?"

"No child of Kev's will ever wear *Predator* ink. *Kev* doesn't even wear *Predator* ink anymore. We carved it off him," I told her, not caring how cruel it sounded to her ears. "And if you actually *want* to be a mother? You'd do well to stay out of my face before I decide I want his whole fucking bloodline wiped from existence; don't push me."

"Why are you so *bitter*?" she sneered, obviously not catching on. Dove grabbed her arm, pulling her backward to step between us. "All this because he was going to break up with you, make us a family? You are one sick bitch!"

"*I'm* the sick bitch?" I countered, waving Keira and Dove away from trying to calm the situation. "That nigga showed up at my house crying about not getting a job; showed up smelling like you, as a matter of fact. It was a goddamn monsoon outside, so I let him in because I felt sorry for him and he fucked me and kicked my ass as a *thank you* for my benevolence. So you tell me who the *sick bitch* is."

Her bottom lip trembled as she clearly grappled with what I'd just revealed. She shook her head. "No. *Nope.* You're a liar. He came to my house after he broke up with you. He was all beat up because you'd sicced those fucking *goons* of yours on him. He told me how jealous you were, how he had to leave because you would send people—"

"Are you *really* this damn gullible?" I interrupted. "Kev and I weren't even a couple, there was no breaking up to do. Glad to know I fought hard enough that he had to lie about getting jumped though; that actually kinda makes me feel good."

"*Where is he*?" she cried, ignoring everything I'd said.

She was holding tight to the false reality he'd created for her.

"Somewhere he can only dream about the sun. Do you want to join him?" I asked, smiling at her. "Go be a happy fucking family? Huh?"

"I'm going to the police!"

"*Do it*," I snapped, laughing. "Please, do it, I want to see what happens. Just a heads up though, that I have video evidence for *my* version of this story, so... do with that what you will." I looked away from her, to Dove. "Get this silly bitch out of my face, I've entertained this too long."

Dove wasted no time.

Even with Sanaa fighting it, Dove dragged her out of the office and closed the door, leaving Keira and I alone.

"You gave her entirely too much," Keira said, shaking her head as I took a seat next to her. "I could've handled it."

"If you'd handled it, she would still feel the urge to seek me out to hear her story. I needed to be cruel to her so she'd know I don't give a fuck."

Keira nodded. "Point taken. You know we're going to have to subsidize her, right? Or elimination is an option too."

I rolled my eyes.

*Predators* had a rule about the children of inked members; we took care of our own. No one who wore ink was doing the deadbeat shit. You did right by your progeny by whatever means necessary or we were taking our ink back.

Most chose the first option.

Sometimes though, they needed help, and of course we gave it. Nobody affiliated with us was going to starve on our watch.

This was a special case though.

"She can make whatever assets Kev has work; that's the absolute most I'm willing to do. Give her his shit." I shrugged. "And I'm only doing *that* 'cause I hope she fucks over it all," I said, as the door opened again and Dove stepped back in.

"I am so sorry about that," she offered, hurrying around the desk to her seat. "She showed up a few minutes before y'all with a sob story and I thought I'd be able to get her out of here. And Tati... I wasn't expecting you at all."

I shook my head. "It's not your fault, D. Let's get into these numbers."


TWENTY MINUTES LATER, we were headed out of the club and Sanaa was nowhere to be seen.

"I'll have to talk to Gavin," Keira complained as we navigated back toward the front of the club. "The other location might require a bit more infrastructure investment than we thought."

I smirked as I met her gaze. "Now *why* do you make that sound like a problem?"

"Don't start..."

"But you had so much to say to me about Onyx, why can't—"

I stopped abruptly, going quiet and still as that same uneasiness from before hit me again. I'd chalked it up to being ambushed by Sanaa before, but... no.

That wasn't it.

My hand was already at my waist, pulling my gun as my gaze scanned the club's midday crowd.

There was *definitely* danger here.

Keira put a hand on my shoulder, letting me know where she was. I didn't have to look to know she'd drawn her weapon too, neither of us making a sound to raise the alarm in the darkened club.

Just when I wondered if maybe I *was* experiencing some sort of post-traumatic paranoia... my gaze landed on her.

Across the room, perfectly illuminated in the indigo and fuchsia ombre lighting of the crowd, there she was, a woman I'd never seen before. Strikingly beautiful, deep dark skin, close faded haircut, nose ring.

She didn't drop her eyes as I stared; she stared right back.

*Who is she?*

She shifted in her seat, offering her gaze to some man who'd approached her; that's when I saw it.

Only barely, because of the way the light blurred the detail, but it was there.

A rose, tattooed near her left armpit.

I only glanced away to tell Keira, "Get Alicia Pelletier on the phone."

By the time I looked back though... the woman was already gone.

# Chapter Seventeen

## NYX

If I couldn't count on *anything* else, I knew how to provoke a reaction when I wanted one.

It was why I'd had the enforcers who'd ridden out with me hang back while I pulled up to the dispensary alone and parked out front, waiting.

I didn't have to wait long.

Jake Lincoln came speeding up to where I was parked. He wasn't alone, but from the way he immediately dismounted to greet me, he didn't seem to be on any shit-starting energy.

When he offered a handshake, I accepted the gesture.

"Haven't seen Tatiana come through in a while," he said, stepping back to leave a good amount of distance between us. "Everything alright?"

"Nothing to tell *you*," I answered. "Why you wanna know?"

He scratched his head. "Well, we ain't *besties* exactly, but I've known her a long time, went to high school with her, all that. I'd like to think we're somewhat friends."

"She doesn't," I told him, bursting whatever bubble of belief he'd built up about his supposed relationship with Tati. "Talk to me about your beef with the *Predators*."

"We don't have one," Jake immediately denied. "I've been trying to say that this whole time. I'm not saying there wasn't tension, or a rivalry, in the past. But not anymore. We just want to coexist."

"Easy to say when *your* father is still alive."

Jake dropped his shoulders. "We didn't have anything to do with that."

"So you keep saying."

"So I'll say until my last fucking breath," he countered. "What can I say that will convince you? We do not want this war."

I shook my head. "There ain't much *to* say, Jake. We're gonna raze your territory to the fucking ground, unless you give me something I can use."

"Like what?"

"Like what the fuck is Rojas up to?" I asked, prompting Jake to glance nervously back at his guys. They were at a distance where they wouldn't likely hear us with lowered voices, so I wasn't surprised when Jake got closer so he could keep his tone low.

"I can't cross Rojas. He's got us by the balls, him and his nephew."

"What nephew?"

"Ivan, *crazy* motherfucker. He just got back to the states from wherever the family had shipped him off to so he'd stay outta trouble."

I sighed. "Let me guess, he didn't stay out of trouble?"

"Not hardly." Jake chuckled. "Trouble goes where he does, and well... he's here."

I didn't have to be a mind reader to tell that even with all the bravado Jake was putting on, this Ivan dude had him concerned.

Which meant we probably should be, too.

"What do you know about the Santiago Cartel?" I asked. "They were your suppliers before Rojas took over, right?"

Jake nodded. "Yeah. I don't know much except where the pickups and drop-offs were though. And Rojas switched everything up, so I don't know how helpful that would be."

"You're right," I agreed. "It's starting to sound like we *should* just wipe you motherfuckers off the map. You're of no use to us."

"Hold on now," Jake insisted, lifting his hands. "I think Rojas is planning to take on a new partner."

I kept my expression neutral. "I'm listening."

"Some French guy, an older Black man, had some brutal-looking guards with him."

*Renard.*

"What makes you think there's a partnership and where did you see them?"

"At the Rojas compound," he said. "We were in the middle of a meeting when they just showed up and Manuel told us he had to convene with his partner. Dismissed us."

"So you literally heard the word *partner* out of his mouth?"

"I sure did." Jake nodded. "Not even two days ago."

*Fuck.*

That was more than enough time to plan out all sorts of havoc, but nothing had happened, which was damn near worse than an obvious attack.

Maybe that was the point though.

To build up anxiety before anybody made a move.

"What does the new partnership mean for your club?" I asked, wondering why – beyond trying not to get killed – he would divulge this information to me. There had to be something more in it for him.

"Rojas hasn't brought it up; it's been business as usual. But I'm not putting too much stock in that. I don't know what he's about to do, but if shit is about to go left, I'd rather have as few enemies as I can get."

The revving of a motor caught my attention before the visual of the bike speeding in our direction did. The gun was the next thing I saw. I was off my own ride, snatching Jake down by the time the first bullet went whizzing by, in the space where my chest had been a moment before.

The rider easily picked off the guys Jake brought, a shame for them, but a blessing for me. The attention he spared to them allowed me a moment to recover from my sudden drop and get my own weapon out.

I moved out of the way just in time to avoid another attempt at a head shot as he circled back—*fuck.*

So it wasn't just a drive by for intimidation; it was a hit.

*But who is the target?*

Beside me on the ground, Jake had managed to get his weapon out, but he was clearly no expert marksman. Still, it was enough to keep the rider distracted, and weaving. I threw myself to the other side of my bike, using the machine for as much of a shield as I could as the rider came in hot, gun raised.

I aimed.

Pulled the trigger.

*One.*

*Two.*

*Three.*

Momentum sent his bike flying into the front of the dispensary as he came crashing down.

Vaguely, I could hear sirens, hear screaming, and I knew a midday show-down would bring cops and who knew who else.

The rider probably wasn't alone.

Still, I rushed over to where he'd fallen, taking note of the *Marauders* jacket he wore.

"You know this motherfucker?" I asked Jake, who'd run up beside me.

"Never seen him a day in my life," he told me, shaking his head.

I believed him.

I reached down, pulling the jacket sleeve off his left arm, hoping to not confirm a suspicion.

Hope rarely worked in my favor though, and this was no exception, the ring of thorns around his bicep was right there in stark black against his pale skin.

"That mean something to you?" Jake asked, and I was still deciding my answer when he spoke again. "Oh, shit. That blood – is that yours or – shit, that's yours! You okay?"

*Fuck.*

Was I okay?

I wasn't completely sure and my brain was suddenly not connecting any dots toward an answer. I could still hear the sirens, still hear the chaos of a gathering crowd, could hear the rev of motorcycles that could be carrying anybody, friend or foe.

And then... nothing.

*"You don't look anything like him. I guess I should consider it a blessing."*

*What was I supposed to say to that?*

*Was it a compliment?*

*Should I apologize?*

*I chose silence, which probably wasn't the right answer either.*

*"Get dressed. And do something with that hair," she demanded, disgusted. By me or my hair, I didn't know. There wasn't much of anything I could do about either, so I just did as she asked without argument.*

*It was usually best to just stay out of her way.*

*She always commented on me sharing her face like it was the worst possible thing.*

*Did she **want** to be reminded of the person who'd forced my creation?*

*I hoped not.*

*She'd once, after a whole bottle of wine, told me a graphically detailed story of killing him with only a knife while she cried.*

*If I looked like him, I'd be scared.*

*But... I looked like her and I was still scared.*

*Scared of the way she looked at me like she hated me for having her face. Did she hate herself? Was that why she was so disgusted?*

*"Come the fuck on!" she yelled from somewhere in the big house and I went running to find her. By the time I did, she was outside by the car.*

*She watched me rush up to her, eyes devoid of... anything.*

*"Get in," she demanded, pointing inside the car. "It's going to be a long trip."*

*"When are we coming back?" I asked, and the question triggered a spark of something, finally.*

*Relief.*

*She let out a breath, looking me right in the face when she answered.*

*"Not for a long, long time."*

Like most people, I hated not knowing where I was.

*Unlike* most people, it was because my chances of whatever unknown place I'd woken up in being hazardous to my health were extremely high.

I wasn't constrained though, and my head was clear. My side hurt like a bitch, but it was the only apparent source of pain. As my eyes adjusted to the dark, I realized exactly where I was.

My bed, in the room at the clubhouse.

*How?*

I closed my eyes, trying to force my mind to connect to the events earlier in the day, assuming it was the same day now. I remembered the mysterious rider, finding the thorn tattoo. Somewhere between the two, I'd taken a bullet to the gut.

*"Fuuuuuuck,"* I groaned as I forced myself to sit up, carefully. I reached for the switch beside the bed that controlled the lamp, flicking it on so I could see.

I was bandaged in the same place on my torso and my back; an entry and exit, which was a good thing, but surprising.

*Thorns* didn't usually mean to maim; they went for the *kill.*

I would've expected the weapon of choice to be something much more destructive.

Or... shit, maybe I'd just gotten lucky. I gingerly peeled back the bandage I could reach for a peek at the stitches; nothing haphazard like what I would've expected outside a hospital. They were remarkably neat.

"What the fuck are you doing?"

*Shit.*

I looked up to find Tati standing in the doorway I hadn't even heard open.

"Just checking on—"

"Uh-huh," she interrupted, stepping inside. "Doc is gonna be *pissed* if you mess up his hard work."

I frowned. "Who the fuck is Doc?"

"Elliot," she answered. "You haven't met him yet. His sister had a baby, so he's been gone midwifing."

"He?"

"The term midwife refers to the gender of the patient, not the service provider," she explained. "Anyway, he's back today, right on time to sew you up. You got lucky; it would've been a Nightmare Before Christmas situation if I'd had to do it."

"Lucky me," I quipped, laying back down to take the tension off the situation in my torso. "What's my prognosis?"

"Four to six weeks recovery, but we all know you won't do that, so... just try to take it easy as much as you can. Next question?"

"What the fuck happened?"

Tati sighed as she crossed the room, taking a seat on the end of the bed. "Not super sure, but... we *believe* Jake was the actual target. He walked away from the dispensary but wasn't as lucky about an hour ago. Somebody hit his house."

My eyes went big. "Did he live?"

"Yeah, he's alive. With a few extra holes now."

"Man... what the hell is going on," I muttered, trying to raise a hand to cover my eyes, but quickly dropping it back down when the action pulled at my torso. "Have y'all talked to him at all?"

She shook her head. "Not really. It's been chaos since this all went down. And now we're on lockdown. Which is why I'm here instead of my cute new house. Thanks."

"You make it sound like it's my fault."

"Isn't it? If you hadn't been going to play tag with Jake, you wouldn't have gotten shot, and I'd be in my freestanding tub."

I shook my head, chuckling at her fake annoyance. "My bad."

"Exactly," she teased, patting my leg through the sheets. "So... did you at least find out something good? We've been waiting. All we know is that both of Jake's guys got wasted, and so did the shooter, but our guys – that could've gotten you out of there sooner if you hadn't made them wait a block away – got you out. You've been passed out since then."

"How long?"

"Eleven or twelve hours. Give or take. Doc said he gave you the good stuff while you couldn't argue about it, since it'll likely be the only pain meds you'll take," Tati explained.

She was right.

But I didn't want to tell her that.

"Jake told me Rojas is taking on a new partner and if it's who I think it is... it won't be good for anybody."

She raised an eyebrow. "Who do you think it is?"

"A man named Renard Belrose, the worst kind of human monster there is."

Her lips parted. "Bel*rose*... is that a coincidence?"

"It's not," I admitted. "He and his brother, they started *The Garden*."

"*The Garden... Thorns* and *Roses*?"

"Yeah."

"What does he want with drug dealers in Vegas?"

"Nothing good."

She nodded. "Okay. Well... shit, I guess it's probably good Alicia is here then."

I almost sat up again, but pain quickly returned me to my back. "What is she doing here?"

"I called her, because she knows you, and... you almost died. I figured I should tell people you know."

I scoffed. "I didn't *almost die*, that's dramatic."

"No, actually," Tati countered as she stood. "You *really* almost did. Doc had to give you a fucking blood transfusion; thank goodness we had a match here. He wanted to keep you in a hospital bed, but we didn't know if you'd wake up ripping out tubes and shit, so we didn't. You... scared us. Scared *me*," she corrected as she walked backward to the door, eyes locked on mine.

"I'm sorry," I told her.

She shrugged. "It's okay. I'm glad you pulled through."

"Why?" I asked, before I could stop myself.

Giving a fuck about people dying was a *very* normal thing, that didn't really require an explanation.

Tati rolled her eyes. "I'm gonna grab Alicia and Blue, so you can tell them what you told me."

"Okay. Answer the question though."

She sighed, shaking her head as she opened the door. "Because... you promised me something, and I expect you to deliver it, which you can't do if you die on me. So... get better soon, okay?"

# Chapter Eighteen

## TATI

"Is there anything sexier than watching two men just beat the shit out of each other?" Jenn asked, her gaze planted firmly on where, across the gym, Onyx and Brandon were sparring.

Shirtless.

In answer, I cringed, not because she was wrong, but because Onyx was still bandaged because he'd *fucking got shot last week.*

Brandon promised me he wouldn't hit him there and apparently *that* was "taking it easy".

*Niggas.*

Still, in the spurts where I managed to push that out of my mind for my sanity, I got exactly what she was saying. Was it kinda toxic? Sure, maybe, but there *was* something mesmerizing about the display of raw power between the two.

I wasn't really looking at Brandon like that. I'd pretty much tuned him out in favor of hyper-focusing on the way Onyx moved around the ring.

He was holding back.

Probably a strange conclusion to arrive at when – again – he was dealing with a fresh gunshot wound, but from a distance, I could tell. Brandon was probably too close to it, to in the moment to pick up on it, but Onyx had clearly clocked *his* caution, and had brought down his aggression to match.

Or maybe he would have done that anyway, since they were having fun, not in a real cage match, with an audience.

And really... knowing they were *both* holding back released me to have fun watching, instead of worrying about it. Not that I was supposed to be watching anyway.

"You ready to get back to it?"

I blinked, tearing my eyes away from Onyx's sweaty body long enough to look to Jenn. Her hands were propped on her hips, a little smirk on her face as she waited for my response, a reluctant nod.

I didn't *want* to "get back to it", but "it" was important.

Brandon, Alicia, Onyx, and Keira had banded together to insist on some "close combat" training for me. At first, I'd been a little offended – and offered to kick all their asses – but common sense had prevailed.

I wouldn't always be in a situation where my guard was up, *expecting* a fight.

Which was a large reason for why Kev had been able to get the best of me.

And honestly... Onyx too, when he'd broken in.

I wasn't great in *caught off guard* situations.

Generally speaking, I could throw hands just fine; it was literally in my blood and I had grown up doing plenty of it—in defense of my little sister and otherwise. As an adult, my father and Jesse – Blue's father – had started the task of teaching me how to *really* fight.

Maybe I wouldn't have this weakness now if their deaths hadn't interrupted that education.

In any case, I had Jenn here now; she was from Alicia's firm, but not a *Rose*. She was the same instructor Keira had gone to years ago when she was doing self-defense classes. Now she'd made the switch to private security but was doing us this favor.

Did I *want* to spend my time doing this?

Not really.

But I'd be damned if anybody got the jump on me again without me being able to give them a run for their money *right then*, not once I found an opening later, like with Kev.

Besides... Jenn was badass.

"It's so much less work to just shoot motherfuckers," I groaned, moving into the stance we'd been working on for the last thirty minutes. "Most people just shut up when they see you've got a gun."

Jenn laughed. "True, but you won't always have a gun," she said, moving behind me to "attack" from outside my sight line. "You need to be able to handle yourself in any circumstance."

*Like weirdo niggas who've decided your body belongs to them...*

I didn't say that aloud so I wouldn't make shit awkward. And sure, my vulnerability was being corrected now, but *shit.*

It kept eating at me.

If I'd decided on my own that I'd needed training months ago, would I have been able to fight Kev off more? Would he have ever even thought he could handle me that way?

*Or,* if my guard had been up like it should, and I'd answered the door still armed... would he just be dead now and I wouldn't have to feel like this?

"I need you *focused,*" Jenn warned, batting me upside the head with one of the mitts I was supposed to be avoiding. "You've gotta be present."

"Yeah. Sorry," I said, shaking off my thoughts so I could give this my full attention. Blaming myself and ruminating about the ways things could have been different wouldn't get me anywhere.

And it wouldn't change anything that had occurred.

No matter how badly I wished I could turn back the clock, there was no dodging the reality of my situation, only moving forward. The issue with that was, it was approaching a month and a half since the assault and mentally... I felt like I was in the same damn place.

Maybe worse.

The move hadn't helped like I thought it would, the whole *hitman shooting Onyx so everybody is on lockdown* thing hadn't exactly been great for my anxiety, and the nightmares I'd been so relieved to not be having?

They'd arrived.

It didn't help anything that not being out and about like I usually would had me bored out of my mind. And the whole *can't turn myself on, can't orgasm* thing?

Well, that was driving me up a wall.

Oddly enough, *that* was the thing that drove me to finally call the therapist Alicia had recommended, someone she used often when bringing her former peers in from the cold. I could only imagine the shit that therapist had heard with former *Roses* and *Thorns* as her patients, so I'd figured *my* situation, as fucked up as it was, might be damn near a "break" from the usual trauma.

Obviously, I didn't ask.

I just tried to lean into it, knowing that professional help was what I needed. I'd only had two virtual sessions, but she'd already got in my ass about downplaying my feelings and thinking something was wrong with me because my process didn't look like the stories I'd seen and heard on the internet.

A kick in the pants I needed more than I'd realized.

Most importantly though, she'd assured me I would be okay – whatever that meant – and I believed her.

I just had to accept that it may not be on any specific timeline, or linear at all.

*Expect bumps,* she'd said.

"Focus, Tate!" Jenn snapped, knocking me upside the head with the mitt again.

*Shit.*

"Sorry," I told Jenn, trying *again* to keep my attention fully on my task. I poured myself so fully into the mental connection between her commands, *"Break the hold – block – cross – dodge – cross – jab – jab – block – cross – dodge – jab – jab"*, and my execution that I didn't even realize Brandon and Onyx had finished up what they were doing and had come to watch me.

"*Whew,*" Brandon whistled, after one particularly sharp jab, once I'd started imagining Kev's face on the mitts and hit it so hard I actually staggered Jenn a bit. "I'd hate for my head to be on the receiving end of *that.*"

"Call one of my bikes ornamental again and I'm socking you," I teased, keeping my attention on him to avoid the powerful urge look at Onyx.

"Oh I believe you." Brandon laughed. "Tati used to hand out two-pieces to whoever wanted one, girl, boy, that shit did *not* matter," he said, talking to Jenn and Onyx.

I raised an eyebrow, using my arm to wipe the sweat off my face. "Oh, *now* you're proud?"

"I was always proud."

My mouth dropped. "You used to tell me to stop!"

"Only because you were embarrassing Tali," he truthfully explained.

"I was *defending* Tali!" was my side of that story, and… both sides were right.

Of *all* the things to pick on somebody for, Tali's PICC line – a medical necessity for her constant transfusions and medicines and whatever else – was the shit those idiot kids chose back in high school.

And I had something for their asses, *every time*, until Brandon and I had graduated and Keira took over, which embarrassed her too. "She never got pissed off when *you* whooped ass over her," I grumbled, rolling my eyes.

"Because I gave her hickies after." Brandon cackled. "You and Keira didn't have any peace offerings she was interested in."

"Who is Tali?" Jenn asked and I sighed, holding out my hands to get my gloves taken off.

"My little sister," I answered. "She passed a few years back."

"Oh my goodness, I'm sorry," Jenn gushed, stopping her process on unstrapping me from the padded gloves. "I didn't know."

"No need to be sorry." I shook my head. "It's not a forbidden topic or anything. Just... a tough one."

"What was her illness?" Onyx asked and I met his gaze, finally, while Jenn finished getting my gloves off.

"Cystic Fibrosis," I said. "She was sick for a long time, but we made sure she lived the best life she could. At least, I like to think so."

"She thought so too," Brandon said to Jenn and Onyx, and then explained further that he and Tali had been boyfriend and girlfriend.

"They were each other's first love," I spoke up, grinning. "He's underselling it."

"Awww," Jenn said. "Is that why you two never had a thing?"

My nose wrinkled. "We never had anything because *eww*," I said, frowning at him. "I still don't know what Tali was thinking."

"You know what, I'm not even going to go there with you today, I've got too much to do." Brandon laughed.

"Or is it that you know I'll roast the life out of you and you don't want your feelings hurt today?" I asked, reaching over the barrier of the ring to push my fists against his chest.

"Sure, let's go with that one." He chuckled, with his usual mush to the side of my head. "Carmen still coming to help you today?"

"Yeah, a bit later," I told him, finally climbing down from the ring to where they were standing. Onyx had still been quiet as hell, and I wasn't sure what it was about.

Was he struggling to keep himself upright after over-taxing himself with shit he had no business doing?

Or did he just not know what to say to me?

It was awkward.

*I was going to fuck you.*

*You promised me something and I expect you to deliver it.*

*Seriously, bitch?*

It was so *old Tati,* the girl who just told a nigga what she expected and he did it because what were his other options? *She* wouldn't be thinking twice about saying those things because *she* was more than confident that they would land exactly as intended and yield the desired result.

Premium dick.

Now?

What would I even *do* with a dick?

How would I *actually* factually respond to sex?

Who knew?

Certainly not *me*.

And yet, I was acting as if getting my pussy knocked off the hinges by a literal killer was not only a foregone conclusion, but something that wouldn't leave me crying in a corner, traumatized.

I had no idea what the hell I was doing.

Luckily, I had other things to focus on, like my new house. We were still on high alert, but with Alicia's people involved now, we were confident enough in our manpower – and firepower – to not be on a full-blown lockdown.

I could go home.

I loved *Predator* territory no doubt, but I also enjoyed having my space where I could just be Tati, instead of *VP*. My mother was coming by the new place today to help me with some projects to help me turn it into something that was more... *me*.

Even though my base pieces, aka my expensive ass furniture, were remaining the same, I felt like it didn't make sense to *not* take advantage of the chance to do some new things with my décor—feature walls, open shelving, cute light fixtures, stuff like that.

My mother had a DIY streak like mine; she was who I'd gotten it from in the first place. And she was worried about me, always wanting to be up under me since the assault anyway. I'd managed to hold her off; 'cause I knew exactly what she'd subject me to, hours of ranting about Kev that I wasn't trying to hear.

Now that she'd mellowed, spending some time together would be a perfect opportunity to knock two things out of the way.

"How is your recovery going?" I asked Onyx, forcing myself to not make it any weirder that we hadn't said anything to each other.

"I've got no complaints," he answered, nonchalant as fuck, with a maddeningly sexy shrug.

"That's really not what I asked you."

"Isn't it though?" he countered and I sucked in a deep breath before I just walked away, ignoring Brandon's quip about a *lover's quarrel*.

Asshole.

Back at my house, I took a good long shower and dressed in clothes I didn't mind getting covered in paint or otherwise; our task list for the day was extensive. Technically the house was a rental, but only in the sense that I'd agreed to that arrangement so I could move in immediately. The purchase was already in progress to make it mine, so I could go ahead and start making whatever changes I wanted. An envelope full of the right amount of cash was good for changing most people's plans and this had been no exception.

A landlord wasn't an option in my position, so Keira made it happen.

I'd been at it for a bit by myself when my mother arrived, breezing in with enough food for an army as usual. Despite my efforts to avoid such a conversation, we went through the usual song and dance of her asking a bunch of questions about how I was feeling, what my plans were, and where Kev was.

She wanted him worse than any of us, honestly, which made me scared of what she might do. In general, my mother was a sweet woman, but she didn't have a reputation for *not* being one to fuck with for no reason.

Age had calmed her, a lot, but she didn't play about her kids.

I loved that – *cherished* that – but still.

She knew Kev was stashed somewhere, but what I wasn't going to do was tell her where. I didn't want her bumping heads with Alicia and her people and I didn't want her "taking care of" Kev in her own way.

I had *my* way, that I was still figuring out.

For now, I was letting him fester.

With a bit of insistence I managed to shift my mother's focus to the actual matter at hand, getting her to give more attention to our list of projects than my trauma.

Aaaand... it took exactly *one* question for me to reconsider the whole thing.

"Are you *sure* about this color?" she asked, referring to the pretty, mauvy gray I'd spent hours agonizing over in front of a wall of paint chips at the store. I'd swatched a big patch of it on the wall so I could see how the color translated once it was dry.

"Yes," I told her bluntly, and she frowned, looking up at the wall of the bathroom I'd already started amending with a decorative wood trim pattern we would be painting over.

"But it's so *bold*," she complained and I shook my head. "You're going to be sick of this in six months."

"It's not bold," I argued. "It's just not neutral. And I don't want neutral, I want it to be interesting and inviting and pretty. And I like it, so..."

"Well I still say it's too much," she maintained, propping her hands on her hips. "We should stop and reconsider."

I pushed out a sigh as I stood, mirroring her stance. "And *I* say, *the paint is already purchased*, and it's what *I* want, for *my* bathroom... so gone and grab a brush, miss mamas."

"*Fine,*" she grumbled, making me laugh.

If there was *anything* Carmen Tate was going to do, it was speak her mind, even if you hadn't actually asked her to. After growing up with her, and surviving my teenage years in her house, I'd learned that I just had to stick to my guns. It was usually enough to overcome her objections—about the small stuff at least.

We were able to get the rest of the trim up and "finished", leaving it ready to be painted before we moved on to the dining room. In there, it was just a simple chair rail molding and the walls would be a super-pale gray; Mama approved.

We were blazing through our to-do list until I realized I had *not* purchased nearly enough of the caulk I'd needed for all the seams and nail holes to make it look professionally finished.

"Let's just run to the store," Mama suggested and I rolled my eyes, because I *already knew.*

"If we leave this house, we are going to end up somewhere having tapas and mimosas." I laughed, shaking my head. "And I really want to get this done today. I'm going back to work next week—like for real, not just stuff here and there like I have been. I want to be able to come home to a space that looks like I want it to."

Not to mention, the level of protection we were under now meant a trip to the store would honestly turn into a whole production.

"Okay so how are you going to get it then?" Mama asked. "You want me to go by myself?"

I sucked my teeth. "If *you* leave, *you'll* just end up going to have the tapas and mimosas *by yourself,* so no, I don't want you to go either. I'll... just call someone."

"Someone" ended up being a whole list of folks, none of whom were truly available.

Not Maite, not Brandon, not Keira.

After that I landed on the person I felt *next* most comfortable asking to come to my home.

Onyx.

*Maybe I can just ask one of the security guys to do it?*

No.

*No.*

I couldn't pull them off their posts for something like this.

"What about that young man that was at the house that day, that big handsome one with the hair?" Mama asked, breaking into my thoughts to suggest the exact person I was trying *not* to call.

But... *fuck it.*

We needed the supplies to finish, and I wanted this done, so... I blew out a sigh and dialed his number. He answered after the second ring and I had to catch my breath a little when I heard his voice.

"What's wrong?" he asked, no hello or anything, just bass and concern, and... *shit.*

"Uh, nothing," I stammered, like the awkward teenager I'd *never* been, so what even was this? "Um...I need you to bring me some caulk."

"Some *what*?"

My nose wrinkled in confusion for a second before I realized. "*Caulk*. C-A-U-L-K. Like the home improvement product. Why would I even use *that* word?"

He chuckled. "You gotta make it plain, after our last real conversation. What do you need that for?" he asked. "You got some plumbing issues? Need your pipes checked out? Got a leak? Something too wet?"

"Funny," I said, even though I really needed him to stop, because the innuendo wasn't helping my flustered state. "I need it for some feature wall stuff I'm doing with my mom. I'm not trying to turn the trip into a big deal for security, so... if you're not busy..."

"I've got you. Text me a picture of what you need."

"Okay. Thanks."

He didn't respond.

Well, he *did* respond, by hanging up, and instead of overthinking it, I just sent the damn picture. Since we couldn't do much until we had the extra supplies, Mama and I broke for lunch. We were finishing up when Onyx arrived and the first question out of his mouth was, "Man y'all had lunch and didn't save me any?"

A response I *really* should have anticipated.

The sound of his voice brought my mom into the kitchen, where she stopped for a moment and stared at him, wearing this strange look. "You're the one who tracked down the motherfucker who hurt my baby."

My eyebrows shot up.

I didn't even know she knew that.

"Uh... yes ma'am," he answered, with a nod.

"Come on in, I'll fix you a plate," she insisted, waving him further into the house. "We got plenty of extra over here in the fridge."

"Nah." He laughed, staying put at the doorway. "You don't have to do that Ms. Carmen. I'm actually not hungry—for a change," he added to the end.

"*Ms. Carmen*," my mom said, with a nudge to my side. "This one's got some good manners, baby. And look at them arms in his sleeves. A man with arms like that—"

"*Okay* that is enough of *that*," I interrupted, drowning out whatever she was about to say. "Onyx, thank you for dropping these supplies off for me. I'm sure you have somewhere to be."

"Not really," he told me, leaning into the doorframe with a grin that kind of made me want to treat him like one of the mitts from earlier. "Things are pretty quiet today."

"Oh good," Mama said. "You and those arms, y'all come on and help hang up some of these sticks Tatiana wants on the walls."

Onyx frowned. "Sticks?"

"They're not *sticks*," I groaned. "We talked about this already, Mama. And he's actually supposed to be taking it easy," I reminded him.

He shrugged, stepping inside. "Can't be any worse than anything I've already done today, right?"

# *Chapter Nineteen*

## TATI

It was quiet again.

Finally.

The whole "low odor" paint thing was mostly a lie, so my house was full of fumes I was currently trying to coax out with open windows, but it looked good.

Or would once I pulled up all the drop cloth and painter's tape.

*I really should have done all this before I moved in*, I mused from the tub. My soak would be *much* more relaxing if I could safely light my candles, but this was fine too. Between me, my mother, Onyx, and then Maite and Keira showing up later, we'd managed to get it all done.

Now, between all that and this morning's training exercise, I was sore and tired.

I hadn't been to *Bottoms* in a long time.

Too long probably, to be second in command of the club.

The first story that spread about my absence was some bullshit initiated by Sanaa, that I was heartbroken and in hiding because of it. The goal was painting me as some bitter chick who couldn't handle being broken up with.

Now, the truth was trickling out, probably thanks to Sanaa as well. This time with the goal of painting me as a liar, but my people knew me too well.

They could easily deduce the truth.

Did I love the idea of everybody and their mama knowing about it and potentially treating me like some victim?

Of course not.

But I also wasn't interested in my assault being some secret to potentially be used against me, like it was something for *me* to be ashamed about.

I wasn't the one who had done something wrong.

Even for the few days I was at the club headquarters during lockdown, I'd kept to myself so much more than I usually would. Instead of being in the mix like normal, I was holed up in my suite, bored out of my mind.

That shit was dead.

No, I didn't want to talk about it, wasn't about to host a damn seminar. I just wasn't going to continue hiding my face and not being visible for my club.

I wasn't going to talk around it.

Yeah, it happened, and I was still *that bitch*.

We could all move on.

I pushed out a sigh.

*Much easier said than done.*

All the affirmations in the world couldn't make up for the fact that I was feeling iffy about showing my face at the bar; it was a little different than the casual environment of headquarters. Typically when I went to *Bottoms*, I was there to represent the club *and* have a good ass time while making sure the patrons were having a good time.

It involved being very, *very* visible.

Which, all things considered... was a little scary.

But by the time I got out of the tub, I'd made my decision.

It had been *too* long since I got myself dressed up to step out.

It was time to make an appearance.

I shot Maite and Keira both texts to give them a heads up that I was going. I knew security would need to know so they could get me there safely, but Keira actually volunteered to pick me up, which I appreciated.

I could use the moral support.

She came through with it too, coming though my door an hour later and declaring, *"Damn bitch, you meant it when you said you were showing up, huh?"*

"So I look decent?" I asked, earning myself sucked teeth and rolled eyes.

"Decent? *Decent*?" she countered, frowning as she shook her head and looped an arm through mine to head out the door. "Stop playing with me and bring your pretty ass on here."

In the car, we fell right into a club-ready vibe—Vanity, Meg, Doja, Nicki, all the usual bad bitch anthems that never failed to get us hyped. Even so, the closer we got to the bar, the more and more nervous I felt, until we pulled into the parking lot.

"I'm going to throw up," I told Keira, who rolled her eyes at me.

"Vomit in my shit and you're gonna have to beat my ass, babe," she said, getting out and then coming around to my side to open my door. "Consider it immersion therapy," she told me, reaching over me to unbuckle my seat belt. "That bar is full of people who adore you; you're going to be just fine. Unless... you *aren't* fine," she said, stepping closer and getting very serious. "'Cause I'll get right back in and drive you home if—"

"No," I told her, pushing out a deep breath. "I can do it. I think I can do it."

"You kinda look too good not to, so..."

"Flattery will get you everywhere." I laughed, not feeling any less like I was about to puke, but still climbing my ass out of the car. "I just need to get it over with."

"I agree." Keira grinned. "Come on."

Inside *Bottoms*, I wasn't that surprised by the reception I received.

I was *definitely* embarrassed about the round of fucking applause, but I swallowed it in favor of smiling and waving and accepting my *welcome back* with grace.

One time, my father had gotten stabbed and had to spend a bit of time out. When he came back, the club members made a sort of fuss about it, which I *knew* he hated. But he grinned and bore it because, as he told me later, a good leader allowed their club to show them affection.

They never *demanded* it, but they *allowed* it, and they accepted it, courteously.

I saw the difference it'd made in our club culture versus some of the others, and I didn't want to be the one to buck the energy. So I accepted the love and I had Erica do a round of shots, for the whole bar, on the house.

People were staring at me, which was initially uncomfortable. I knew the club members weren't the only patrons, and some of these people were likely confused as to why my presence was a big deal, but damn.

I had to remind myself though, that people *always* stared at me, because I was big and fine, I made a fucking impression, I got attention.

What was new?

I perched myself at my usual corner booth with Keira and no more than a few minutes had passed before Brandon showed up with Nessa on his arm.

"*Hey!*" I greeted her warmly, honestly excited to see her after what felt like a long while. I kept expecting to feel weird about Brandon getting serious about someone else, considering that he'd been so close with Tali, but I really loved Nessa for him. She'd passed nearly four years ago at this point; he needed someone, in my opinion. There was a weird bitch he'd dealt with not long before Nessa who I *thought* was going to be a problem. Luckily, that was short-lived and then this one came along.

*This one* was really good for him.

She gave him balance.

"Listen to me," Nessa said, bending to give me a hug, "I know Brandon already passed this message along, but if you need *anything* from me or mine? Just say the word." She leaned in a little more, telling me in my ear, "I've got people too, okay?"

"I appreciate you," I told her, squeezing her tight before I released her so she could stand up. "Brandon finally let you come back out here, huh?"

She rolled her eyes at him as he hooked an arm around her shoulder. "Girl. All over me about *security* as if the Hamiltons don't shoot back."

"I keep trying to get you to understand, these ain't the usual shooters, gorgeous," he said. "This shit is different."

"Two to the dome takes anybody down, doesn't it?" she asked, innocently batting her eyelashes at him as he bit his lip.

"What have I told you about talking like that?"

"What the fuck you gone do about it?"

"Oh my *God*, get a room." I laughed, waving them off. They did indeed head towards the back, to do God knows what, and a moment later Keira jumped up, rattling off something about catching Gavin to talk numbers before he left. She gave a quick hug to Maite, who was approaching the table as she rushed off.

"Ahhh, you look cuuute," Maite gushed, excitedly taking a seat beside me. "You okay?"

I took a deep breath, really considering it before I nodded. "Yeah. I am."

"Good. Let me tell you *this* shit."

I sat back with my drink and listened as she regaled me with too many details about the things she'd been doing with Trinidad.

"Maite, we're supposed to be on lockdown, you know that, right? We're *this close* to launching a damn assault on the *Renegados* and you're fucking that man's wife still?!"

"I can't help who I love!" she whined.

"Bitch, you're gonna get your ass killed, talking about *love!*"

She huffed, sitting back with her arms crossed. "We're being careful, damn! Do you wanna know what I have to tell you or not?"

"I wanna know why you don't think it's risky as fuck for Trinidad to be sneaking you into that house—which, how? *How?*" I repeated, legitimately confused. "Manuel is gonna go upside *both* your heads, if I don't first."

She sucked her teeth. "And I'll have something for his bitch ass if he tries me. But *listen!*"

"*What?*" I asked, glaring at her.

"While I was there, Manuel got a visitor. I had to wait until those scary niggas was *all the way* gone before I could leave."

My eyebrow went up. "Scary?"

"Girl... *Terrifying.* Some old fucking French dude and some younger guys with tats like the one Nyx has. I don't know what that shit means, but I know it ain't good; those niggas were dead in the eyes."

"You saw their eyes; so they saw you?" I asked, chest tight.

"One of them did, but he just didn't react, like *at all.* Like some kind of brainwashing," she said. "I just acted like I was supposed to be there and didn't say anything. But I'm telling you, something about this shit is *not* right."

She had no idea how correct she was.

"Did you overhear any of the meeting?" I asked, already picking up my phone to shoot a text to the group chat with Brandon, Onyx, and Alicia. I didn't know *everything* about *The Garden* and all that, but I *did* know enough to deduce that Maite had probably seen Renard Belrose, in yet another meeting with Rojas.

After their last meeting, people had died.

"No, sorry," Maite answered. "I would've tried to get closer, but I was afraid of getting caught."

"You did the right thing. *Keep* being afraid your ass is going to get caught and stay out of that man's house," I told her as my phone lit up with notifications.

The fervor died down quickly though because all we could really do was exactly what we'd *been* doing.

Speculating.

"I see you decided to pop out looking good," Onyx said, appearing seemingly out of nowhere at the head of the table. "Why you hiding back here?"

"How did you know where I was? Stalker much?" I asked, as he slid into the empty space on the other side of me in the circular booth.

He looked at Maite. "You going to tell her you told me she was here or not?" he said to Maite, who rolled her eyes.

"I would think getting shot would calm you down, but there's never any chill with you, huh?"

"A bullet doesn't mean shit to me." Onyx grinned. "If I don't die, they are, and if I die... well, I won't know any different, will I?" he asked her and then turned to me. "You good?" he inquired, gesturing at my drink. "You want another one?"

"No thank you," I told him, shaking my head. "I popped out to get a *little* loose. Just a little."

He nodded. "Understandable. Special occasion I don't know about?"

"Nope. Just felt like being out."

"And that's a good sign, right?"

I shrugged. "Yeah, I would say so. What are you doing here? Other than stalking me."

"That's the only reason I'm out," he said. "I heard you were out here fucking 'em up, I had to come see for myself."

"Who said that?"

He chuckled. "Everybody in this motherfucker."

Maite groaned. "Okay, y'all are on the cute shit, so I'm out," she said, removing herself from the booth before I could even argue.

I... hadn't realized we were on any "cute" shit. I was just enjoying being among a crowd.

And having a certain man's attention.

"Am I?" I asked Onyx, going back to the conversation we'd been having.

"Are you what?"

"Fucking 'em up?"

He leaned in a bit, peeking around the table to give me another slow perusal. "You are. I like the boots."

"Thank you."

They were actually brand new—gorgeous burgundy thigh-high beauties I'd been waiting on an opportunity to wear. An opportunity that likely would have come much sooner if my social life hadn't been completely derailed thanks to Kev's inability to keep his dick to himself.

*Shit.*

I wasn't supposed to be thinking about that tonight.

I looked good, I felt good, and I didn't intend to let anything throw that off.

"You having a good time?" Onyx asked and I nodded.

"I am. Do I not seem like it?"

"You seem a little quiet. More lowkey than the last time I saw you here."

I raised an eyebrow. "You know... you're right," I told him. "Let's do something about that," I said, grabbing his hand to slide out of the booth. Onyx didn't really have a choice except to give in to my tugging at his hand, following me to the other side of the bar where the dance floor was set up.

"You said they trained you in how to be good at everything right?" I asked, pushing up my toes to talk to him over the music.

"I did say that." He chuckled, probably already guessing where I was going.

"Well then," I said, stepping right up against him. "Let's dance."

Well... I don't know if what we did out there on the floor could really qualify as dancing *with* each other. The DJ started playing Vanity and I went straight into the twerk that was just my body's natural reaction, grinding my ass on him.

So it was more like *I* was dancing and he moved right along with it. A group of women passed by, hyping me up, which did exactly what they'd intended it to do.

Hyped me the fuck up.

Exactly the energy I needed.

I went from having a lowkey good time, just glad to be back in the mix, to having a fucking *blast*.

I *did* have that other drink and I didn't regret it.

Because I knew Onyx and the others wouldn't let anything happen to me.

Kev had invaded this place so much seeking attention that I'd nearly forgotten before he ever came along, this was *my* safe space. For the most part, the only people in here now were *Predators* and *Bottoms* regulars, and a few brave tourists who'd been warned about the potential for more than the usual trouble popping off.

Everybody here was vetted and approved.

So I had *another* drink.

And I got really damn goofy behind it, then promptly danced it all out of my system. It wasn't until I was exhausted and ready to go that I remembered I'd shown up here with Keira, who'd been ghost since she... went to find Ghost.

When I went looking, her office light was on, but the door was closed, so I assumed they were talking business, which I didn't want to interrupt. And if they *weren't* talking business... I didn't want to interrupt *that* either.

"Hey... I need a ride home," I told Onyx after I'd hunted him down again, at the bar talking to Teo. "If that's okay with you."

"It's definitely good with me," he said, leaning in to speak to me. "But you should know, I rode here on my bike. So if you want a ride from me, you have to put your arms around me and get *real* close."

I bit down on my lip, holding his gaze. "Wouldn't be the first time, but uh... how about *I* drive and *you* ride on the back?"

He smirked. "We can do that too, sweetheart. I got no problem being the big spoon."

I laughed. "You are such a damn fool."

I grabbed a spare helmet from my office before I followed him out to his bike, and minutes later, we were whipping through the desert, heading back to the city. I couldn't front like it didn't feel good being this close, with my arms tight around him to keep myself secure on the bike.

It was...cozy.

Even with our security escort.

I tuned them out, pretending they weren't even there so I could just mentally settle into the moment. That cozy feeling didn't subside even after he'd parked and walked me to my front door. I'd had a full, busy ass day today, leading into a good ass night.

One I wasn't quite ready to be over.

"Thank you," I told him, pushing my key into the door instead of using the keypad, just because it took a few seconds longer and I was trying to prolong saying goodbye.

"For what?" he asked, frowning like he was confused.

"For contributing to... a normal-feeling night. A *great* night. And of course, for your help with the house stuff earlier. I know you had better shit to do than paint."

He shook his head. "I didn't."

"That's *not* what Brandon said." I laughed, smiling up at him. "*He* said he was going to have to lock me up somewhere because I was ruining a perfectly good lieutenant."

His eyebrows went up. "Oh, *lieutenant*? I'm moving up in the world from a corner boy recruit, huh?"

"You would *never* be a corner boy," I reminded him.

"Tell me anything, Tati."

I stayed quiet for a moment, just looking at him. And then I pushed the door open behind me and stepped inside, without turning around. "I want you to come in."

There was nothing but the loud ass crickets for what felt like a long time.

And then he asked, "Are you sure about that?" His eyes narrowed as he leaned in my doorway. "You know what's going to happen if I come inside?"

"I've already been accused of ruining you," I countered. "So... I may as well."

He ran his tongue over his lips. "*Ruining* me. Wow. You're *sure*?"

"Will you just get your ass in here?" I asked.

He battled with himself. I could see it in his eyes; he knew the same thing that I did, that whatever might happen between us, there was never any *real* hope of it being "just" a casual thing.

It was probably a fucking mistake, honestly.

But I didn't care.

He came in.

He closed the door, locked it, and then... silence.

Neither of us moved.

Until...

"Can I touch you?"

Was he joking?

Him touching me was the *only* thing in the world I wanted.

I nodded, hoping it would be enough to get him to take things real far, real fast, but instead he just closed the distance between us and cupped me under my chin, tipping my face up to his.

"I need you to say it," he murmured, with his face close enough for his lips to brush mine, but not quite kiss. "No ambiguity, sweetheart. I need to hear it."

"Touch me," I said—*begged.*

That was all the permission he needed to grab me at the waist and snatch my body against his, his dick pressing into my stomach as he kissed me like it was a moment he'd just been fucking *waiting for.* His tongue in my mouth, his fingertips gripping my waist, then my ass, the smell of him, feel of him...I wanted it all.

I wanted everything.

I didn't usually like being picked up; at my size, it had a tendency to feel like a precarious situation. But when Onyx hiked my thighs around his waist, I wasn't sure I'd ever felt more secure and I didn't even flinch about it when carried me straight to my bedroom.

Whatever was about to happen, I was ready.

I was willing.

*I think.*

Shit.

*Was I ready?*

Instead of stripping me, licking me, fucking me, like I needed him to,

Onyx deposited me on the bed, and then just stood there at the foot like he was waiting.

Like he'd picked up on the sudden doubt coursing through my brain. *Shit.*

I needed one of us to be confident about this and lead the damn way.

"What is it?" I asked, sitting up on my elbows, panting. "You changed your mind?"

"Fuck no," he replied, shaking his head. "I'm just not about to do a damn thing that you don't tell me."

"What?" I asked, eyes narrowed in confusion. "Is this… about consent?" I appreciated him seeking certainty, but, "You've got it. Let's do this."

"No." He chuckled, grabbing me by the ankle to do a slow unzip on one of my boots. I felt *every* molecule of the action; his fingers at the zipper, his hand holding up my leg, the slow journey of heat from my thigh to my heel. "I know I have your consent, Tati. I'm waiting on your direction."

"Direction?"

He nodded. "Use your mouth, sweetheart. Tell me what you want." He made that demand with my calf in his hand, holding me as he pulled off the boot. He raised an eyebrow at me, still waiting for me to say something as he moved to the other one. "If you're not *sure*…" he started, when I still hadn't offered anything with both boots on the ground, and my legs haphazard on the bed, but I stopped him.

"No, I'm sure," I said.

He raised an eyebrow. "Okay. So…?"

"Your mouth," I told him. "I want your mouth."

"You want me to sing to you?"

"No, I…" I pushed out a sigh, fighting my frustration to meet his gaze. "I want you to eat my pussy."

He smirked. "Gladly."

I let out a sound that was half giggle, half scream as he grabbed the waistband of my jeans, using it to pull me closer to the end of the bed. I was still laughing when he stepped between my legs, winking at me as he unbuttoned and unzipped, then took them off me with my panties still tucked in them.

Baring my pussy.

He blew out this… *grateful* sort of sigh as he stared between my legs, his eyes full of something like hunger.

I sucked in a breath.

I didn't know how this was about to go.

Could he *feel* the tension emanating off me as he knelt before me, ready to give my pussy whatever veneration he'd been considering in his spare time?

It was another layer of anxiety on an already fraught experience.

I couldn't relax.

Not through the feeling of his lips on my inner thighs, his teeth on my ass cheeks, his fingers digging into my hips. Somehow, I managed not to burst into tears as he made his way to the center, and then, finally, pressed his lips to the folds of my pussy.

It just felt good.

I didn't black out and mentally transport back some horrific memory.

It just... *felt good.*

And once I realized it?

The tension drained out of me like a switch had been flipped.

Onyx pressed his face deeper between my legs, putting his tongue to work as he propped my thighs over his shoulders. I let my eyelids droop but kept them open, keeping my gaze on the top of his head, fingers buried in his locs as he licked, teased, *devoured.*

And... *holy shit*, there it was.

Finally.

The fucking *build up.*

I'd missed it, so much.

Onyx chased it easily with a perfect cadence of his tongue, lapping and prodding, intercut with slow, deep sucks on my clit that made me feel like I was coming unglued.

And his *fingers.*

God, those long, thick fingers that pushed deep, stroking in tandem with the rhythm of his mouth, seeking and exploring my pussy.

My head fell back, and I let my eyes close, fully giving myself to the impending orgasm. I yelled, moaned, whimpered, let whatever came to my mouth come right out, committed to not holding back a goddamn thing.

And when it hit, finally?

*Finally.*

Unquestionable bliss, washing over me, through me, an underestimated storm surge that just kept going, and *going*, exacerbated by Onyx's tongue, his fingers, his *teeth.*

When it did eventually subside?

My whole body just felt like... jelly.

Euphoria had me damn near humming a tune as Onyx kissed his way up my body, over my stretchmarks and rolls, happily giving them his attention, only stopping to help me out of my shirt and bra.

"What's on your mind?" he asked once he'd made it in line with my face.

*I love you*, I thought, but – thankfully – knew *that* shit was a temporary, insane byproduct of him giving me the orgasm that had been out of my reach.

"Not much," I said instead. "You uh... took a lot off my mind," I breathed.

"Glad to be of service," he murmured, still smelling like my pussy as he brought his lips to mine for a kiss.

I didn't care.

I just wanted his tongue back in my mouth, and his fingers back inside me, so I told him that and he obliged.

I wanted his clothes off and he obliged.

I wanted his naked ass in my carefully chosen dressing chair, his dick sitting straight up, long and thick, waiting for me.

And he obliged.

I felt very powerful.

And a little terrified.

His mouth was one thing, his fingers another.

His dick?

Something else entirely.

*You want this.*

No question.

I did.

I was just a little afraid of the possibilities.

*But you're not a punk.*

I wasn't.

Really.

So, I took a deep breath and I climbed on, knowing I had all the power, all the control in this situation. His gaze stayed on my face as I lined him up with my pussy and... sank down.

Just a little.

Just to get acclimated.

Once again... it just felt good.

And then even better, once I let myself sink down a little more, releasing the breath I'd been holding as I met Onyx's eyes. After a moment, his hands moved to my hips, stilling my movements.

"You okay?"

"Yeah."

"Good." His hand came to my neck, dragging me forward so my face was right in line with his. "So fuck me like you mean it and stop playing."

He wasn't *rushing* me.

It was an encouragement, and I took it to heart.

I didn't have to be afraid, I could just... ride him in this chair, an option I'd chosen for good leverage, so I could really get into it.

So I got into it.

Hands gripping his shoulders, feet planted on the ground, I *rode him like I fucking meant it*, until we were both breathing hard and barely keeping it together.

"*There you go,*" he grunted into my ear, his fingers digging into my ass cheeks. "*Just like that.*"

Why did that make me ride him harder?

Less about the bouncing and more about the grinding in my hips, creating a delicious friction against my clit.

"*Goddamn,*" Onyx growled, gripping my ass even harder, with no attempt to alter my pace. "What the fuck are you trying to do to me?"

I just grinned.

This was *wonderful.*

Onyx went back and forth between my breasts, little nips and hard sucks that hit me right between the legs, making me wetter and wetter. His hand went between us, finding my clit to offer a more concentrated stimulation than what I could do on my own while I rode him.

Harder.

Faster.

"*There* you go, sweetheart. I see you."

*Harder.*

*Faster.*

"Your fine ass knows *exactly* how fucking good you feel, don't you?"

I gave up on any semblance of rhythm, just doing whatever the fuck felt best as Onyx groaned and cursed into my neck.

"Tati. Ta—*shit,*" he groaned. "I'm about to—"

"I'm on birth control," I told him, not stopping, in fact, I went *harder,* as he pinched down on my clit, and then...

Another wave.

Another flood.

His arms wrapped around me, holding me tight as *his* hips surged.

I couldn't focus on him though.

I was reeling from what had just surged through *me* and I had to give my attention to *that*. I was all out of breath, trying to get myself together, which Onyx thought was funny.

He picked us *both* up from the chair like it was nothing and deposited me on the bed. He walked away and I heard him in my bathroom a moment later, first in my towel cabinet, and then running water.

*What a gentleman*, I thought, and then laughed, closing my eyes.

I felt good.

I felt fucking *amazing*.

All that drama in my head, for nothing.

It was all *fine* and I was perfectly okay.

Until... I wasn't.

The change was swift.

With my eyes still closed, I tried to wipe away sweat I logically understood was only my own but didn't feel that way. My euphoric, post-orgasm feeling was rapidly replaced with an encompassing sensation akin to disgust, making my stomach twist in a knot.

All the praise Onyx had offered while he was buried in me, that illicit pride he'd induced had slipped away, leaving behind a feeling of being used that snaked around my throat, making it hard to breathe.

I *couldn't* breathe.

I couldn't—

I can't...

"Tati—*Tati—open your eyes*. Hey—*Hey*."

I forced myself to heed the voice, peeling my eyelids apart to find Onyx in front of my face in the dark.

"Breathe. *Breathe.* In through your nose. Out through your mouth," he insisted, several times before I could actually pull together the synapses in my brain to actually *do it*. "Sit up," he said, and I did, but it was a struggle, with my lungs on fire the way they were. Once I was upright, he pulled my freshly redone braids up off my neck, helping me feel instantly cooler as he kept talking me through the breaths.

*In through my nose, out through my mouth.*

Over, and over, until I'd finally calmed.

Momentarily.

My breathing difficulties were replaced with sobs—deep, wracking sobs I couldn't just breathe through and couldn't seem to stop. Sobs I didn't even understand, which made them even more fucking... embarrassing.

"Tell me what you need."

I pulled my head up from where I'd buried myself in my covers, looking into Onyx's face.

"I don't know."

"What usually makes you feel better?"

I shook my head, confused at how the hell I was supposed to answer that, but I managed to blurt out one thing, "*The shower.*"

"Can I touch you?"

The same question from before.

Completely different context.

It made me cry even harder, but I nodded.

He didn't *help* me to my shower, he picked me up and took me there, depositing me on the wide bench seat that had sold this place for me before he turned on the water.

Then sat down beside me.

Neither of us said anything.

We just sat there, until my tears had subsided, and then I got up, stepping under the water to let it wash me clean. I couldn't bear to even look at Onyx, terrified of the inevitable pity I knew I'd see in his eyes.

That thought had barely finished crossing my mind before he was behind me in the water, arms around me, lips against my shoulder. "I know you're upset. I know you wish it didn't have to happen, but... it did. Now tell me... was it as bad as you expected?"

I shook my head, sinking into him. "No."

# Chapter Twenty

## NYX



*No.*

A SEARCH-AND-DESTROY MISSION with half my senses dulled by sleep put a stop to clumsy fingers at the waistband of my boxers.

I squinted as my eyes adjusted to the barely-there morning light peeking through the window and a muffled "*oouuucchhh*" from underneath the covers drew me out of my nightmares and into reality.

"*Oh, shit,*" I hissed, releasing my hold on Tati's wrists, and flipping the covers back. She immediately sat up, hands massaging the places where I'd been holding her too tight.

"*Sorry,*" she breathed, braids all over the place as she met my gaze with puffy, contrite eyes. "I wasn't thinking."

I sat up to join her, taking over the massage of the sensitive flesh I hopefully hadn't bruised. "*I'm* sorry." I pushed out a sigh. "I don't even know what the fuck that was," I admitted.

"It wasn't a great idea... all things considered," she said, accompanying the words with a dry laugh. "I shouldn't have assumed that was something you would even want, especially without any sort of warning, while you were *asleep*. Wow, I really fucked—"

"Stop," I interrupted, dropping her wrists to pull her into me. "It's not like that."

"How would you know?" she drew back, raising an eyebrow at me. "You just said you didn't know what happened?"

"What if I figured it out though, smartass?"

"I'm listening."

"What's up with the attitude?"

"I don't *have* an attitude."

"So you're a liar now."

"Nigga..."

"I'm just not used to waking up to anybody," I said before I *actually* pissed her off. I knew her well enough now to tell the "attitude" was just anxiety, which wasn't something I cared to cultivate between us.

Her expression softened. "So... you're telling me you haven't had a lil girlfriend, sneaky link, none of that?"

"Do I seem that fuckin' domesticated?" I asked, making her laugh.

"No," she conceded. "You are... quite the feral big cat."

"You calling me pussy?"

"*Stop*." She laughed again. "No, I'm saying you're... used to being a lion in the wild. One with no pack. Unsustainable. You belong in a group. Pack hunters."

"I thought hunting was a lioness' job in the wild."

"*Not* the point, sir," she teased, playfully jabbing me in the chest. "You know that, right?"

"I do."

"Okay." She nodded. "So... come to the bathroom. I want to look at your bandages. Doc asked me to keep an eye on you."

"I'm pretty sure I can take care of myself," I called after her. She was already off the bed, heading for the door.

"Says the man who went to sleep with those bandages wet. Bring your ass to the bathroom," she demanded, naked, wearing an expression that really invited no nonsense, so...

"Whatever," I grumbled, like I wasn't *very* willing to have a fine ass, nude woman tending to me.

I couldn't let her think it was *too* easy.

"So…" she started, once she'd gotten yesterday's still damp bandages off, and done a little examination of my external wounds. "You wanna talk about what happened a few minutes ago?"

"Not particularly."

A soft sigh pushed from her throat as she taped fresh gauze around the small wound on my torso. "I'm sorry. Again."

"You're good. It's fine."

"It's really not though," she insisted, nudging me to turn around so she could tend to the exit wound. "I understand that you're not angry with me, but… it's not okay. Knowing what you've been through."

"You don't know what I've been through."

"I know enough," she argued, peeking around my body to meet my gaze. "We… have some uncomfortable… *traumas,* in common. At different degrees, different circumstances, but in common still. I was so wrapped up in using you for my own rehabilitation that I wasn't thinking about *your*… triggers. And that's not cool. So I'm sorry."

I nodded. "I appreciate that, but seriously… I'm good."

Done with the bandages, she stepped in front of me, eyebrow raised. "So you're cool with me treating you like an emotionless piece of meat?"

"It's how I prefer being used to be honest," I teased her, wrapping an arm around her waist to pull her into me. "All jokes aside, chill. I wouldn't be here if I wasn't comfortable."

*Which was exactly the fucking problem.*

I was entirely *too* comfortable.

And here she was apologizing to preserve *my* feelings, as if *I* wasn't the one keeping secrets. If anybody had reasons to be repentant…

"I've got something I've gotta do," I told her, breaking the connection I didn't deserve, to put some space between us.

Her eyes went wide. "That sounds pretty ominous…"

"Nah, it's nothing like *that,*" I assured. "I just… I have a routine I'm trying to stick to."

"Oh. Do you need anything?" she asked, pushing her braids back from her face.

"Just space. You mind if I use your courtyard?"

She grinned. "Sure. Have at it."

She slipped out of the bathroom, leaving me to take the heavy breath I desperately needed. I wasn't fronting about the routine; it had been doing a masterful job of keeping me in a good place mentally.

Today, it was definitely needed.

She was in her closet when I left the bathroom, so I was able to grab my boxers and some other paraphernalia to head to my destination—the courtyard in the middle of her house. It was one of the things I'd liked most about her new place, outdoor space with no way to access it from the exterior of the house.

A perfect place to blaze up and meditate.

Tati kept a little basket of throw blankets right next to the door, so I took one with me to spread out on the grass. The sun was finally making a real impact on the sky as I took my seat.

With my eyes closed and a few puffs down, I let myself sink into my thoughts.

Kind of a dangerous place.

But, as I settled into myself here in Vegas, joined a pack, as Tati had phrased it, it made the things in my head much less dire.

The whole world wasn't against me.

There were people who gave a shit if I lived or died.

Maybe I *wasn't* just a nightmare come to life.

*Fuck.*

I wanted to bury that thought, but I was coming to understand that burying shit didn't really do anything. At best, it remained under the surface, waiting to bubble up at an inopportune moment.

At worst... it *thrived* there, making deep unshakable roots and you ended up growing something you never wanted to nurture.

I didn't need either of those.

I took another puff – another *few* puffs – and managed to settle back into my meditation. I was immersed for a while before I felt a shift in the energy around me.

Not a disturbance, just a shift.

I opened my eyes to find Tati peeking through the closed atrium door. Raising an eyebrow, I gave her a little wave that seemed to embarrass her. Her eyes went wide like she hadn't expected to get caught watching me.

Instead of walking off, she slid the door open. "I am *so* sorry. I was just peeking to make sure you were okay. I didn't think you'd noticed me," she explained.

"You're a hard woman not to notice," I told her. "You want to join me?"

She lifted an eyebrow and her gaze fell to the joint I was holding. "Is that ours?"

"What kind of product ambassador would I be if it wasn't?"

She laughed. "*Product Ambassador.* I don't think that job title exists in our organization."

"Well, while we're waiting on the dispensary to be cleared as a damn crime scene, you can think about why maybe it should be. Come here," I told her, patting the ground next to me.

After a short moment of hesitation, she padded over to where I was in an oversized t-shirt, and took a seat on the blanket with me, willingly taking the joint when I passed it her way.

I watched as she sucked the smoke in, holding it for a moment before she blew it all out in a perfect stream before she handed it back to me for my turn.

"This might be a pretty solid way to start the day," she mused, after a couple rounds.

"I was just thinking about that." I chuckled.

"You do this every morning?"

"Most mornings, the last couple weeks. Sometimes a bit of light yoga, meditation."

She smiled. "Yoga and meditation? I can't say I would have predicted that."

"Why? I don't look like I do yoga?"

"You look like you kill people." She laughed. "Which... I guess wouldn't exclude you from yoga."

I shook my head. "I *look like* I kill people? Damn, here I was thinking I was incognito."

She reached out, grabbing my hand. "Let me rephrase that. It's not that you *look like it*," she explained. "More like...you have this certain energy."

"All the time?"

"Not all the time." She shook her head. "Not right now. You're very... Zen right now."

"That's the whole purpose."

"Right," she nodded. "You're out here...getting lifted."

"Gotta stay balanced somehow."

"Yeah," she agreed. "So... tell me, what do we do? I want to join you."

"What, with the yoga?"

She nodded, a timid grin spreading over her lips. "Is that okay?"

"Yeah," I told her. "Let's get into it."

She was right there with me and it was... nice.

Inviting somebody into this with me had never crossed my mind but working through the poses and all of that with her felt effortless. There wasn't much talking between us—just enough to communicate the pose. Other than that, we were each in our own heads, sharing space in a way that felt almost instinctive.

*This shit is dangerous.*

In the last pose, which required us to just lay out on the ground, I started picking up a bit of a different energy. At first, I thought I was maybe imagining it, but then I felt the shift beside me as Tati adjusted her position, and then a moment later she was hovering over me, straddling my lap.

"Is this okay?" she asked, not actually lowering her body until I gave her a simple nod, not knowing how to articulate that it was *more* than okay now that I was fully awake.

"I want to try again," she murmured, apprehensive for whatever reason.

I didn't have to ask to know what she was talking about.

We hadn't talked about it much, but I knew the way the night before ended had bothered her, probably why she'd woken up before me with a redo on her mind.

One I'd disrupted.

I met her gaze and shrugged. "Do whatever you feel."

My body had already reacted—that "shift" before she even climbed on top of me? That shit was electric. I'd felt it. Unlike when she'd caught me by surprise, my dick was rock hard when she pulled it from my boxers.

I didn't know she wasn't wearing any panties underneath that damn t-shirt until she was able to slide right on me, no need to move anything aside or slip anything off.

"*Mmmmmm*," Tati sounded off in a leisurely, throaty moan as she sank further down on me, circling her hips.

"Shit," I grunted, damn near as gratified by her reaction to my dick as I was by the glory of being inside her.

She felt good as *fuck*.

No different from last night, only *this* time I didn't have to offer any encouragement for her to really get after it. She'd been cautious then, damn near like she was scared to ride me.

This time?

She had no such hesitation.

She peeled her shirt off, completely baring herself to me as she rolled her hips, grinding on my dick. I caught her ass cheeks in my hands, caressing and squeezing, but no attempt to adjust her speed, her depth, none of that.

It was her world.

I appreciated that it seemed she was fully invested in exactly that, her pussy clenching around me as she bounced up and down. My hands went up, further, going for full breasts as they bobbed in my face, large areolas tipped in perfect chocolate chip nipples I pinched between my fingers, to make her gasp and ride me harder.

*Damn she's beautiful.*

"That's right," I murmured to her, ignoring the nagging pain in my core to pull myself up, so I could get right in line with her face. "Give me all of it. Every drop."

She stared for a second, still moving, and then her mouth was on mine as she rode harder still. Faster and faster, as both of our pleasures built.

It didn't take long before she lost her rhythm because it was too good, and... *shit*, I was losing my ability to hold out too. I grabbed her hips, doing the work of moving her up and down as I felt the shift in tension in her body.

"*Do it,*" I urged her.

She opened her mouth to say something, but the orgasm hit, making her scream instead as she gripped my shoulders tight, nails digging into my skin.

Good thing there was no need to pull out.

That was a mission we would have sorely failed, cause my hips surged up instead of away, burying myself as deep as I could get as I released inside her.

For a long moment we just laid there.

Both of us... *waiting.*

I wrapped my arms around her, feeling every twitch of her pussy as her body calmed, and we waited. For the orgasm to finish sweeping through, for her breathing to even, for her to... be okay.

When the heaving of her chest against mine had long leveled out, I cupped her face in my hands, turning it up toward me, "Hey... You good?"

She lifted her eyes to mine, biting down on her lip a bit before she gave me the tiniest nod. "Yeah. I'm good."

"You sure?"

Another few seconds passed before a wide grin spread over her lips and she gave me a more enthusiastic nod. "Yeah."

"Proud of you," I told her, bringing my mouth to hers.

"Proud of me for riding your dick?"

"For doing it so damn well." I chuckled at the very obvious reaction she had to those words—a little shudder that made her wiggle in my lap as she moaned into my lips.

"*Mmmm.* We've got to get cleaned up," she said. "As much as I think I'd enjoy just being complimented on my pussy for the rest of the day."

I agreed – with both statements – but told her, "I need a few minutes," as she climbed off me.

"Of course, I interrupted *your* flow," she said, leaning to snag a quick kiss before she grabbed the shirt she'd discarded. "I'm getting in the shower."

When she left, I breathed out a sigh that wasn't really relief, but something adjacent. Not that her presence was something I needed to be "eased" from; it was more along the lines of being glad that moment between us had been able to complete the circle.

Without the interruption of trauma.

I laid all the way back, knowing I needed to get up and clean myself up too, but I just needed a minute. A moment to come back into myself and resettle my thoughts for the day—especially knowing what my plans were.

Blue had asked me to meet Manuel Rojas with him.

After hearing that he'd met with Renard again, we *needed* some answers; we couldn't keep watching and waiting. Maybe it didn't have anything to do with the *Predators* and I was going to be exposing myself to unnecessary danger. Or maybe they were counting on us remaining in the dark so they could have the element of shock.

Either way… the level of uncertainty we were under now wasn't something we could sustain.

Fuck the foreboding, we needed answers.

Yeah, by keeping cool so far, we'd been able to avoid causing any type of flare-ups, which would likely only lead to more bloodshed.

But there was no way anything a monster like Renard wanted was good for the *Predators*.

He was already on my hit list.

If I had to eliminate him earlier than planned… so be it.

After spending the next several moments trying to put myself in a head-space for dealing with the *Renegados* in a way that wouldn't incite a war in the middle of the afternoon, I pulled myself up in search of a shower like Tati had.

No guest room for me this time—I took my ass right back to her room, where she was getting dressed for the day, with a perky energy that answered a question I hadn't yet verbalized.

There was no way she'd be *this* light if she knew what Blue and I were about to get into.

I wasn't about to be the one to kill her vibe. I flirted a bit, then went and took my shower, irritated that once again I was putting the same clothes back on that I'd worn the previous day.

*I've gotta start keeping a change of clothes in my saddlebag for when I come over here.*

*Shit.*

There it was again, that fucking *comfort* that I didn't deserve.

What the hell was I thinking?

Tati left out another fresh toothbrush for me, so I took advantage of it, cleaning myself up as much as I could before I went off in search of her. She'd disappeared to somewhere else in the house, and just like before, I followed the smell of food and the sound of her music blasting to find her in the kitchen.

With Blue.

"Where ya clothes at, nigga?" he asked, scowling at me from the other side of the counter where he was seated, with a plate in front of him.

*Oh, shit.*

I had put on my boxers and jeans, then went sauntering into the kitchen shirtless because I was only expecting Tati.

Not a meeting.

"Brandon..." Tati warned, pushing out a sigh.

"Don't *Brandon* me," he grunted. "I knew his ass was here cause I saw his bike, but I come in and this motherfucker walking around your house like he owns it!"

"He owns my pussy, so now what?" she argued, making my eyes go wide, cause... *damn she really said that shit to him.* "He's my guest; he can be comfortable."

Blue looked at me.

Tati looked at me.

And I... didn't say shit.

I just went to where Tati was sitting and leaned down to kiss her temple. "Good morning again," I told her and Blue burst out laughing.

"Wow, nigga. *Wow!* You are bold as fuck. *Brave* as fuck," he jeered across the counter.

"My man, that's not new information for you," I told him with a shrug.

"Fair enough," he conceded, meeting my gaze. "But you know I will fucking kill you over my sister; you understand that, right?"

I didn't back down from his glare, fully understanding that he wasn't threatening me for my current actions, but for what I could potentially do to her.

"I'm aware," I told him, then looked to Tati. "I'm going to the clubhouse to change. I'll see you later. You still coming to pick me up from there, right?" I asked Blue, whose only answer was a grunt.

"What are you picking him up for?" Tati asked and I didn't waste any time getting out of there.

He could be to the one to tell her.

I shook my head, moving back to Tati's room for my shirt, shoes, and other shit. I was seated on the chair she'd rode me on last night, thinking through the good memories while I put my shoes on when she appeared at the door.

"Be careful today, okay?"

"I'm always careful."

She sucked her teeth. "I mean... *for real* though. Blue just told me what y'all are getting into, and you need to understand, even without whatever influence this foreign motherfucker has, Manuel is... petty, vindictive, and very smart. *On his own.* He needs to be handled delicately." She stopped, pushing out a sigh. "I know me being out of commission...that kind of threw a wrench in things."

I cocked an eyebrow at her. "Out of commission? That's how you're phrasing it?"

"How else should I?" She shrugged. "I haven't been available, that's a fact."

"Well yeah, but it's not like..."

"What are you even saying?"

"I don't know," I admitted, tossing up my hands. "I just don't like you framing it like you blame yourself for the shit or something."

"I'm not blaming *myself* for anything other than not taking it as seriously as I should've when everybody was trying to tell me that nigga was bad news. I should have been—I *am* smarter than that. What he did is what he did, but I let my guard down with somebody who didn't deserve that kind of courtesy from me. It won't happen again."

I scoffed. "That's just how niggas like that operate; they make themselves seem like somebody you can trust, when they're not."

*Huh.*

I had a lot of damn nerve, stating the obvious when it came to Kev, but not myself.

As if my presence here had ever been altruistic.

"You didn't do anything wrong by thinking you could trust him," I told her, pushing away my guilt for another time.

"I know that," she huffed.

"Are you sure?"

"Yes," she told me. "I'm *very* sure."

"Good. *Stay* sure," I countered, honestly not even *sure* myself as to why I was pressing this so hard. I just hated the idea of her feeling like there was something she could have – should have – done differently.

Was it important for her to be mindful of her surroundings and all of that?

Of course.

Especially when niggas like Kev existed.

And honestly, niggas like what *I* used to be too.

It wasn't pretty, but it was true that people would make calculations, mental and otherwise, on which targets to prey on. However, no amount of imprudence would make you a victim if there wasn't a perpetrator around.

It wasn't on *her* to do this or that, to "protect" herself from becoming a victim.

It was on *him* to not fucking victimize.

She wasn't trying to hear a lecture though, and I wasn't trying to give one, so I didn't. I finished getting dressed, kissed her, and headed out to get ready for this meeting.

If any sort of luck was on my side, I'd see her tonight.

# Chapter Twenty-One

## NYX

I was going to kill Manuel Rojas.

And his bitch ass nephew.

Wipe his whole bloodline off the collective consciousness of the general public.

It was only a matter of when, *not* if.

And the answer was *soon*.

It didn't even take a full minute in his presence for Tati's description of him — petty, vindictive, too smart for his own good — to prove mostly accurate.

I actually felt she wasn't harsh enough in describing this devious motherfucker.

We'd agreed to meet at what was supposed to be a neutral location, but was really *Renegados* territory, a nice restaurant, packed with patrons. We were taken to a private room, tucked away from the unsuspecting guests; a more trusting person would take it as a good sign.

Surely there wouldn't be too much trouble in a public place.

The thing with that was only certain people were bound by that type of moral constraint.

I wasn't one of them.

Undoubtedly, there were other shooters in the building, but the guards Manuel kept close weren't *Thorns*, a good sign, but confusing.

If he was working with Renard, it was idiotic not to take advantage of the *Thorn* level of security. Less for him meant more for us though, so I wasn't complaining.

I just didn't understand the reasoning.

"I was so saddened to hear about what happened to Tatiana," Manuel said as we took seats around the private table. "Such a beautiful woman like that, so unafraid to flaunt it; it was only a matter of time before someone couldn't help themselves, no?"

I looked at Blue, because there was no way this motherfucker had just said what I thought I heard.

Right?

He was looking at me too, as if he was making sure *he* hadn't imagined it.

He hadn't.

Before I could react, with my hands around Manuel's throat, Blue was already on his feet.

"I will burn your whole motherfucking life down," he said, looking Rojas dead in the face as he spoke, paying no mind to the guards who'd stood at the same time. "Keep her name out of your mouth."

Manuel raised his hands. "I meant no harm, or to suggest anything malicious," he claimed, stammering over those insincere words as he looked to his guys for assistance that would never happen before I acted. "I—"

"How the fuck," I interrupted, still seated, "is it *not* malicious to suggest it was some unavoidable reality that she was going to get raped because of how she looks?" I asked, very quietly, trying to keep myself calm.

Under the table, my hand was already going for the blade they'd failed to notice on their little pat down.

One move to grab it.

One move to get my hand up.

And then, just a little flick of the wrist, and he'd be gone.

I visualized it over and over as a soothing mechanism to keep me from actually implementing it as he faltered through some weak explanation about men's moral failings and some other shit that was true, but not the fucking point.

He was just saying the shit because he got challenged.

Saying whatever he thought sounded good.

I wasn't falling for this shit, though, and neither was Blue. We'd anticipated it, preparing ourselves for the possibility of him trying to goad us into something he could take as aggression.

"This woman he mentioned, she is important to you?" Those words came across the room from a man I presumed had to be Ivan, who'd opted to stand. I remembered Jake Lincoln's mention of him, remembered the characterization he gave.

*Volatile.*

That... wasn't what I got from him though.

Dangerous, maybe.

Calculated, for sure.

But I had a feeling he didn't make a damn move without first thinking it through.

"Why?" Blue asked, still standing as Ivan made his way to the table.

He still looked like he might go across the table at any moment and I wasn't particularly inclined to stop him. At this point, I'd decided for us, Manuel was no ally. And I was just shy of coming to the conclusion that *he* was the one who'd murdered the *Predators* leadership.

In service to Renard.

"My uncle, forgive him," Ivan said, a hand to his chest, performing contrition. "His generation, they have no concept of the level of civilization we millennials have evolved to, you know?"

I narrowed my eyes.

*Bullshit.*

"I am sorry for whatever offense he caused; can we start over?" Ivan asked, looking between me and Blue. "We have business to discuss and I'm sure you gentleman are very busy."

"Who the fuck are you?" Blue asked.

"Ivan Rojas," he answered immediately, extending a hand across the table. "I believe you are well acquainted with my half-brother, Teodoro. We share the same errant paternity if you don't know the story."

"I know exactly what the fuck goes on in my club," Blue snapped. "I know all about your wayward-dicked father; good thing a little blood doesn't *really* make you family, huh?"

Ivan smirked. "Right. Teo always did feel slighted that he wasn't embraced, but wasn't that to be expected with... what is the term? Project twins?" He laughed. "But again, we're off path from the matter at hand. Please, sit," he said, taking the seat beside Manuel, who'd smartly not opened his mouth again.

Ivan was slick too, but I was *really* wondering now about ol' Manny.

If he was the one who'd levied the attack on the *Predators*, it didn't matter whose protection he was under, who he brought on to do his dirty work.

He was going to pay for his shit soon.

For now, it was imperative for him to believe we were still looking at the *Marauders*. It probably looked suspicious that we hadn't made a move on them while they were weak, still reeling from the attempt on Jake.

But, between the work we were doing to build income streams and the need to give Tati whatever she needed in the way of time and space, our lack of movement could easily be explained away.

That didn't keep them from questioning it though.

"The last I heard from your people; you were planning to interrupt our supply chain, what happened?" Manuel asked.

"I'd think you would be glad we hadn't made any move yet," I answered, glaring across the table at him. "Doesn't it make you more money, if the *Marauders* can continue moving your product?" I asked.

"They haven't been moving anything anyway; they're tucked behind their walls, afraid of themselves," he said. "Bunch of pussies."

"So why don't *you* take them out; clearly that's what you want," Blue spoke up. "Or what, you *are* afraid to fuck up your income?"

"Money isn't everything," Manuel replied, glaring right back. "I need assurances on the timing. If you're disrupting my profit, I need to know when to expect that, so I can plan accordingly."

"The chain is already disrupted, thanks to the hit attempt on the Lincolns," Blue told him. "Why are we beating around the bush instead of you just making shit plain?"

"Clearly you have something to say, so maybe *you* should be making things plain," Ivan spoke up. "What is it you think you know?"

"We know you've found yourself a new partner, a partner with goons that tried to kill one of my lieutenants," Blue said.

Manuel's eyebrows went up. "If I wanted any of your people dead, they would be, I assure you."

"And yet, here I am," I said, complete with a little wave just to get under his skin. "It's a bit convenient that word gets out that you have a new business relationship and suddenly people are getting shot at in public places."

"Why do you think *we* have anything to do with an ambush?" Ivan asked.

I chuckled. "I'd hardly call it an ambush, but your hitman had some pretty distinctive ink, ink associated with *your* new partner."

"How would you know anything about that?" Manuel asked, and I narrowed my eyes before yanking my jacket off my shoulder, baring my arm.

My ink.

"I know a helluva lot more than he's telling *you*, I guarantee."

"Que es esto?!" Manuel exclaimed, immediately pushing back from the table as he registered what he was looking at.

Ivan was shook too; he hadn't given any outward reaction, but the alarm was apparent in his eyes. "This is some kind of setup?" he asked.

"You tell us," Blue countered. "Y'all are having the fucking secret meetings, not us."

"I am *done* talking," Manuel huffed.

Blue scoffed. "Motherfucker, you're not done with *shit*."

"I sure the fuck *am*," Manuel bellowed, standing up.

From the faces around the room, we were *all* caught off guard by his anger.

"I will *not* be manipulated or disrespected by the likes of you. I have done enough. I have sacrificed enough!"

"The *Predators* haven't asked you for shit; let's make that clear," Blue told him, sitting forward across the table. "The only thing the *Predators* need from the *Renegados* is respect, and you've been riding the line too fucking long— let's talk about *that*."

Manuel crossed his arms, glowering. "I'm sure you've heard more than once that respect is not simply given; it's earned."

"Right, so what the fuck have you done?" Blue asked. "Exactly what have you done that you deserve my undying respect?" He stood too; face pulled into a scowl. "You're the one talking slick about my vice president. *You* hopped up like you want something to pop off."

"Do you not know what that tattoo on him means? He is one of the Frenchman's people," Manuel insisted, looking to me like I was a damn ghost.

"I belong to no one, *especially* not Renard Belrose."

Manuel sneered. "I've seen what he can do to people with those tattoos."

"That doesn't have shit to do with me," I denied, even though I knew there wasn't much I could do to avoid *exactly* what he was talking about.

The only thing I'd *maybe* had on my side thus far was anonymity and I was pretty sure I could consider that blown now.

"I'm sure you've noticed a different energy in this town. I noticed it as soon as I returned," Ivan spoke up. "Getting under everybody's skin, tempers running hot."

"Yeah, we noticed," Blue spoke up, with a warning edge to his tone. "But if you've got no problem, we've got no problem. If you *do* have a problem...

you make sure you don't hesitate to let us know. Let's get the fuck out of here."

With that, Blue stood up from the table, damn near knocking his chair over as he strode out. I was close behind him, keeping my eyes open for all possibilities as I followed him out through the back of the restaurant and into the parking garage.

"You did good," he told me in the car. "You kept it balanced."

"I didn't have a choice." I chuckled. "Were you *trying* to piss the dude off?"

"A little bit," he admitted. "Trip him up, make him sweat. We need to know what he's got going on, so if I can get him hyped up enough to reveal anything about his plan while also getting what I really feel off my chest, well... that sounds like a win-win, doesn't it?"

I nodded. "I follow you. But we still didn't find out what he has going on with Renard."

He shook his head. "It wasn't happening. Not once he saw your ink and got spooked. Which is interesting..."

"If that's his partner, why is he so tense?"

Blue nodded. "Exactly, what the fuck is he so worried about?"

As Blue pulled up to a stoplight around the front of the restaurant, I looked out the window, taking inventory of faces in the crowd. It was something I did often—part of my training to avoid being tracked without noticing.

A couple of times after they'd snatched me from the bar, I'd locked eyes with a *Rose* or *Thorn*, and today was no different. They knew when the meeting was and they'd been in the restaurant too, unbeknownst to Manuel and his people.

We weren't stupid enough to walk in there blind.

We had Alicia's people and our own, in addition to the escort riding a few cars ahead of us and a few cars behind. If Manuel *had* decided to turn the meeting into an event, we were ready for it.

What I wasn't ready for was contact with a familiar face. My eyebrows shot up as I took in those deep brown eyes, deep brown skin, button nose, full lips.

*Margeaux.*

I made the mistake of blinking, but I *needed* that blink to confirm it wasn't just some illusion of the mind. When I opened my eyes and looked again, she was already gone.

*Fuck.*

I hurriedly pulled out my phone, gesturing for Blue to give me a second while I dialed Alicia, who picked up on the first ring.

"How did the meeting go?"

"About as expected," I answered. "I thought you were sending somebody to get Margeaux?"

"I *did*," she groaned. "He had her, and then... he lost her."

"Here in Vegas?"

There was silence for a moment and then she answered, obviously frustrated. "She's a *lot* slipperier than we thought."

"I could've sworn I told you that." I chuckled, shaking my head.

"Yeah, but you didn't say the extent of it," Alicia argued. "I knew she had *Rose* ink, but damn, I didn't think she had the full training. We need to find her. You said she was at Rojas' restaurant?"

"Outside it, but yeah. Which would make sense if he's working with Renard."

"It *doesn't* make sense though," Alicia mused, almost like she was talking to herself more than me. "Why would she be on Renard's side?"

"Who says she is?" I countered. "Maybe she wants his head. Would you blame her?"

"Not remotely," Alicia said. "I'm surprised you aren't chomping at the bit to get him yourself."

I pushed out a breath. "In due time. That aside, we need to know why she's here; she's another loose end."

"True. Are you also a little scared she wants *your* head?"

"Why would she?"

"Didn't you break her heart?"

"That accusation assumes she has one and I'm not so sure."

Alicia chuckled. "Heart or no heart, she knows something. She was outside that restaurant instead of laying low for a reason. And whatever that reason is, we're going to have to figure it out."

We hung up after that.

"Who is Margeaux?" Blue asked, navigating us back toward the clubhouse.

*Shit.*

"She is... Renard Belrose's niece," I answered. "I think I saw her on the street just now."

"Shit." Blue shook his head. "These motherfuckers are just coming out of the woodwork, huh?"

I chuckled. "Uh... Like I was telling Alicia, I don't think she's on Renard's side. Maybe not ours either, but definitely not his."

"Why not? Aren't they family?"

"Yeah," I confirmed. "But that only makes what he and her father did to her worse," I said, pushing out a sigh as I dropped the phone into my lap. "She... does some fucked up things, but it's barely her damn fault, honestly. She never had much of a choice."

With his gaze turned out the window, he nodded. "Sounds like you know her pretty well."

"Well enough."

"Sounds like you care about her."

I frowned, but he still wasn't looking at me when I shrugged.

"I'm not sure it could be called that. Trauma bonded, maybe," I said, with a dry laugh. "Or... shit. Maybe I did care about her at some point."

"But then you left?"

My eyebrows furrowed together. "What? Nah, if anything, *she...* wait a minute. What the fuck is this about?" I asked.

"Well... It's about you getting involved with Tati even though you're planning to leave after this shit with whoever-the-fuck is over. Or did you forget you told me that shit?"

*Fuck.*

*Fuck.*

"I didn't forget," I answered honestly. "I just..."

"Figured she could handle it?" he interrupted, finally looking over to fix me with a scowl at a stoplight. "Well guess what, motherfucker, I don't think she can."

"I wasn't thinking that shit anyway," I denied. "I... wasn't thinking about it at all, actually, if you want the truth."

"She's not worth that?"

"That's not what I said."

"You don't have to," he barked. "Your fucking actions did!"

"You were all gung-ho about this shit I thought?" I asked him, confused by his energy. "You were acting like you approved."

"Before I knew about this Renard, *Garden*, *Renegados* connection and all this other shit," he explained. "When I thought we could talk you into hanging around, yeah. *Before* I saw how she fucking looks at you, *yeah*. Before I thought I might really have to throw hands with your stupid ass, *yeah*."

I blew out a sigh. "Listen, I would *never* hurt Tati on purpose. You know that, don't you?"

Blue shook his head, returning his attention to the road. "I'm not worried about what you might do on purpose; it's the unexpected shit."

I swallowed.

What the fuck was I supposed to say, when he was giving voice to exactly what I'd already feared?

"Let me say this," he spoke up again. "If you leave – if it *hurts her* – you better go where I can't fucking find you."

# *Chapter Twenty-Two*

## TATI

Ozias said, peeking into the office to deliver the news.

News I was too plugged in to not already have. Hell, I knew before he did.

But Ozias always found a reason to come talk to me, a reason to seek me out since according to him, I didn't "fuck with him", so he had to make sure I understood his usefulness.

As if I were going to make him disappear or something otherwise.

If I were going to do that, I would've gotten it over with already.

"Thank you," I told him simply, instead of making him privy to everything rolling over in my head, shit that had nothing to do with him.

Brandon and Onyx had both, separately, let me know things were "fine", but *that* shit was so beyond relative.

*Fine* for other people meant everybody was cool, things were peaceful, etc.

Around here?

*Fine* just meant nobody had picked up any new holes.

"Ay, boss lady," Ozias spoke up; his voice startled me at first, but I quickly realized he'd never actually left the door.

"Yes?"

"Shit's getting a bit out of hand around here, don't you think?" he asked, stepping into the office now. At Brandon's insistence even before his meeting with Rojas, we were back on lockdown, so I was posted up at the clubhouse.

I raised an eyebrow. "You think it's more than we can handle?"

"Never that," he denied, gesturing with his hands like he was pushing that thought away from him. "Just a little more heat than usual."

I turned away from my computer to give him my full attention, with a smile. "Ozias... how about you just tell me what's on your mind?"

He reached up, scratching underneath the old-school Kangol he always wore, covering his almost fully-grayed ponytail. "Well, baby girl..." My breath caught in my throat. I'd been *baby girl* for years, and years, and *years* before the tragedy that turned me to "boss lady". "I've got that feeling like I did before... you know."

I did.

Ozias was an OG, one of the few in our chain-of-command who'd not been caught up in the massacre. As road captain, he never stayed behind, but that day he literally *couldn't* ride.

So he'd been right here in the clubhouse as so many we loved died.

It wasn't his fault.

I knew that.

*Everybody* knew that.

And yet, because of his role, I'd lowkey held it against him at first, because how could he not know?

It was *literally* his job to predict and perceive the threats against us, to make the battle plan, to ensure shit like this *didn't* happen.

*That* shit, though?

It was something else.

Something he couldn't have known.

"What do you think it is?" I asked him.

Ozias had top notch instincts; it was why he held the position he did in the first place. I didn't *want* to believe we should be on higher alert than we already were, but if that was the situation we were in, I needed to know.

"I can't call it," he answered, shaking his head. "It just don't feel right, you know?"

I nodded. "Stop walking on eggshells around me like you think I'm mad at you; I'm not," I told him, cutting through tension that had been hovering between us for months. "Keep me updated, whenever you *can* call it, I need to be first to know."

He grinned at me, giving a little tip of his hat before he said, "Yes ma'am."

This time, he actually stepped away, leaving me wondering what the hell might be going on. Ozias wasn't the type to arouse unnecessary panic, so him being worried was... a lot.

I couldn't focus for shit after that and didn't relax until I got word that Onyx and Brandon were back on site. I went straight to the garage when I heard they were pulling in, but when I got there it was just Brandon talking to Teo.

"Where is Onyx?" I asked, confused about where he might be.

Instead of his usual sort of ribbing, Brandon didn't crack a grin. He dismissed Teo with a nod, then turned back to me. "We need to talk about that nigga."

"Don't do this," I groaned, letting my head fall back to stare up at the ceiling. "Can we skip the protective big brother shit? *You're* the baby, by a good three wee—"

"Did he tell you he was leaving?"

I stopped talking, dropping my gaze back to his, eyes narrowed. "What?"

"Did Nyx tell you he wasn't going to be around?" Brandon asked, the same confusing fucking question, with slightly different phrasing.

My heart had immediately seized up in my chest, but I tried to keep my expression neutral when I asked, "He left?"

"Not yet, no," was the answer, a relieving one. "But he will. He's going to."

I swallowed the lump in my throat and nodded. "Well… he never made it seem like he was going to hang around beyond the thing with *Marauders*, right?"

Brandon frowned. "So you *did* know. Then why are you getting involved with him?"

"Did something happen?" I asked, returning his frown. "'Cause you were definitely team Onyx before."

"*Before* I knew your feelings might actually get hurt," Brandon countered.

"Okay… what changed to make my feelings getting hurt more likely? I've never been *that* girl before, so what makes you think I am now?"

"Because now you're—shit, you know what? Never mind." He shook his head and started to walk off, but I got in front of him, not willing to let it go.

"Nah, Brandon —*say it*," I insisted, shoving his chest. "Now I'm what?"

"Just leave it alone, aiight?"

"Hell no," I snapped, not getting out of his face. "What am I, huh?"

"*Fragile*," he growled, glaring at me as he leaned in. "You're *fragile*, emotionally. And you should be, with what you've been through. You get to be that, and I get it," he added, trying to soften the blow, but I'd already bristled at the insinuation that I was *weak*.

I got even closer into his face, trying to get inside his goddamn skin as I looked him right in the eyes to tell him, *"Fuck you, Blue."*

"Fuck me?" he asked, giving me a gentle shove away from him. *"Blue? Wow."*

"How *should* I react to this? Should I be jumping for joy that you just looked me in the face and called me pussy?"

"That's not what I said."

"It's *exactly* what you said!" I snarled, closing the space between us again. *"Baselessly."*

*"Baselessly?"* he shot back. "Tati, you've got this nigga *spending the night,* comfortable as fuck in your house, like a month ago you didn't get..."

He couldn't finish it.

I crossed my arms. "It's okay to say it, *Blue.* I was raped. Fucked without permission—"

"Don't say that shit."

*"Fuck you!"* I screamed, doubly frustrated, by him, and by the tears that had broken free. "I will call it whatever the fuck I want, frame it how I want, because it happened *to me,"* I told him, slapping my chest. "I could be curled up somewhere in a fucking ball and it would be valid. I could eviscerate that motherfucker and spread his pieces all around this city and it would be valid. I can reclaim ownership of *my* body, and do what makes *me* feel normal, and it's *valid! Fragile?!* You're really saying that shit to *me?!"* I growled and then my hand was back before I could catch myself, smacking him across the face.

And he let me.

"I'm sorry," he spoke, his tone so much softer than just a moment before, and I...

Immediately broke down in tears.

"I'm *sorry,"* he repeated, wrapping his arms around me to pull me into him as I sobbed. "You're not fucking... *fragile, you're* just... my goddamn sister and I'm worried about you," he muttered into my hair. "That night when you called me... I've never seen you like that before."

I lifted my head, not caring that I was a snotty mess. "Like what?"

With his arms still heavy around me, he sighed. "...Broken. I know, I wasn't the injured party, but *shit.* You don't know how that felt for me," he said, eyebrows furrowed. "You've always been bulletproof; I needed you to be bulletproof, 'cause we were still in recovery mode. Then seeing you like that and not being able to undo it... It's a mindfuck, Tati."

"I *know* that."

*"Do you?"* he countered. "Cause if you do, it shouldn't be a surprise for

me to see you as *delicate*. Not unbreakable, not anymore. Yeah, I thought Nyx would be good for you because I saw the care he took for you that night, the way he stepped up, knew he was fucking solid."

"All of that is still true."

"Except, for how long?" he questioned, letting me go. "Tati, you're not... the lovey-dovey shit ain't you, but I've seen how you've been responding to this nigga, seen how you look at him. And that shit this morning? He *owns your pussy*? Really?"

I shrugged. "What can I say, the dick thus far has been amazing. And his mouth? I don't have the words."

"I don't want or need to hear that shit."

"You've gotta be kidding." I laughed. "I know much too much about the sexual proclivities *you* stepped into when you were grieving over *my sister* for you to be acting like this."

"That's not the point."

"Isn't it?"

"The *point*," he said, scowling at me, "is that I expected him to... shit, at least take it slow with you or something?"

I raised an eyebrow. "You expected gentleman behavior from a quite literal shooter. Is everything okay with you, Brandon?"

"Oh I'm Brandon again now?" he asked, hand to his chest. "That's a relief."

"You're on thin ice, nigga," I told him. "Call me *fragile* again and I'm squaring up."

"Oh shit, it's getting domestic!"

"Shut up!" I laughed, swatting his arm. "I guess I'm sorry for slapping you. Aww, your face is red," I gushed. "You should've hit me back."

"Bullshit." He cackled. "So your nigga could come ziplining out the ceiling on *me*? I think the fuck not."

"He's *my nigga* now? Do you trust him or not, damn?"

Brandon blew out a sigh. "Trust ain't the problem; it never was," he said. "I just know he's already flipped his hourglass. You've gotta ask yourself, are you comfortable getting close to him not knowing when it's going to run out?"

I HAD to pull myself together after the conversation with Brandon *before* I sought Onyx out. Once we'd made it past the blowup, I'd gotten my debrief about the meeting with Rojas *and* Brandon's gossipy recap of a phone call with Alicia afterward.

Who the fuck was *Margeaux?*

*Why do you care?*

This deeper involvement I had going with Onyx was supposed to be about my sexual... therapy, nothing more. I'd never had an issue compartmentalizing my emotions where men were concerned and this wasn't supposed to be any different.

Except... *compartmentalizing my emotions* was... not exactly what'd been happening.

To compartmentalize them, I needed to *have* the emotions, and in past experiences, that wasn't exactly the way it went down.

Not with Kev, nor the guy before him, nor the one before that.

Honestly, the last man to have me in my feelings was a college boyfriend I'd thought I'd wanted to marry, until he switched up after learning of my "gang" involvement.

*Bitch.*

That was when I'd learned an important lesson; not everybody was built for this and that was fine. After Tali died though, it wasn't even about finding that diamond in the rough, that rare breed who could handle it.

I didn't *want* to find anyone because I didn't want to lose anyone because losing people... hurt.

Losing my father only further cauterized my heart.

That was where Kev had come in.

Perfect face, perfect dick, *perfectly* uninspiring in every other category.

No chance that once the inevitable end of our affair came, I would miss him.

Which... shit, was still true, although him being a *literal* sexual predator was certainly not what I'd expected. In most cases like mine, there would have been some level of grief, for the loss of the relationship the target thought they had with their abuser.

I'd gotten lucky.

I got to skip that part because I really didn't feel anything for him in the first place.

This thing with Onyx, though...

*Fuck my life.*

This was something else.

Something alien.

Probably why I'd gotten so pissed at Brandon for questioning it. He was poking at something I didn't understand well enough to offer much in the way of a rational defense.

I stood by *every* word I'd said to him, but thinking back on it, I'd gone straight from zero to ten, unnecessarily. But I'd held *him* down through plenty of moments when he was at a twenty even though a three was more appropriate.

We balanced each other.

And I knew, beyond *any* doubt, that he had my back. Brandon wanted the absolute best for me and I trusted his judgement, implicitly.

He was right. I needed to be careful of my feelings where Onyx was concerned, the chances of some sort of toxic, trauma bonding shit was *high*.

That night, he and Brandon had been my heroes, and *obviously* I wasn't going to latch onto my damn brother in an intimate manner.

That savior attachment shit was real; my therapist had warned me about it.

But whatever this was, it wasn't *only* about that night.

I wasn't sure it was about that night, which I only remembered in bits and pieces now anyway, at all.

It was about everything in between.

It was about him fucking *listening* to me, and not treating me like I was made of glass, and not downplaying my feelings. It was about him not seeing me as some sort of damaged goods and still wanting me.

And... yes, the dick had been as immaculate as he'd teased.

So I rejected the idea that being drawn to him had anything to do with *fragility*.

It was the opposite, really.

I was giving in to it because I knew I had the strength not to crumble when he did, inevitably, leave. Would it be rough initially? Yeah, probably so.

But I had to believe I'd be grateful for the memories.

Just like with my father.

Just like with Tali.

Now that most of the day was gone, the clubhouse was full of people and Ozias had decided to fire up the grill. Lockdown meant that we had more than usual on site, including our surviving OGs, which meant things were about to turn into an event.

I hunted Onyx down in his room to pull him into the mix.

He was more subdued than usual but warmed up quickly enough. I could tell he was worried about something though.

"Whatever's happening in your head, tuck it away until tomorrow," I insisted, leaving him in the main room with Teo at the pool table to track down my mother.

A plate of food would probably perk him *right* up.

"Hey," I greeted her in the kitchen, with a kiss on the cheek. "I have an urgent request for a little taste of something from your stove," I told her.

"Lil girl, you know the rules," she scolded, smacking my hand with a silicon spoon.

"It's not for me, it's for Onyx," I whined, rubbing the spot where she'd hit me. I rolled my eyes when her expression immediately changed and she reached for a sectioned Styrofoam bowl.

"Grab me a corn muffin from over there," she directed, already spooning greens into one side of the bowl, then moving to the fridge to put potato salad in the other. I brought her the cornbread and then tried to take the bowl from her, but she smacked me again, then grabbed a plastic fork. "Where is he with those arms?"

"I hope you know this is unacceptable," I told her, laughing as I led her out to the main room. As I'd hoped, he was already embroiled in conversation with the other guys in there and I turned to my mother to point him out.

Except... something was wrong.

"You okay, Mama?" I asked, stepping backward to where she'd stopped in the doorway, her expression inscrutable.

She blinked, looking at me. "That tattoo he has; do you know what that is?"

I raised an eyebrow. "... do *you*?"

"I know it's a mark of something dangerous." She nodded, and I frowned, confused by the shift. I'd only seen my mother shaken up a handful of times and I'd seen her *scared* even less than that.

Which had *me* concerned.

"Mama, he's *always* had it," I explained, as a weird feeling swept over me. "Why is it a problem now?"

"Well it's *my* first time seeing it, so I don't know what you're expecting from me," she snapped, puzzling me even more. She kept glancing at him, backing away like she thought he was going to sprout another damn head.

"I... want you to keep the same energy you've always had about him and help me perk his ass up," I explained, grabbing her free hand to keep her still and calm her down.

She pulled away from me, shaking her head. "You stay away from him, you hear me? And anybody else with a mark like that," she demanded, jabbing a finger in his direction. "And you keep him the hell away from me."

With that, she turned and went back down the hall, dumping the bowl of food in a trash can as she passed.

"Well *damn*," I muttered, baffled by what had just happened. "Is it just the *Everybody Hates Onyx* show around here today?"

I started to follow her, to push the issue, but... *no*.

Not today.

Not with everything.

This was supposed to be my safe space, my natural fucking habitat, yet it felt like being here was attacking my sense of peace from all sides.

*Fuck.*

I tried not to dwell on it, instead venturing back into the crowd to pull Onyx away. Except now it seemed like people – the ones who'd been close enough to overhear my mother's outburst – were staring.

Exactly the shit I *didn't* want to deal with.

Not right now.

"I wanna go home," I told Onyx, pushing up on my toes to speak into his ear, voicing the suddenly overwhelming need. "Like, right now."

Immediately, he shook his head, rightfully looking at me like I'd lost my mind. "Nah, sweetheart, you know we're on lockdown, right? After Rojas was talking crazy?"

"I do know that and I also don't care. I want to sleep in my own bed tonight. And... I want you there too," I told him, meeting his gaze before I leaned in to press my lips to his.

I... don't know why I *wasn't* expecting that to set off a chorus of whistles and shit exactly like it did, since we were in a *very* public setting.

"This is how you get what you want?" he muttered, uncharacteristically flustered as he drew back, but didn't completely pull away. "Do some shit to make it unsafe for me to stay here?"

"What are you talking about? This is the safest place on earth for you right now."

"I thought you wanted to go home though," he countered and I grinned.

"I do. You're not... *scared*, are you?"

He shook his head, swiping a hand over his face as he stepped away. "You're a fucking menace, you know that?"

"I am an *angel*, excuse you," I teased, winking at him before I turned. "Grab your stuff. I'm gonna go let Brandon know."

Onyx scoffed. "Better you than me," he said, and… that was true.

While our conversation from earlier had ended on a good note because *we* were family, it stood to reason that Brandon might not really be feeling Onyx right now.

Still, he knew like I did that there were few safer places than my house if Onyx was there and a couple of enforcers would jump at the chance to get out and about to be on standby, instead of hanging at the clubhouse going stir crazy.

There was really no convincing necessary.

I felt like a teenager with a freshly extended curfew.

*Giddy.*

And… *relieved.*

The car ride back to my house was quiet, but not uncomfortably. There was no handholding or anything corny, just a cozy silence that gave me, maybe too much, time to think.

Thinking was dangerous.

*Thinking* made me wonder if all of this was just… *too easy.*

The confidence that Manuel Rojas or Renard Belrose wouldn't dare bring out their full firepower and just end us all tonight? Too easy.

The distance I'd traveled in coping with the assault? Too easy.

This effortless shift into intimacy between me and Onyx? *Too fucking easy.*

It had never, *ever* worked out like that for me.

But as soon as we were on the other side of my front door, breathing in the lingering smell of paint… I just didn't give a shit.

I chose *easy.*

I chose Onyx's mouth on my neck and his hands gripping my ass and unzipping my jeans, not even bothering to make it to the bedroom before his fingers were in my panties and then my pussy.

"*Mmmmnh,*" I groaned into his mouth as he kissed me, as his skilled fingers went *straight* to exactly the right place, found exactly the right pace to have me arching my body into his.

He stopped long enough just to strip me down to nothing and pull me to the floor, spreading my legs wide open before a headfirst dive.

I cleared my head of everything.

*Everything.*

Nothing but *this* allowed.

Nothing but the heat and rasp of his tongue on my clit, while his long, thick fingers stroked.

His soft lips on my soaked lips, the gentle heat of his breath on my skin.

His satisfied grunts and groans as he enjoyed his meal.

The build of pressure and pleasure.

My nerve endings going haywire.

His locs gripped in my fists.

Noise and static.

Bliss as the orgasm hit.

Nothing but the sound of his clothes hitting the floor.

His lips on my *other* lips.

The deliciously gratifying stretch as he sank into me.

His tongue in my mouth.

His fingers on my clit.

The delicious friction as he pushed as deep as he could get.

His whispers about the perfection of me, the perfection of my pussy.

Nothing but his declarations of how good I looked taking his dick.

Oh, it was *fucking magnificent.*

Afterwards though, I was restless.

He was snoring away beside me, after we'd finally made it to bed, but my mind was on overload. Between Brandon and my mother, the *Never Mind About Onyx* contingent was firmly in my head.

They'd loved him for me, had encouraged it until *I'd* wanted him.

Which was bullshit.

I understood Brandon's concern even though I refused to agree, but I wasn't so sure about my mother. I wouldn't dare discount her alarm over the ring of thorns on his bicep since I'd had the same suspicions not that long ago.

But that flipped switch?

*That* was weird.

So weird that the discomfort over the whole situation had driven me to the silly, risky decision of coming here, instead of staying put in *Predator* territory. Which... now that I was thinking about it with a clearer mind... I wasn't that sure why Brandon let that slide.

Even if he didn't give a fuck what happened to Onyx, his concern about *my* safety was without question.

Maybe I was overthinking it and too focused on the negative.

Keira liked Onyx, and so did Maite.

And really, so did everybody else whose opinion I cared about.

The *Predators* had embraced him, which one of the biggest checkmarks a person could get. Notably, damn near everyone had been a little iffy about Kev.

*Tali would've hated him*, I thought, then smiled over the visual.

And my *father?*

Man... Kev was the kind of *wannabe* he couldn't stand.

Onyx, though?

Tali would've had a crush.

Even though she likely would've been married, assuming her and Brandon had stayed together, which there was no doubt in my mind they would've.

And my father?

All his concerns about *a sturdy nigga my ass won't run into the ground* would've been more than alleviated.

*Shit.*

Now I was missing them again.

I left Onyx in my bed, snoring, heading to the room that would be my studio eventually. I hadn't brought over any of the tools and stuff yet, so for now it was a catchall.

I hunted through the marked boxes until I found one that I'd never actually unpacked at my old house either, full of albums.

I wasn't the most sentimental girl, but... I just wanted to see my people.

I sat down on the floor, flipping through the albums.

One of just Tali, one of just me, which I skipped, and then one featuring the *Predators* over the years.

I laughed my ass off at one of Ozias posing with his bike, *way* before the gray and the ponytail. I set *that* one aside, so I could snap a picture of the picture to show him next time I saw him. Then I picked up an album I hadn't seen in forever, one of me and Tali as kids.

Pretty quickly, I realized I'd actually *never* seen this one; it just had the same cover as the one I was expecting. This one was grainy ass pictures of me as a baby, that made me chuckle.

I was juicy back then, too.

Tears sprang to my eyes as I came across one of me and my father when I couldn't have been more than a year or two old. It was obviously old, but not as grainy as the others.

It almost looked like he was singing to me. His face was angled away so I couldn't completely tell, but he was definitely smiling and I was smiling back, *clearly* in love.

I started to turn the page, wanting to see more, but an obscure detail made me flip back to it, bringing the album up to my face to see closer.

*Is that...?*

"No way," I said aloud, shaking my head as I squinted at the picture, trying to see better. Panic built in my chest as I flipped through the pages, searching out another picture of my father.

Then another.

And another.

Then back to the first one.

I... wanted to vomit.

Slowly, I pulled myself back to my feet, carrying the album open, but tucked under my arm, back to my room.

Onyx was awake now.

"I was wondering where you'd gotten off to," he said, completely relaxed. He hadn't even looked at me; his attention was on the sports highlights on the TV.

I didn't say anything. I went to my bedside and picked up my gun, aiming it at his bare chest before I tossed the open photo album at him.

"Yes or no question," I said, hating the crack in my voice as I spoke. "Did you come to Vegas to kill me?"

Confused, he frowned at me. "*What?*" he asked. "Tati—"

"*Yes or no question!*" I screamed, willing my hand to stop trembling.

"*No,*" he answered emphatically. "Why the fuck are you asking me that?"

I swallowed the nerves threatening to overtake me and gestured at the album. "Look at the picture. And tell me I don't see what I *know* I see."

Reluctantly, he tore his gaze away from me to look at the album. "I see a picture of a man and a baby; you and your father, I guess. What does that have to do with me?"

"*His arm,*" I hissed, aggressively wiping away tears of frustration, and fear, and... shit, I didn't even know.

Onyx looked at the picture again; still confused at first, but then he did exactly as I had a few moments ago.

He pulled it closer.

And then, there it was.

*Clarity.*

"All my life," I spoke. "I remembered it being a snake. A mighty anaconda, a predator, wrapped around his arm. But that's not a snake, is it?"

He looked at me, met my gaze, and shook his head. "It's not a snake."

"What is it?"

"You see what it is, but I swear—"

"*What is it?*" I asked him again. "Just... say it."

"Thorns, Tati," he admitted. "But I *swear to you*... I don't know shit about that. It doesn't have *anything* to do with me."

I shook my head. "How am I supposed to believe that? This is just a fucking coincidence? Did *you* kill him?!" I shrieked, brandishing the gun so wildly in my chaotic state that I was actually relieved when Onyx finally reacted, easily taking it away from me.

"Your father was killed before coming to Vegas was ever even a thought for me," he said, holding my wrists to keep me still. "And I did *not* come here to do you any harm. Okay?"

"How the fuck would I know?" I asked, both of us glancing to the other side table as his phone rang.

*Alicia.*

"I need to get this," he told me. "And then... we can talk."

"Or we can talk *now*," I countered and he pushed out a breath, clearly overwhelmed.

"Tati, please, you know she wouldn't be calling me at this time if it wasn't something pressing."

*Fuck.*

*Fuck!*

"Take it," I told him, snatching away. "And then you have some shit to answer for. You're gonna tell me *everything*."

He ran his tongue over his lips, pushing out a sigh. "Okay."

I shouldn't have agreed.

That was so fucking stupid.

But I just... *fuck*... I needed a second to breathe.

He stepped out of the room, the phone already up to his ear as he moved down the hall in just his boxers, and I... could just *scream*.

What the hell was even *happening*?

I picked up the album again, my eyes going straight to the spiky vine of thorns circling my father's arm. It had been there all along, hidden in the scales of that snake.

I shook my head, questioning everything I knew as I tried to make sense of it all.

And then *my* phone rang.

*Alicia.*

Dread swept through me as I dove for my phone, snatching it off the charger.

"Hello?"

"Where is Nyx?" Alicia asked immediately, sounding worried.

"He... was on the phone with you, I thought," I answered, standing from the bed. I grabbed my gun from where he'd left it, balancing the phone against my ear as I moved into the hall to follow him.

"Yes, he was. He stepped out to your porch, he said, but then he heard something. The call dropped and I tried to call back, but he's not answering."

"*What the fuck*," I muttered.

Not to her, just... into the ether.

I spent the next few minutes searching every inch of my house, walking outside to see where he could have possibly gotten off to.

His clothes were still in my living room and I found his phone smashed in my driveway.

Other than that... nothing.

"Tati, I need you to talk to me," Alicia said. "What do you see?"

I shook my head like she could see me, staring into the dark from my empty front porch. "Nothing. He's gone."

THE END... FOR NOW.

<h1 style="text-align:center">Afterword</h1>

Yes, the end, but just for now!
    Look for book two in early March.

If you enjoyed this book, please consider leaving a review at your preferred retailer - including the CCJ Romance site!

# Acknowledgments

To my betas, for reading this twice.
To Nicole & Alex for gassing me.
To LB & Phyl for keeping me upright in more ways than they know.
To Leila for coming through.
To my family, for making room.
To my readers, for rocking with whatever wave I'm on.
To God, for never moving.

I love you.
-CCJ

# About the Author

Christina C. Jones is a best-selling romance novelist and digital media creator. A timeless storyteller, she is lauded by readers for her ability to seamlessly weave the complexities of modern life into captivating tales of Black characters in nearly every romance subgenre. In addition to her full-time writing career, she co-founded Girl, Have You Read – a popular digital platform that amplifies Black romance authors and their stories. Christina has a passion for making beautiful things, and be found crafting, cooking, and designing and building a (literal) home with her husband in her spare time.

*Also by Christina C Jones*

(Links and more info for all titles can be found on my website.)

THE CLARKE BROTHERS

Collision Course

Controlled Chaos

Close Contact

THE WRIGHT BROTHERS

Getting Schooled

Pulling Doubles

Bending the Rules

THE LOVE SISTERS

I Think I Might Love You

I Think I Might Need You

I Think I Might Want You

SUGAR VALLEY

The Culmination of Everything

The Point of It All

INEVITABLE SERIES

Inevitable Conclusions

Inevitable Seductions

Inevitable Addiction

THE TROUBLE SERIES

The Trouble With Love: a tale of two sisters

The Trouble With Us

The Right Kind of Trouble

IF YOU CAN SERIES

Catch Me If You Can

Release Me If You Can

Save Me If You Can

HIGH STAKES SERIES

Ante Up

King of Hearts: A Short Story Collection

Deuces Wild

EQUILIBRIUM SERIES

Love Notes

Grow Something: An Equilibrium Novelette

In Tandem

Frosted.Whipped.Buttered: An Equilibrium Short

Plus One: An Equilibrium Short

Bittersweet

Press Rewind: An Equilibrium Short

SWEET HEAT SERIES

Hints of Spice

A Dash of Heat

A Touch of Sugar

SERENDIPITOUS SERIES

A Crazy Little Thing Called Love

Didn't Mean To Love You

Fall in Love Again

The Way Love Goes

Love You Forever

Something Like Love

CONNECTICUT KING SERIES (Collaboration with Love Belvin)

Love on the Highlight Reel (Book 2)

Determining Possession (Book 3)

Pass Interference (Book 6)

STRICTLY PROFESSIONAL

Strictly Professional

Unfinished Business

TRUTH AND LIES

The Truth: His Side, Her Side, and The Truth About Falling in Love

The Lies: The Lies We Tell About Life, Love, and Everything in Between

FRIENDS & LOVERS

Finding Forever

Chasing Commitment

ETERNALLY TETHERED

Haunted

Coveted

STANDALONES

Mine Tonight

Wonder

Equivalent Exchange

Love & Other Things

A Mutually Beneficial Agreement

Relationship Goals: a novella

Anonymous Acts (Five Star Enterprises)

The Reinvention of the Rose

Me + Somebody's Son: A Heights Story

The Rose That Got Away

9 781953 214324